# PRISON CLOWN

# RICHARD KEITH

# PRISON CLOWN

## RICHARD KEITH

Green Bay, WI

*Dedicated to Steve Arwady*

*And for my mother Sandra who passed about a year ago from Alzheimer's and gave me the inspiration to always do my best and not to listen to people who say I can't. Love you, Mom.*

*For my dad Seymour who has always taken an interest in everything I do and never stopped believing in me.*

*For my kids Gary, Bary and Heather, David, Mike and Lindsay and Danielle, and Jackie who stood by me when I got cranky, and was always there with the encouragement I needed.*

*To my father-in-law Jerry who I miss so much and who believed in me always and who without, this book would not have been written. To my mother-in-law Lorraine who I miss dearly, and Papa Roy, for all their support and love, and for my brother and sister-in-law Larry and Jodie who supported me in writing this book.*

*For my brother Paul, who I love with all my heart, and who listened and helped guide me in every step of this long, difficult process.*

*For my loving wife who is my world and I thank God I found, and who without I would be a lost soul.*

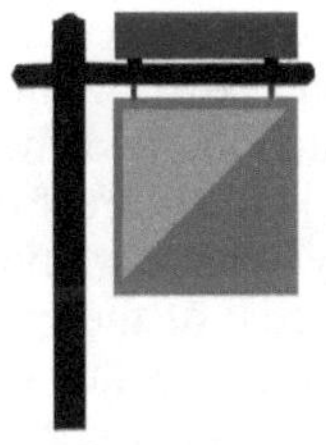

# Preface

It's a common phrase: *If it could happen to me, it could happen to anyone.*

This is often a handy cliché and we don't actually mean it. But sometimes, the old adage proves true. In my case, my "happened to me" story revolves around the legal system. It's not surprising to say that a run-in with law enforcement can have far reaching consequences, whether it's a routine traffic stop gone bad or, in my case, a situation categorized as "white collar crime."

My story begins at a point in my life—2003 to 2009—when I was a successful entrepreneur investing in Chicago real estate. The year 2008 was pivotal because of the real estate crash. I'm sure most adults remember that bleak time.

Then, in 2009, I became one of the Federal government's backlash victims. It's no exaggeration to say that everything in my life changed drastically and it will never go back to the way it was before 2009.

My financial goals were simple—to increase property values and earn profits for my investors. At first, I could do no wrong. I hired a contractor who became a friend. He would do the work on his own dime and then sleep at the house to make sure no one broke in and stole anything from our work-in-progress.

Rather than borrowing money from banks to purchase starter properties, I contacted a company purchasing properties at Tax Sales and Foreclosure Auctions. I'd found two companies that bought properties at tax auctions and then sold them to me on land contract. A land contract allows a rehabber to work on a property with a minimal down payment. The balance of the cost of the property is paid when the rehab is complete and the sale to a third party buyer takes place. The land contracts allowed me to start the repairs and upgrades, so we could then flip them in quick sales. The buyers obtained their loans from mortgage brokers. When I started out, flipping properties had not yet earned its negative reputation, but was considered a smart real estate move.

Within the first year, I built up my business to a point at which my investors earned quarterly interest of 15%. My investors were friends who lent me money to do the rehab, and also enabled me to buy properties (not on land contract). It was easier to acquire investment money from private parties then banks, but because I borrowed money for short periods of time, I had to pay a healthy interest to entice my investors. Since, I was providing such a great return on investment, I decided to do business with family and friends instead of giving strangers this return. My business was going great and life was good.

This brings us to 2008, when the real estate market collapsed and the Federal government sent its agents to go after the perpetrators of this collapse. But did they target the banks that held millions of mortgages? No. They targeted the investors, lawyers, small brokers, title companies, and the borrowers. They targeted business people who, like me, had dealt in real estate.

The Federal Bureau of Investigation targeted *me*. And the family and friends I loved became their "civilian" casualties. Had I thought for a *nanosecond* my family and friends could *possibly* be hurt by investing in my company, I never would have involved them in my business dealings. Never in a thousand years could I have guessed the crosshairs of the FBI would focus on me: investigating, charging, convicting, and ultimately, imprisoning me.

After my shock, disbelief, and anger settled down some, which began to happen once I was in prison, I begin writing. I described all the events that led to this nightmare and I acknowledged my state of mind. Writing became my release, my desperate search for a way to express the reality of my circumstances after facing all the lies, snares, and betrayals.

In prison, one has plenty of time to write so I took advantage of the situation. I had to use a pen to write longhand because there were no computers. It was also against prison rules to write anything involving an inmate's story. No free speech in prison.

The impetus to publish my story is to give my perspective (and my abject horror) about the current state of our judicial system, top to bottom, including the U.S. Department of Justice. This important arm of government has the shockingly easy capacity to *betray innocent citizens and use its agents and employees to ruin law-abiding citizens' lives*.

In telling my story of arrest and imprisonment, I expose the dreadful consequences, not only for me, but for my family and friends, too. I'm also motivated to tell my story in order to introduce readers to a few incredible men I met while serving my sentence in a Federal Prison Camp, which I'm calling the "Franklin Prison Camp." These men made mistakes that landed them in prison, some for very long periods of time, often in the prime of their life. In some cases, like mine, the men weren't guilty of scheming to hurt any person or entity. In either case, these long sentences could break any person's spirit.

As my story unfolds, I believe you will understand how the same thing that happened to me could happen to you. I also hope you take away insights into what the justice system has become and how so many people of all description end up entangled in that very system. That includes people like me, who, I suspect, are much like you.

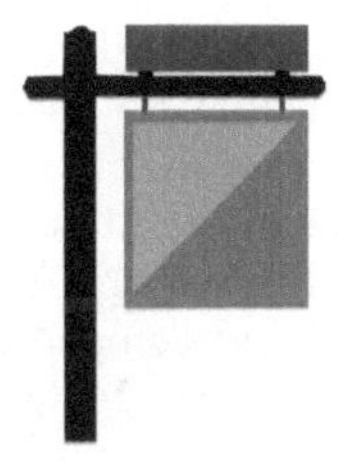

# Chapter One

## The Hole

Chuck and I were doing our usual pre-chow smoke outside by the tennis courts. That's where the inmates usually smoked. They also smoked by the baseball field, but that made me nervous because the guard towers overlooked that area. I had never smoked a cigarette in my life until I came to prison. Now I smoke like a fiend, mainly because I'm so damn bored all the time.

I used to smoke cigars, but that would be impossible to get in prison. Plus, the fact that smoking a cigar is harder to hide because of the strong smell. The cigarettes we were smoking were skinny like a joint. The inmates would share between two guys every time they smoked. The cost of a cigarette hand-rolled by an inmate was two stamps a piece.

I passed the cigarette to Chuck when all of the sudden we heard "Get against the building and spread 'em."

Holy shit! It was a guard walking the perimeter of the camp. The guard was about half a block away, so Chuck had time to put the cigarette out and bury it in the stones with his shoes. This was something we always practiced just in case we got caught.

We stepped up to the gym building and placed our hands on the brick wall. The guard told us to follow him to the bubble and we would be going to "the hole."

The hole was basically a dungeon with no windows. There was nothing to do there. You couldn't read or watch TV. There was no companionship. It was very much like the hole Steve McQueen stayed in the movie *The Great Escape.* The lights are on all day and all night. You sleep on a cement slab. Many inmates came out with bad backs and needed a cane the rest of their sentence.

They let you out to exercise one hour a day. You get two cold showers a week. When they release you, sometimes after a year has gone by, you are usually shipped to a prison far away so it's difficult for your family to visit.

Going to the hole was not a good thing. I was scared out of my mind.

Chuck, being twenty-two-years-old and having the experience that comes from being in the army, was not scared at all. As we walked thru the halls, my friend Pete Strand was telling Chuck to take care of me and keep me calm. Pete knew I had claustrophobia and would climb the walls in the hole.

When we got to "the bubble" (the camp office), the guard sat us down and asked where our floor was. Then, he and the other guards went there and looked through the entire floor for cigarettes and tobacco pouches. Every time an inmate gets caught smoking, the guards go through the belongings of all the inmates on the same floor. Not a good way to get popular with your fellow inmates.

As we sat in the bubble, inmates said their good-byes to us, figuring we would not be back.

Chuck told me over and over, "Keith, do not say you were smoking."

The arresting guard came back and apparently found nothing on either of our units or floors. He also couldn't find the cigarettes we had been smoking because there was hardly any of it left and Chuck had buried it.

The guard looked at me and said, "Tell me the truth and I'll let you go back to your room. Were you smoking a cigarette?"

I looked at Chuck and looked back at the guard and replied, "Could you ask him first?"

The guard looked at Chuck and asked the same question. "Were you smoking?"

Chuck answered yes quickly.

I was confused because we were supposed to say no. I took his lead and yelled out, "I was smoking also."

They told us to wait and we sat, relieved that we were going back to our rooms and not another prison.

I looked around the bubble and saw President Obama's portrait along with the head of the BOP's picture. Now that I could breathe again, my mind started flashing back to how I got here in the first place. How did a guy who never committed a crime in his life for 59 years get thrown in prison?

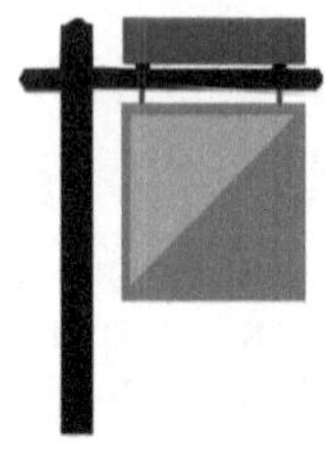

# Chapter Two

## The Calm Before the Storm

While holding a checklist in his hand, my friend Cliff was indicating items to be marked OK before takeoff. I'd never flown in a 4-seater plane, and since I was deathly afraid of flying in the first place, I had begun feeling nervous. I tried to hide it because it was important that Cliff not think I didn't trust him—simply because he'd just received his pilot's license. Cliff shared my uneasiness about flying, but he thought a great way to conquer his fear was to learn to fly.

We both got into the plane, and Cliff called to the tower, speaking words that made no sense to me. Meanwhile, I thought my stomach might fall out, the kind of feeling I had before a rollercoaster ride. Cliff started to taxi and soon the plane lifted off the tarmac, and seconds later so did we. The clouds grew closer and closer and the roar of the engine became a steady, loud hum.

Once in the air, I began talking to Cliff about my business dilemma, but he gently chided me, saying, "Why don't you just relax and enjoy the sky?"

And so we did. The flying was so quiet and tranquil it seemed I was leaving all my problems down on the ground. We flew over my house in Buffalo Grove, Illinois, and around my neighborhood. I opened the window and let the air rush into my face.

Cliff let me take the wheel and it gave me a sense of security, even safety. My friend was a no-nonsense guy when he had to be, and I respected his ability as a pilot. He was one of those guys that make you feel safe. He also had a good head on his shoulders.

We flew for a couple of hours before we started descending to the airport in Milwaukee. Cliff talked to the tower before his picture-perfect landing.

As we taxied down the runway, I was struck, hard, and jolted into my reality and the need to get back to work. The plane stopped, and as we got out and headed toward his car, my cell phone rang.

My wife Julie was on the phone. She told me to get back home *fast. The FBI was waiting for me at my office.*

"Why?"

She had no idea, but there was nothing for me to do but head home and find out.

Cliff dropped me off at my house.

Julie had left and we arranged to meet in the bowling alley parking lot a block from my office, about 15 minutes away. Julie got in my car and we drove the block to my office together.

When we arrived, we stared out the window. We counted *20* FBI officers in front of my office building. All my neighbors were outside, looking towards my office.

When one of the FBI agents approached me, I said, "Did you think I would resist?"

She remained stone-faced, pretending not to hear me.

We were directed to go into the office and sit down while the officers began opening my office cabinets and desk drawers, removing and packing up all my office files.

I asked the same agent if she could please tell me what was going on.

"If you talk with me, I'll tell you what is happening," she said.

Being an attorney, Julie immediately transitioned to lawyer mode. "We are not saying a word to you. Where is your warrant?"

Frowning, the agent handed Julie an envelope that we were instructed *not* to open. Apparently, this was a type of warrant we were not allowed to see or read.

"Now, do you want to talk?" the agent asked, her voice cool.

Just as coolly, Julie replied, "No. We have nothing to say."

It's a good thing Julie handled this. If it had been left up to me, I'd have poured them coffee and told them my life story! Later on, every lawyer I spoke to was relieved we didn't talk to the Feds.

Rule #1: Don't talk to the Feds. In case following Rule #1 is not possible, go to Rule #2: Don't talk to the Feds.

I pulled Julie aside and asked why we shouldn't speak to the FBI agents? I was keenly interested in learning what they were doing at my office and why they were boxing up all my files?

Julie explained it was important not to say a word because anything I say would be used against me. Julie practiced real estate law and was my company lawyer. She was focused on protecting me, but later we learned, she was protecting both of us.

Finally, the agent told us we were both going to be indicted for bank/mortgage fraud.

"Mortgage fraud! (Really just another word for bank fraud.) But I'm not a mortgage broker and I don't work for one. I don't even borrow money from a bank."

"You headed up a scheme to defraud many banks out of ten million dollars," she said, not backing down.

So, in less than a full day, the FBI closed down my company and told us to get a lawyer. We did as we were told and contacted a friend of Julie's, who worked at the United States Attorney's office. This person recommended a lawyer whom we called immediately.

Looking back, I realize my life was doomed as soon as I contacted the first lawyer. The way the justice system stands today, the only reason to bring in a lawyer is to negotiate the length of your prison stay. Once the Feds think they've got you or believe what they believe, that becomes the truth. The truth is what they believe happened. There is no way out. You are royally screwed.

After those events unfolded, I can fast forward to today. The truth is, I live the life of a post convict. Generally, when the public is watching breaking news on TV and someone has been indicted, the viewers assume the person is guilty. Otherwise, why would the powerful United States government prosecute in the first place?

Once the sentence is served, the former convict's life never returns to what it once was or might have been. Employers don't want to get involved with a past criminal, and this is true for those convicted of white collar crimes as much as it is for those involved in other crimes that result in incarceration.

This was true for me. To make a living, I ended up starting a steel brokerage company on my own, and I also sell as a rep for a friend who got me started in the construction equipment field. I lease construction equipment for his company out of California, and broker steel at the same time.

Given the internet, it's even more difficult today for a past felon to conduct any business whatsoever. It takes only seconds to look me up and find my criminal history posted for anyone who wants to see it. Each time I fail to get an order, I believe it is because my buyers were scared away because of what they learned on the internet. It's like living with a ghost of your past. If you looked me up, you'd see the government perceived me as the largest bank criminal since Dillinger.

In spite of this, I'm aware I'm one of the fortunate ones. I have a family that loves me, believes in me, and knows the truth. I have a house, and luckily, no assets in my name. I'm also sixty-four-years-old, at the end of my career, but I pity the younger inmates

I came to know; these men face decades of problems ahead of them.

I have a $4,000,000 debt to the government, which is called restitution. They computed this figure by taking the price of the buildings I sold (without the fixtures yet installed) and subtracting that from the price it should have been without the fixtures installed. The problem is, I ended up always purchasing and installing the fixtures. (I'll go into greater detail about this later.)

So, although the government realizes I can't ever pay the total restitution figure, I have to pay a percentage of my earnings after tax. Because our justice system just looks at the cold hard facts of the law, the ability of the felon to survive this hardship is not taken into account. Since this fine doesn't go away in bankruptcy, I find myself branded as a felon with a debt large enough to choke a horse.

Despite that, I look at life differently today. Of course, I realize how precious freedom is. The inmates used to say, "Each inmate should be made to spend some time in 'the hole,' so when they come out, they can realize how lucky they are to be able to enjoy the freedom of walking and talking to other inmates in the prison." The same thing is true in "regular" life. Once a person's freedom is snatched away, one realizes just how precious it is.

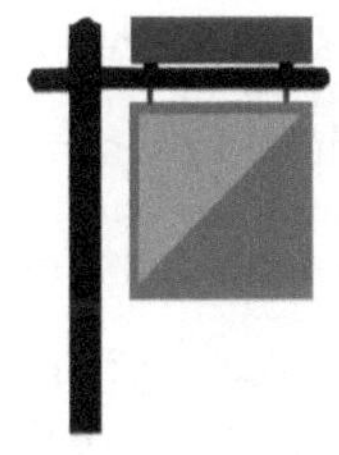

# Chapter Three

## "Englewood, the War Zone of Chicago"

So, what was the actual basis of the government's case against me? If you're confused, I understand. Many people are, including lawyers and law professors I've spoken to over the years, because the case was so convoluted even legal experts have had difficulty. So, here is the "raw material" for my case.

### The background

Englewood is one of Chicago's rough Southside neighborhoods, and it was here that I purchased buildings on land contracted from a private company that handled tax sales and foreclosures. I also bought property from real estate agents. I purchased some on land contracts and some for cash borrowed from my friends. I repaired each house by hiring a single contractor to install sheet rock, paint, repair plumbing, replace electric service if needed, and replace old fixtures and windows. I also hired contractors to install sturdy indoor/outdoor carpet with padding, along with tile flooring.

One of my contractors, Gil Pearson, slept in the

property undergoing the work. I was fortunate not to have much theft and vandalism. With Gil sleeping in the property, once it had been renovated it remained renovated. It was a good—and simple—arrangement all around, and Gil was paid on completion. Financially, it was a Fin-Fin.

I spent approximately $20,000-$40,000 for an entire rehab on an apartment building. This flipping practice became hugely popular, even to the point of generating a TV program called *Flip This House*. It never occurred to me I had anything to fear from the law.

I located buyers by running ads in the *Chicago Sun-Times* for about $200 a week. The newspaper was full of ads declaring, "Purchase your dream home! No money down. No closing costs."

When I received calls from buyers, they came to view the home and purchased it with no money down. I worked with a few different banks and mortgage brokers and often closed the loan in 45 to 60 days.

The land contracts were good for 60 days, so time was of the essence when closing loans. If the loan did not close within the specified 60 days, I could lose the house, plus the cost of labor and materials that I had already spent.

In a typical closing process, the bank or mortgage broker would write the loan and then call my lawyer to schedule the closing, held at a title company. Since my wife is a lawyer, she usually represented our company at the closing, but if she couldn't make it, I sent another lawyer in her place. Again, trying to keep the money in my family, I hired my cousin. Luckily, he didn't get in trouble when all hell broke loose. Looking back, I wish I hadn't involved either of them. I'd rather have paid the $300.00 to another closing attorney not in my family.

The seller cannot supply the down payment to the buyer, since it's illegal for the seller to help with 100% of the down payment. However, some avenues were available to assist the buyer with the down payment.

Gift letters must be from a relative, FDA loans, or high credit lending programs that allowed for 0% down payment.

And finally, "no source" loans meant the bank didn't ask where borrowers got their down payment, which the Dodd-Frank law made illegal. (Its future is in question, nevertheless.)

Even at the time, however, the banks were offering these programs while the Feds assumed they were illegal. Banks always want the buyer to have skin in the deal, something to lose if the loan goes into default. Today, because of the 2008 and 2009 economic recession, almost no loans exist where the seller can help the borrower with all of the down payment. This is also true of the so-called "no seasoning" loans, which mean the funds don't have to be in a savings account for a specific period of time. The brokers that were closing my buyers' loans were using these programs. Once the loan was secured, the buyer would then close the loan without closing costs, earnest money, or down payment. At that time, the buyer could close a mortgage loan with only a valid driver's license.

Before the regulations were tightened, the banking programs were so lenient, that a monkey could buy a home. Prior to these new lending programs a bank would never have thought about loaning money this easily or loosely. (Again, the future of financial regulation is still in question, and some loosening of lending guidelines has already taken place.)

Sometimes a buyer would bring an attorney to the closing, but most of the time not. Once the property was flipped to the buyers, I directed them to a real estate agent who worked with Section 8 tenants. Section 8 tenants are those whose rent is subsidized by the Federal government. The amount of rent was determined by the number of bedrooms in the property. At the time, the average property owner would clear $800/month profit above their mortgage payment on a newly acquired house rented to Section 8 tenants.

The value of Englewood properties were derived

from the property appraisals. Most often, the mortgage broker hired the appraiser, but it was not uncommon for the seller to work with the appraiser hired by the broker. Today, the appraiser can only be hired by the broker or bank.

Here is the core of my Fin-Fin plan: brokers and banks earned their fees, and the buyers earned profits from the rents; the neighborhood, in this case, Englewood, benefited from rehabilitation of its older buildings. I brought in approximately $40,000 gross per property. Out of this, I paid overhead and payroll. Overall, my program made business sense and brought in a very solid profit.

Later the Feds would use the fact I made a healthy profit against me. When a defendant is in front of a jury, the prosecutor always brings up the fact that there was a lot of money made. All of a sudden, making a profit in the U.S. took on a dirty connotation. Maybe, the Feds already knew some jurors who were jealous when they learned the defendant made money.

The funding of down payments was provided by long-term friends of mine, who earned a healthy return on this short-term investment. Because there was room in my rehab-then-sell (flip) formula for a healthy earned interest, I decided to share the wealth with friends and family rather than strangers. Later, I would regret this.

The high interest stemmed from my short-term need for the money. As soon as the loan closed, the money would be deposited back into the company account. Later, when I began buying properties outright, I used friends' money for 90- to 120-day loans. It made no sense for a private investor to take a risk of lending $70,000 for a 1% interest rate per month. Instead, I'd pay 15% for a three-month loan.

## A turn for the worse

Things went well until my General Contractor,

Gil Pearson, died. I had *no idea* his death would ultimately lead to my financial demise and shockingly, dreadfully, a head on collision with a train I never saw coming—prison. After Gil's death, I needed to hire other contractors, some by referrals and others by way of newspaper advertisements. Those who placed advertisements in the *Chicago Sun-Times* were mostly experienced rehabilitation contractors, so I thought I had "easy pickins'." I was very much mistaken.

It wasn't easy to find a trustworthy contractor on the south side of Chicago, and building trust all over again also wasn't easy. A government organization for low income housing, Chicago Housing Authority Commission (CHAC), asked that I draw my labor from Chicago's South Side. None of the contractors were able to front money for any portion of the labor draw, which Gil Pearson had done.

In addition, if I'd hired outside of the Englewood area, the cost for the fix-up would have been way out of my budget. This meant I needed to front all labor expenses until the loan closed. So, I obtained the necessary labor expense funds from an investor and repaid him when the loans closed.

Without Gil, I began to experience theft. Furnaces, windows, cabinets, toilets, tubs, sinks and copper wiring, and copper pipes were being stolen hours after installation. The first time this happened, I was shocked to turn over a house to a buyer and found nothing inside. Every fixture had been stolen—even the outside siding was gone.

This meant I had to buy fixtures twice, or even three times, for each house. Hiring an armed guard was way too expensive. Since the appraisal kicks off the loan process, I'd have had to keep an armed guard around the premises for 60 days or so. There was no way I could turn a profit using an armed guard for that long of a time.

My new general contractor and I attempted to find a solution, first installing burglar alarms. But the thieves stole the alarms. Then, we placed a live-in house sitter to watch the property, but the house sitters couldn't remain on the property all of the time, and thieves ended up watching the houses and timing their break-ins. We even had a few house sitters who worked with the thieves and helped them remove fixtures.

Next, we tried boarding up the windows with heavy wood and carriage bolts, but vandals pried off the boards. We put up VPS (Vacant Property Services) on the entire first floor of unsold properties. VPS is an expensive steel structure covering windows and doors and needs a series of color codes to unlock. The system costs about $1,000 per month to install. Almost unbelievably, the thieves were able to get under this steel structure by using crowbars and wire.

We tried guard dogs and burglar bars, and made deals with the neighbors in the area to help watch the houses. Nothing worked.

By this time, I'd borrowed a great deal of money from many good friends. My parents and my wife pressured me to get out of Englewood and return to the safety of the suburbs, but I'd involved my friends and family. I couldn't quit and leave.

After conferring with other friends in the rehab industry, I met Jim Hayman, an expert appraiser in the Englewood area. Jim knew all the troubles involved in building in this troubled area. He said, that although properties must be 100% complete at closing, he didn't see a huge problem withholding fixtures until shortly after closing. "Just get them in quickly," he said.

Jim's appraisal would declare the property complete, and as long as I installed fixtures shortly after the title transfer, he saw no problem. After all, who were we hurting? This would allow fixtures to be installed *after* the title transferred to the new buyer. The new owner would then be responsible to protect the property.

This sounded plausible and we decided to operate this way going forward, at least for a while until I could find a way to stop the theft. The problem? The theft still occurred. (Once I'd closed on the property the owners had to worry about theft.) I thought the new owners would make arrangements to protect their property.

I was wrong. Some of the new owners didn't show up to the house for months. The theft problem was still bad and getting worse.

It began to develop that the owners had no means to pay mortgages, because they couldn't rent houses without fixtures installed, and theft remained. This put the owner in a disastrous financial situation, because tenants paid rents to cover the mortgage. But, there were no tenants, because without installed house fixtures, Section 8 would not inspect the house. With no inspection, no owner could rent the property to tenants. In the end, the banks' predatory lending programs gave loans to people without money in reserve to pay the mortgage. Thus, if there was no tenant, the house would ultimately go into foreclosure.

I began to look for *any* means of succeeding in this Englewood endeavor. I went so far as to ask Jim if I could place fixtures in buildings 60 days prior to closing for him to take photographs for the bank, then remove them until the buyer held title. This 60-day time period began at the appraisal and ended at the closing. I learned this would not work, because a seller may not install fixtures, have an appraisal written, and then remove them. This was looked upon as fraud.

I found myself under such a load of crippling stress over what seemed like insurmountable challenges I began taking hydrocodone acetaminophen like it was aspirin. Not only was I paying for the material and labor over and over, but I was forced to pay the buyer's mortgage. According to the deal, buyers were supposed to make money each month after receiving rent and paying the mortgage on the property. Since the fixtures were stolen even after I was no longer responsible, I felt obligated to reinstall them at my cost, not my legal obligation, but a moral one. At least that's how I saw it.

I also had to keep these properties from going into foreclosure, because if they did, I'd have a more difficult time getting loans from my broker. The broker would sign a contract with the bank that made them liable for the money lost due to a foreclosure and would be obligated to pay the bank back on the defaulted loan. In short, I had to keep my customers' buildings out of trouble.

I ran into all kinds of other problems. For example, I couldn't find an insurance policy that would replace stolen fixtures. They covered vandalism only, and they paid for broken door jams and locks, but not stolen items. Even if I'd found insurance to cover theft, the policy would have been discontinued because these were multiple thefts. To this day, I believe that if I'd had an insurance policy to reimburse my buyer for theft, the Feds would have gone after me on insurance fraud. After all, I knew we'd have theft on every single house I rehabbed.

In addition, Section 8 was creating other problems for rehabbers. Because Englewood was a high crime area, the CHA (Chicago Housing Authority) were no longer interested in placing Section 8 voucher holders in the area where I had my houses. Maps were dispersed in the market place, with undesirable areas shaded, and that included the blocks my houses were on.

Next, the banks no longer offered loans for building or rehabs in this area. The banks had to be careful not to enter into the illegal practice of what's known as "red lining," defined as a bias against a specific neighborhood, not unlike a bias toward certain people. If a bank didn't want to underwrite loans for a particular neighborhood, they had to pull out of the entire state.

Section 8 already had established rules about quality standards, including room sizes and basement-ceiling height, for example. However, to keep their voucher holders away from the Englewood area, Section 8 rules instituted more strict standards. These standards affected low-income areas, and included lot sizes, number of vacant lots on each block, number of vacant properties in the area, and so on. They even monitored the ceiling height of the bedrooms. As a result, I had properties to sell that no longer met Section 8 standards. Now, the difference left over after the mortgage was paid (profit) was considerably less than before the new Section 8 standards.

As properties were getting harder to sell, I felt the weight of the world on my shoulders. After all, good friends and relatives had money invested in my company.

You may remember that in 2007 the entire housing market was slowing down. Buyers were becoming more and more difficult to find. The so-called real estate bubble was about to burst.

Banks began restricting lending to the mortgage industry, and even individuals with strong credit found it nearly impossible to obtain a mortgage. Many buyers all over the U.S. had been purchasing property with Adjustable Rate Mortgages (ARMS), from 90 days to five years. Now when it came time to refinance, they could no longer afford the house they'd bought.

When I first offered my friends the opportunity to invest in my company, they usually asked about the chances the company would fail. But I was spending $80,000 for fix-ups and selling at $160,000, so my answer was always, "There would have to be an economic disaster not seen since the Great Depression."

I couldn't run because I would be running from everyone I cared deeply about. It would have been like trying to run from my own shadow. And I'm not accustomed to giving up, so that was not an option. If I continued operating the way I was, maybe I could pay the mortgage payments on the properties and keep them out of foreclosure long enough to solve the problems I faced.

But, I had no idea that the entire economy was about to drown me and everyone else. As I said, the bubble was about to burst.

## The worst recession since…

Unless you're very young, you probably recall 2007, the year the housing market completely *died*. For me, that meant no buyers were taking numbers and forming a line to talk to me about buying a building. My phones completely stopped ringing. The company that sold me properties on land contract was calling and faxing inventory lists that now had eight times the number of buildings it used to have. Prices that had been rising at 20% per year were coming down fast. Frighteningly fast.

Housing values were plummeting, along with housing starts. The banks started pulling loans and not lending money. Major Wall Street firms had been buying bundled loans and were now stuck with tons of "bad paper." Banks were foreclosing on properties like never before.

Now what? I had properties to sell and properties that were still unfinished, but I paid mortgages without any income flowing into the company, because no loans were closing.

During this rapid move toward economic collapse that culminated in the fall of 2008, economists and journalists called this period, "the worst since the Great Depression." The ongoing economic disaster matched what I had unknowingly declared to my friends as the only reason they'd lose their money. Sadly, I'd been disastrously prophetic.

I had experienced serious pressure from my buyers when they first bought the homes, then experienced pressure closing the loans, and finally underwent pressures from the countless construction problems caused by contractors' poor quality work.

I had hired Larry, my cousin, and Sean, Julie's uncle to manage problems between buyers and contractors. Several contractors caused problems because they focused on filling their own wallets rather than doing an honest job and producing quality work. Sadly, these contractors were more "street smart" than Larry and

Sean, and me. By the time we caught up with them the damage had been done. The situation was out of control and I was left with many unhappy buyers.

Of course, predatory lending practices were already in the air and gaining exposure in 2007. The Federal government stood by banks, however, and cast them in the defendant role. Illinois Attorney General, Lisa Madigan, worked with other states to develop a formal inquiry into the predatory lending programs banks instituted in the subprime mortgage market. State politicians would find themselves powerless before the Federal government, as this inquiry delved into banking procedures and consequences.

Subprime lending was presented as a way of allowing those with lower incomes to own a home. Instead, subprime lending resulted in tempting lending officers to become greedy. Perhaps, banks promoted greed by creating commission structures that made it lucrative for brokers to pressure high yield programs on inexperienced, unsuspecting borrowers.

A borrower who qualified for a low-rate program loan would be *intentionally directed by mortgage loan officers* to enter into a subprime program because the commission structure in subprime was lucrative. Now, these loans were proven dangerous to borrowers, with the Feds blaming everyone but the banks themselves.

Before the bubble burst, the mortgage lending market was inviting, flying high, booming. Real estate values were climbing each quarter. Banks bundled these high interest loans and passed them off to Wall Street just two days after closing. Adjustable Rate Mortgages (ARMs) were offered left and right, intimating (or stating) that the borrower could refinance "down the road."

As you probably remember, problems intensified in early 2008 when the market slowed and slowed and slowed and banks and brokers ran for the hills, until there would be no more "down the road." The bubble burst and we experienced a crushing recession with millions of jobs lost.

# Chapter Four

## A Full-time Job

"We're not telling the children." Julie's voice was unnaturally calm after our silent drive home from our now closed up office. We no longer had a business, our main source of income.

As for me, I felt scared—and angry. But Julie's words grabbed my attention. Oh, my God! Our four children were uppermost in Julie's mind as we started our drive back home. David and Mikey were already adults in their late twenties, but the girls, Dani and Jackie, were sixteen and thirteen, respectively.

At first, I agreed we should stay silent and not burden the children with our troubles. At that point, though, we had no idea then that this situation was completely out of our hands.

The following week I happened to watch an interview with Patrick Fitsgerald, the U.S. Attorney at the time. He was talking about devastating consequences of mortgage and bank fraud, and mentioned that just that week the FBI had closed in on the picture-ready bandits of mortgage fraud perpetrators in Chicago. He explained how the crooks schemed and took interior pictures of one house and used them for another house. This is something my appraiser did when the bank asked for interior pictures. The crazy thing about that was that when the bank had their own appraiser go into the subject property, they never stopped the loan. I never could understand how they let my buyer close even though the bank's appraiser physically went into the house and saw there were no fixtures.

Was he kidding? I'd never stolen as much as grapes from the grocery store, and now the head of the FBI was taking credit for apprehending a bunch of criminals and he was including my wife and me in this "fraud" case.

My first thought was to pack up and leave the country. Where would we go? Israel? No, they extradite indicted people back to the U.S. and Mexico? No, in the movies everyone flees to Mexico.

Then it hit me. Julie and I hadn't been convicted of a crime, at least not yet. In fact, we weren't even indicted.

At that point, I knew only this: investigators had something I actually did confused with something they *thought* I did. I believe early on, the Feds got wrong information and thought I was selling unfinished houses and never finishing them. It was this misunderstanding that got them eager to stop me and spend money on prosecuting me. However, what I was *actually* guilty of was knowing the appraisal said the property was 100% done, the sales contract said the property was not done, and then physically the actual property was not done. The cabinets, sinks, toilets, and so forth were always put in the house but not at the time the appraisal said it was.

**It's not about the truth**

Julie and I started interviewing lawyers, with the help of her Uncle Manny, a criminal lawyer. At a party for Julie's stepmother, who had just received her doctorate, I approached Manny to ask for his opinion and for direction. As soon as I told him what had happened, his eyes lit open as if he'd been hit with a jolt of electricity. He was nervous, too. Although I could see him trying to keep his cool as he managed to say, "Stay strong for your family." Those five words carried me through more misery and anxiety than I'd expected to handle in an entire lifetime.

Manny passed along names of lawyers to interview, and when we followed up with them, they offered a mix of advice. One said the key issue was who signed what documents. Another lawyer laughed when I said, "This was not a scheme but a misunderstanding. The truth is, there was no intention to defraud or hurt anyone."

That lawyer responded with stark words. "This is not about the truth." He spoke as if I was a naive child living in a dream world.

Finally, we spoke to Tom Bradley, a lawyer who had been in the business for more than forty years and came highly recommended by Uncle Manny. Tom was a no-nonsense guy. He explained the facts, and they weren't good.

First, Julie and I were both going to be indicted for mortgage fraud. This, he told us, was 100% certain. Next, we were both going to prison. That also was 100% certain.

Confusing. Why was he so sure? After all, we had the right to a trial—to tell our story. Why was he certain we'd go to prison when there was no intention to defraud? What was I missing here?

Tom didn't win any points with Julie and me. When he asked Julie how much money we had saved from our "scheme," she answered, none.

He lost his temper and cried out, "Don't lie to me!"

"Zero dollars," Julie repeated. That was true, since we spent the profits on mortgage payments and fixtures for the buyers.

This time, he calmed down and set his face in a Denny frown, which told us nothing and wasn't reassuring. But we decided to hire Tom, because Julie's uncle said he was the best.

Our first move was to meet with the FBI agents reviewing our case. The FBI set up a meeting with us, which stipulated that we couldn't talk, just listen. We consented and agreed upon a date.


## The conspiracy


When we arrived at the United States Attorney's office, we were greeted by the same female agent that had run things the day the FBI met us at my office. She didn't have a gun now, and her hair was down. She smiled and shook my hand. Then she turned to Julie and said, "I'm so sorry, Julie."

What did that mean? Why was she apologizing to Julie?

We all sat around a table with other FBI agents and our prosecutor, Mr. Ruttles, a bald guy in his mid-fifties or so. Frankly, he brought to mind the judges on all those Nazi documentaries about the trial of the Valkyrie conspirators, the men who attempted the assassination of Adolf Hitler. They were on trial, in a Kangaroo Court—you know, a court in which all the defendants had their belts taken away, so their pants would fall down.

Ruttles told us he knew about the deal with our lawyer to remain silent. With that, he laid two loan applications on the table. Both applications were customers of Michael Nash at what I'm calling the XYZ Mortgage Co. (who was a broker I'd told my buyers to go to for their loans). The next paper we saw was the buyer's bank statement showing that the down payment amount had never existed in their account. Then, Ruttles showed a VOD (verification of deposit), which verified a deposit coming out of these two borrowers accounts. The numbers didn't jive, Ruttles explained, saying, "This is bank fraud."

Ruttles showed Julie and me a copy of the buyer's W-2 Form. The income on the loan statement Ruttles showed us did not equal the income on the buyer's

W-2. The incongruence between the figures appeared fraudulent, true enough, but I didn't understand why he was showing this to us. We were the sellers, not the mortgage brokers. In other words, we had nothing to do with this transaction, so Julie and I had no responsibility for these documents.

Then, Ruttles showed us the HUD statement. Speaking directly to Julie, he said, "HUD says money from borrower where the down payment is listed, but, the money came from the real estate, and was drawn on your bank. As you know, Mrs. Keith, the seller cannot supply the down payment. This is an illegal act and it is bank fraud."

The Feds were correct. It was true that in the past, it was illegal for a seller to pay the buyer's down payment. However, as far as we knew, the broker was using a new loan program that allowed the down payment to come from anyone. Julie brought a certified check to the closing and handed it to the closing agent. Julie told the closing agent that this was our company check and we were giving it to the buyer for their down payment. In addition, everyone at the title company was able to see that each time we closed a loan, the buyer used a check from the same bank. The chances of 300 buyers all banking at the same bank is impossible. (Julie brought in a cashier's check from our company feeling confident she was doing nothing wrong by placing the down payment for the buyer. The broker said he was using a program that allowed the seller to place the down payment.)

When there was an overage from the estimated down payment, Julie asked for it because it was her money. What idiot would divulge all of this incriminating information to the title company which is supposed to protect the bank's interest? If the broker was lying about the bank program he used for my buyer, how did the unseasoned and unsourced loan get through the title company? Or for that matter, the bank itself? If the down payment was handled incorrectly, why didn't the title company or bank tell Julie there was a problem with closing the loan?

If a seller wants to fraudulently give the down payment to the buyer, he would deposit cash into his buyer's account so there would be no paper trail of this deposit ever being made by the seller. However, in our case, nothing was concealed, and it was all transparent to the title company.

Next, Ruttles played a tape of the appraiser asking me questions at a lunch meeting. By the time we met with Ruttles, I'd learned that the appraiser, Jim Hayman, was helping the Feds make a case against Julie and me. Hearing the tape, I recalled the lunch meeting in which Jim asked me leading questions about putting fixtures in after the closing. Jim also spoke about taking interior photos of finished houses and not photos of the subject property.

"You lied to the bank," Ruttles said, "and this is called mortgage fraud."

The accusations Ruttles made about the numbers not jiving on the mortgage application and the bank account didn't concern us. It meant only that information listed on mortgage applications by the mortgage broker was falsely inflated so the buyer could get the loan. We had no knowledge of any of this. However, this one accusation was true: I had been installing fixtures after closing. I would have admitted to this and explained about the theft issues I endured in Englewood, but my attorney told us to keep quiet. My explanations would have to wait.

As the meeting went on, I was dying to ask the prosecutor questions. What were we doing here? Where was the mortgage broker? Why are we being blamed for his paperwork with his borrower? As the seller, I was not allowed to be privy to any of this information. A seller can't know any financial information about his buyer from the broker or bank. That's against the privacy laws, so there was no way I could have known any of this was going on. If we had known this program was illegal, we certainly wouldn't have flashed everything in front of the title company and the banks. That would have been like asking a cop to watch you rob a bank. But, Julie and I were not supposed to say a word. It was like a stupid game designed to frustrate us.

I grew angrier by the minute, but Ruttles insisted he had us dead to rights, and if we wanted to keep our prison time to a minimum, we had better step up and help them indict Les Raymond of the title company we used. If not, we would be going away for a very long time.

When Julie and I exchanged a glance, we were thinking the same thing. Not only did we not know what Raymond had done, we weren't aware of anything we'd done that linked us to any of this. What I hadn't learned yet is that the Feds have something called conspiracy. It's a magical instrument for them. They wave it in the courtroom and presto, they don't need any evidence to convict, just a story that can possibly tie the defendants together. As you'll see, this "instrument" is powerful in today's justice system.

Ruttles then threatened us again. "If you don't cooperate with us to get Raymond, we'll put you at the head of the scheme."

Ruttles was finished and so were we.

When the Feds left us alone in the room, Tom said, "I think it would be wise for you both to accept a plea agreement."

I looked at Tom, and I thought he was nuts for saying such a thing. Hadn't he read my letters to him or heard *anything* I said in our office meetings? He was ready to give up at the drop of a hat. I was disgusted. I couldn't believe how fast he sold us down the river. We left the meeting and went home.

Feeling helpless, Julie and I wondered how we'd fight the United States Government. The entire ordeal was frightening. We were in for a long, hard fight that would cost money we didn't have. On the other hand, the government had unlimited resources on its side.

Later, when we sat alone in our library, Julie was pale with stress. Neither of us could possibly begin to express our feelings. Finally, I looked up at her, pleading, "You're a lawyer. What's going on here?"

She looked at me, her eyes soft. "You're kidding, right? What's going on here?" Her tone turned serious when she added, "I have absolutely *no* idea what is happening here."

As hard as the situation was for me, it was even harder for Julie. It was my real estate company and my program. Julie was involved only in the closings. As far as the HUD statement and the down payment issue, Julie had no reason to believe the bank program was incorrect, since the title company and bank kept closing the deals.

Uncle Manny's words hung heavy on my mind and in my heart. "Stay strong for your family!" That's the moment I decided to put every drop of energy into researching mortgage fraud and the facts of our case. I started by firing Tom, our attorney, whose only advice was to cut our losses and help the Feds. If he'd listened to my story, he'd have come to a different conclusion. It seemed he was helping the Feds, not us. I wanted a lawyer who wasn't afraid to fight for what was right. A lawyer who would go all the way and never stop fighting.

Although I didn't know it at the time, I was being an idiot.


**Finding the right lawyer**


In our Federal justice system, defendants lose 98% of the time. If you're lucky enough to win, the Feds try to get you on another charge. If they don't get you right away, they have the right to keep trying until they win or an entire jury votes against the Feds and with the defendant. Good luck.

Intention doesn't mean much, either, and we had no intention of defrauding anyone.

1.     The title company (Raymond) was aware of Julie providing the down payment for the buyer. Whenever there was an overage due back from the down payment, Julie asked the closer to make the check out to her personally. This would constitute self-incrimination if Julie were intentionally hiding the source of funds.
2.     We had samples of bank programs and matrices showing the down payment could originate from anyone. No source. No seasoning.
3.     The funds for down payments did not need to remain in any bank account for a specified period of time. Hence, no seasoning of funds. Usually banks frown upon large deposits being shown for short periods of time, and then used for a down payment. This program allowed for it.
4.     The seller's attorney is not liable for the buyer's side of the HUD.
5.     There were other attorneys at each closing that could have questioned the program.
6.     The down payment checks were all written on our bank. How could every customer use one bank? How could they *all* use our bank? With the new Patriot Act laws, one would have to have an account in the bank to obtain a certified check for a down payment. None of our customers had an account at our bank. Why didn't the title company closer question the fact that all the down payment checks were written from the same bank?
7.     Regarding the issue of finishing the property after the closing, I was very open on this fact. My contract stated that if the property was not finished before closing, I would be responsible for the monthly mortgage payments. This would lead the bank to see there would be a possibility of the fixtures being installed post-closing.
8.     The type of insurance demanded by the bank was Homeowners Insurance. My insurance was called Builders Risk (a type of insurance used for unfinished buildings). This should have sent up red flags to the bank that the property was not finished at closing.

9. The *Chicago Sun-Times* carried advertisements every day offering competitive programs to mine.

10. I had cancelled checks totaling $5.5 million in construction costs. I had $1 million in mortgage payments paid to the various banks because the houses were not 100% finished at the closing. This would prove no intention to defraud banks.

I fired our attorney because he didn't consider the facts that I gathered in order to show that we had not intentionally done anything wrong. Only later did I come to realize Tom's advice was correct.

Meanwhile, Julie called her father, Freddy, to discuss finances and tell him we were in the process of finding another attorney. Freddy was committed to helping us and offered to help us pay for the best attorney we could find. My father-in-law never wavered in his belief in us.

My father-in-law is a doctor/inventor, mostly inventing various medical devices, and was called the resident genius in the family. Back in the 1970s, he was featured in the *Wall Street Journal* for inventing the transmission of the EKG through phone wires. He also developed the software which made it possible for the machine to explain the findings instead of the doctor having to decipher them himself. Fortunately, he had the means to offer unconditional help to Julie and me, and his kindness opened doors I couldn't have opened on my own. After all that happened in the real estate market all over the country, my business was no longer financially sound.

**All by myself**

At some point, Julie fell into denial. The stress of imagining not being able to see our kids if we went to prison, being labeled as a crook, losing our house and savings, along with wanting to strangle me for getting her mixed up in this mess was too much for her to cope with, at least at that time. That left me to go it alone, starting with choosing an attorney.

I received referrals from various friends and I looked for characteristics and expertise I thought would help our case, but it was difficult to find an attorney with knowledge of criminal mortgage fraud. Subprime lending, a relatively new concept, had started in the 1990s when President Clinton tried to make the "American dream" of owning a home achievable to everyone. With subprime lending, mortgage brokers and the borrowers didn't have to prove things like income and employment, or show where the down payment came from or bank account information. All they had to do was state the information. These were nicknamed liar loans and stated loans.

These newer guidelines led to everyone jumping on the bandwagon, but somehow, the banks created these predatory bank programs without the FDIC and the Treasury Department being fully aware of what was happening. Or, so they made it seem. Then, when the agencies became aware of subprime, they went ballistic when they realized what had been going on.

The Feds considered almost everything the banks were doing in the subprime market as fraud. Prior to subprime lending, it had been illegal to approve a loan without pay stubs or income tax returns. Prior to subprime lending, it was unheard of to lend money without checking out the borrower's job. It was unheard of for a bank to ask how much the borrower had in the bank without verifying the information. But, when the bubble burst, the Feds didn't look to the banks, but went after everyone else instead. They looked at Julie and me as if we masterminded all these subprime programs. I was just a seller, not even a real estate agent.

Julie and I were telling and showing everything we were doing to everyone in the mortgage chain. The buyer had my contract, the broker had my contract, and the bank had my contract, too—either from the broker or the buyer. The bank even went out and did a field review where they went inside the house and saw there were no fixtures installed. Why did it take the Feds' prying to stop my business? And why did they let me run my program for years if they thought I was defrauding my buyers?

I needed to determine if attorneys I interviewed would admit their lack of knowledge about mortgage fraud. It also was important to see how early in the meeting attorneys brought up their fees. If they started the meeting with their fees, then I sensed that's what would guide their efforts. I also tried to determine which attorneys were fighters and who were not.

Through all of this, I still found it difficult to explain exactly what the FBI told us we did wrong. That meant finding out if the attorneys could follow the threads of the story. Of course, I asked about their successes with whatever crimes they'd defended. I was curious about their opinions of the Feds and the climate at the Justice Department. Finally, could they keep us from going to prison? I never got a straight answer on what their win ratio was. Later I found out why. Their win percentage was all of 2%.

Sherry and Gary Trains had been two of my best friends ever since they moved next door. The Trains were lifelines to me during the time the Feds made my life miserable, and I visited them often. They referred me to the attorney we ultimately hired, Dan Purdom.

Once Dan learned as much as I knew about our case to that point, he said time was of the essence and we needed to stop any indictment process. He wanted to concentrate all of his efforts on that issue. What really sold me was the value he put on freedom and family, calling both priceless.

Also, Dan was honest in saying that if the indictment went through, we had a 98% chance of going to prison. It's weird that even with that slim chance of beating the system, I still thought we'd at least try, logical or not. However, realizing my chances were slim, I supported Dan's idea to kill the indictment, whereas our previous lawyer wanted to wait for an indictment so we'd know the direction to take.

Dan wanted to act *now*. I was impressed by his salesmanship. He knew all the right things to say. If my wife and I were going to prison if we were indicted, why not try and stop the indictment? I hired him immediately.

Although interviewing lawyers was one of the most important things I did, it was an ordeal and took a devastating emotional toll. By this point, Julie and I were dealing very differently with the crisis that hit our family. Even the possibility of being taken away from our children had caused Julie to emotionally shut down. When we were faced with these legal problems, Julie was so freaked out she believed she could will this nightmare away. On the other hand, was I running so fast with all my might because I thought hard work and long hours would make it go away?

Dan wanted Julie involved, but it was no use. Julie could have brought a lot to the table, because she knew the issues involved in the charges we faced. But the more I begged her to help, the angrier she got. She didn't read reports I sent to Dan, and if I waited until midnight to ask her, sometimes she'd agree to read them in the morning. Maybe she would follow through, maybe she wouldn't.

This was a nightmarish time, with me up working late, shouldering the weight of blame for what had happened. True, I wasn't guilty of intentional wrongdoing, but I was the operator of the business, and Julie was the closing attorney. It was a part-time job, and her other work was being a stay-at-home mom and a volunteer, not involved nor interested in the details of my business. To say Julie isn't greedy is an understatement. She preferred her charity work to earning money, so the FBI was really stretching when they went after her.

In the middle of all this, Robert, a very close and dear friend, was losing his company to bankruptcy. He would come over and talk to me about another friend of ours who wanted to buy Robert's business for a song. If the company made a certain amount of profit, Robert would benefit with a small percentage of it. During the due diligence period, our friend learned the landlord was kicking Robert out of the office because of non-payment. This crushed the deal.

Robert's family and my family were close. Our little girls had grown up together, and even had their bat mitzvahs together. Our wives were closer than sisters. I felt compelled to help. This situation came at a good time, because I needed a job to support us since my company had been shut down.

Meanwhile, it was difficult to see Robert losing his house and his business and now riding a bicycle to work. Seeing him on the bike broke my heart so I lent him a car for six months so he could get around. Then, I introduced him to a friend who could help keep him from complete financial ruin by using a type of bankruptcy used in business.

After reviewing Robert's financials, I determined his company needed a good salesman who could work with Robert and the floundering company and supply a shot in the arm. So while all this was going on between the Feds and me, I was trying to concentrate on building up a company from the ground floor. It was hard to concentrate, although looking back, I helped Robert reach monthly sales figures never seen before. Not bad for a person trying to tread water in a criminal investigation.

One day, a Federal agent came to our office and I told the receptionist to let him in to my office, which was inside Robert's suite. I was surprised to find out that the agent was there to see Robert about a case he had before I came to the company. Robert apologized for scaring the wits out of me.

While I was trying to build back a company, I also had to deal with our crisis. I had no alternative but to be a lawyer and businessman while helping Dan help us. My mission was to save Julie's life-as-she-knew-it and preserve our children's well-being and at the same time grow a successful business. But could I pull it off? I had to teach myself what I needed to know in order to direct my lawyer.

I'd never needed to turn to God for help more. If He would direct me and give me the strength, I would work until I dropped. Not that I'd been a religious man before, although I believe in God, had a bar mitzvah, and went to temple on the high holy days. That was the extent of it. But I learned, like many people do, the irony of turning to God when we're in serious trouble.

With Dan in place as my attorney, I started learning everything I could about mortgage fraud. During this time, I was very fortunate to have Steve, another close friend who knew a lot about financial law and came with me when I met with Dan.

As I've said, the principle of "innocent until proven guilty" doesn't match the reality we faced. As the accused, Julie and I had to prove our innocence. On the Federal level, the burden of guilt doesn't really rest with the prosecution, and it's not easy to prove a negative—as in, "I didn't do" whatever the charge is. The need to prove my innocence was endlessly frustrating. I soon found out that facts positive for the defense can—and will—be spun by the prosecution to take on a negative meaning.


**Is this on?**


Most every criminal case has snitches who wear a wire—there're not just devices on TV shows. In my case, the appraiser wore a wire. The problem with a wire is that everything said on it tends to sound incriminating. The things said on the tape can take on many different meanings, and wires don't pick up body language, including facial expressions. Without body language cues, it's difficult to tell if the words and true meaning match.

Nodding or a simple spoken "Yeah," may send the

wrong signal on tape, not to mention that the way a question is asked may be intended to confuse the targeted person. Confusion tends to sound negative. Even a question can end up being incriminating, because a long answer can sound like a lie just because it is lengthy. The "air" or silence between questions can take on a negative connotation. The shock to the defendant upon hearing a question and then answering it may convey a negative tone to a jury listening to the recording.

Dan and the others on my legal team spent many hours discussing the meaning behind each recorded statement. I was certain about one thing: the real meaning will be spun by the Feds during trial to suit their intention.

Again, it's a scary reality that 98% of Federal indictments result in convictions. From our first meeting, Dan always brought up the possibility of prison for Julie and me. We were attacking the problem on the indictment end, as in avoiding it, because by this time, I knew that to exercise our right to a trial was an act of insanity. That's one reason the conviction rate is so high.


**Beliefs die hard**


It's difficult to give up the belief that we in the U.S. can always get our day in court. If we're wrongly convicted, we'll surely get another day in court. But it's not true. Your lawyer and the Feds will tell you this: if you dare go to trial, and waste the good people of the United States' time and money, and *are* convicted, you will be incarcerated not only for two to four times the length of time, but sometimes in a higher security prison than if you plea.

There you have it—and in the starkest of terms. That's the reality of our twenty-first century courts.

When I first became aware I'd landed right in the

Feds' radar, I held onto the belief that I'd be able to make everything okay. I counted on having my day in court to explain the truth and reasons for the confusion, and then go home to my family.

Sadly, in reality, after an indictment, no opportunity exists to tell the prosecutor or the judge *anything*. As a matter of fact, the first things lawyers do is swear their new clients to secrecy. And they mean it.

Once someone is indicted, the government has already spent money on the case. So, once expenditures have been made, the person is condemned. Astoundingly, it takes relatively no effort to indict someone. You've no doubt heard the common adage of TV lawyers say, "Prosecutors can indict a ham sandwich." Could be it's true, because the indictment proceedings don't include representation for the defendant. The prosecution states their case, and that's it!

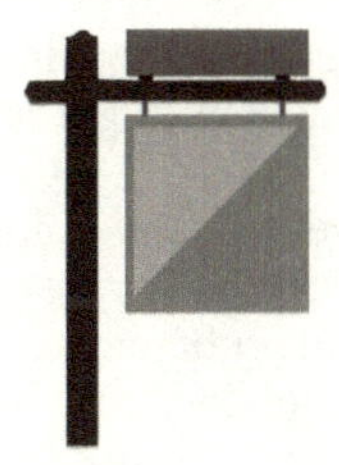

# Chapter Five

## Indicted, Tried, and Done

I was at home playing with our golden retriever pup when Dan called and gave me the news. Despite his efforts of explaining the truth to the prosecutor and his boss and how Julie had nothing to do with the running of the business, Julie and I would soon be indicted. My heart sank. Somehow, I never imagined this would *actually happen.*

With heavy hearts, Julie and I decided we needed to tell the girls. They'd already been affected by our troubles, anyway. Our thirteen-year-old, Jackie, had recently come home from school and asked why a kid at school ragged her with, "Your parents are going to jail for thirty years!" Julie brushed it off as a ridiculous rumor. Sometimes, parents don't use their brains when they open their mouths.

In as convincing a tone we could manage, we told Jackie and Danielle that because we were innocent of any intentional wrongdoing, we would be acquitted of all charges. We desperately *wanted* it to be true. Both girls believed us, but that also sparked their interest in our case.

As I looked for helpful information online, the girls continued to ask questions about the case, always wanting reassurance that everything would be all right.

And then, things began to get interesting—and not in a good way.

Since the Feds were finally going to indict us, they had to reveal the counts against us and what they entailed. Prior to our indictments, Prosecutor Ruttles grimly notified Julie and me by saying, "You're cooked!" We were going to prison for a long time, he maintained, but if we helped get the title company we could help ourselves. Apparently, this was considered good news. We had some idea about this "good news," but we had to be sure. This prosecutor provided a rough outline of why he expected we'd go to prison.

1. I'd told buyers not to bring a lawyer to the closing. (In fact, there were closings with the buyers' lawyers present.)

2. I never finished rehabbing the houses.

3. Teaching the brokers how to falsify bank documents.

4. Money laundering.

5. Manipulating bank programs to fit my buyer, so the buyer could purchase the house.

6. Falsifying values of houses.

Ruttles cited these things, but never offered evidence to prove the allegations. I spent countless nights, well into the wee hours of the morning, trying to prove Julie's innocence. At one point, I told Dan that everything Julie did, she did with the full knowledge of the title company. This meant Julie was open and honest with the title company when acting with the bank's agent. Upon hearing this, instead of dropping charges against Julie and me, Ruttles went after the vice president of the title company and threw her under the same bus. Instead of seeing that what happened was not a plot against the bank, they just pretended our alibi was also a crook. You can't win with these guys.

On one occasion, Ruttles told Dan that I took the banks to the cleaners and then ran the hell out of town. Ruttles claimed I thought I could run far away and get away with it.

Immediately, Dan pointed out that I was so consumed with the fact I had to pay my friends and family back that I was still writing mortgage payments and replacing fixtures right up until the time I got arrested. Dan said, "Richard Keith  never ran anywhere. He would have kept rehabbing and buying buildings in Englewood until he dropped.

When hearing this, Ruttles exclaimed, "Well, then he was so greedy he never would have stopped the fraud scheme unless we stopped him."

What he failed to mention is that he let me go on and on doing these so-called terrible things for years while he gathered his evidence.

When Ruttles found out that my contract stated the house would not be finished until after the closing, he insisted that it was all part of my scheme. When the FBI closed in, he said Richard Keith would be able to offer up the contracts and use them to protect himself.

This is our justice department.

Our indictment included 22 counts of wire fraud. The counts ranged from money laundering, faking bank deposits, placing fraudulent down payments on behalf of borrowers, and helping to falsify information on the loan applications. Ninety percent of the counts were referring to duties of a mortgage broker, *not the seller.* The main counts charged were related to finishing the building *after* the closing. Julie was charged for giving the buyer the down payment.

## To plea or not to plea, that is the question

Julie is a determined individual who believes in truth and justice. There was no chance she would plead guilty, because she thought pleading guilty would constitute lying to the judge. If you did not commit a crime and you say under oath that you did, you're lying under oath. Our attorney, Dan, agreed. Julie should go to trial. He still couldn't believe the government was going after her in the first place. However, Julie's Uncle Manny begged with Julie to plead guilty. He was concerned about the risk of the jury not understanding the case, which meant the Feds would spin facts and evidence to sway the jury into a conviction. The government also had deeper pockets.

It all came to naught. Not even Uncle Manny could move Julie. She was going to trial. Man, she was so stubborn. You could not talk her out of it.

Prosecutor Ruttles seemed to think Julie and I were like a Bonnie & Clyde team, but I was the worst. Since I was more involved in the business, I believed Julie had a better chance of an acquittal, which meant the girls wouldn't lose their mother. That's what made me decide, with trepidation, to plead guilty. It seemed the only way to minimize the damage to our lives.

So, I pled guilty to installing the fixtures after the closing and giving the buyer a down payment. Later, I found out my plea involved admitting to a lot more than I thought. Apparently, you can't just pick the part of the crime you agree pertained to you. You have to fall on your sword for the entire complaint. If I didn't plead guilty, Julie's chances of winning would have been even worse.

## Julie's trial

The courtroom was much larger than any traffic court I'd seen. Twelve seats for the twelve jurors were on one side, and there was room for forty or so observers in the back. The broad and imposing judge's bench dominated the front of the room.

Everyone was quiet.

Ruttles entered the courtroom like he owned it. He walked past Julie and me and sat to the right of the judge's bench and closer than Julie to the jury. Dan sat with Julie farther away from the jury on the left side of the judge. Being a lawyer herself, Julie appeared confident and calm, as did Dan's assistant, Brian, whose briefcase held the mountain of documents required for our trial. Everyone was shuffling papers and talking to their respective teams.

Before the trial, the FBI had transferred 100,000 documents to Dan. There were also files they'd scanned into their computers when the FBI agents raided my office. When the Feds give you their evidence, they throw so much at you it can't possibly be deciphered.

Judge Conners, a tall, middle-aged man, began explaining the workings of his courtroom and then introduced Julie's case. My thoughts were focused on the reality that this man possessed the power to change our lives for the better or worse. I wasn't even certain he would understand the charges in our case.

As for the jury, I had no hope of them understanding the inside look at subprime lending, a fairly recent way of borrowing from a bank. Even the courts had little information about it. The crime I supposedly committed was done in an arena so new there were no set precedents yet.

Scanning the courtroom, I spotted Ms. Wilkton, a schoolteacher who'd wanted to subsidize her income with real estate investing. She bought a two-story frame house on Woodlawn Avenue that my general contractor had remodeled. A quality rehab, I'd thought of it as my trophy house. Wilkton wanted special details done for her, and because she was relentless in her requests, the contractor had given her what she wanted. However, a roof leak occurred and Wilkton demanded the entire roof be replaced. I refused to do that, and she wrote me a letter stating the quality of workmanship on this house was inferior.

When Wilkton took the stand, the trial started. Ruttles began his direct examination and let her speak at length about the terrible quality of the construction of her house. She elaborated, saying I was difficult to deal with, and she couldn't get tenants to rent because it looked so terrible. Suddenly, she began to cry like she was being stabbed by a knife and went on about her life being over because of this ordeal.

On cross-examination, Dan asked what she did for employment. She said she was a schoolteacher and mentioned some other jobs. Dan asked her if she was leaving anything out and she said no.

Then, Dan asked, "What about being an actress?"

She blushed and said nothing. Dan thought it was quite a coincidence that she was crying profusely and forgot to admit she was also a trained actress.

The next witness told the same kind of story about me. She said Julie passed the down payment check under the table to the title company representative, acting like she was doing something sneaky. And so, it went.

Dan presented the closing documents as exhibit A. He showed the judge the date of closing and then handed the documents to Ms. Pickens. Did the date of the closing match what appeared on the documents? She agreed it was the correct date. Dan explained that Julie Keith was not available on this date to close, so she wasn't there at the closing in question.

"Why did you lie to the court?" Dan asked, repeating the observation about passing papers under the table when Julie wasn't even present.

Dan asked the judge for a mistrial because so far both witnesses had lied, but the judge turned him down.

Another witness, Mark Largo, claimed I never gave him enough money to do a good quality job on the houses he rehabbed for me. He never mentioned on the stand that he'd told the Feds that he took some of the funds I gave him and spent it on his own houses. He did admit this in the meeting he had with the Feds, but it never came out on the stand.

When Dan was walking away from the bench, Mark also suddenly blurted that Julie knew everything and was part of the "scheme."

Dan asked Mark if the Feds told him to say that—the statements were that far out. It was obvious he was told to get that out into the courtroom. It would have sounded better if he'd patiently waited until the subject arose, instead of blurting it out in the courtroom for no apparent reason. The judge just allowed this circus to go on.

The government's expert banking witness testified next. After dispensing with the questions about credentials, Ruttles asked, "Have you ever heard of a program that would let a seller provide a down payment for the buyer without a gift letter?"

The witness considered his words and said, "No, not where the seller can gift it without a gift letter."

When it was Dan's turn, he asked the witness again to verify he'd worked for the same bank for 30 years, and the witness said that was true. He then asked the name of the bank, and the witness indicated he'd worked for Countrywide. (A bank implicated in the mortgage crisis, and ultimately, became unviable as a business and was sold.)

Dan then said, "You told Mr. Ruttles that you never heard of a program that would allow the seller to gift the down payment to the buyer without a gift letter, correct?"

"Correct," he answered again.

"And so, Mr. Keith would be committing fraud if he gave the down payment as the seller to the buyer without a gift letter, correct?"

"I guess so," the witness replied.

"What if I told you there was a subprime program that allows the seller to gift the down payment without a gift letter?"

Looking down, the witness said, "I would say that's impossible."

Dan handed a document to the judge and asked it to be entered as an exhibit. He then asked the witness to read it aloud.

The witness began reading the document about a program that offered no sourcing or seasoning of funds, which contradicted his testimony.

This meant Dan had the basis to get the witness to admit ignorance of these programs and admit he'd testified in error. The witness admitted not having worked with sub-prime lending.

"But, you were eager to say what the Feds told you to say," Dan challenged, "and thus, send an innocent person to prison."

"Well, I never heard of this no source, no seasoning program before."

Dan pointed at the document and said, "Tell the jury the name of the bank that offered this program."

The witness turned pale and then under his breath he said, "The name of the bank is Countywide."

"Louder, please."

This time he said it louder. "Countrywide Bank."

"No further questions," Dan said.

And so, it went.

This exchange was an example of the lies the witnesses told while the judge sat and listened.

Finally, one of the Feds who showed up at my office on the first day got up in front of the courtroom and started reciting the Hud1, which is a standard form used to itemize services and fees the lender charges to the borrower when applying for a loan to purchase real estate. She read about 15 HUDS to the courtroom.

This portion of the trial focused on the down payment funds, with the Feds trying to show how the down payment was listed as coming from the borrower but actually provided by the seller. Dan proved to the court that there was a program that let the seller give the down payment for the buyer, but the FBI agent kept harping about the HUD. It seemed the Federal agents, who then testified, couldn't or wouldn't believe there was such a program under sub-prime lending.

I came to understand that if the Feds say it's illegal, *it's illegal*. If a defendant gets a loan by doing what a bank says to do and the Feds say the bank is wrong, they can place the defendant in prison without the bank. In other words, following directions can end up being doing something illegal. Then, the Feds take you away and leave the banker to his job.

During this financial/housing crisis, few bankers went to prison and they were the ones reviewing their own programs—the fox watched the hen house.


## We'll get you


Our friends in the courtroom were hopeful about the jury's decision, and we all thought Dan had done a superb job of discrediting the Fed's witnesses. No compelling evidence existed that portrayed Julie as doing anything wrong when she gave the down payment check to the buyer. The title company saw that all the checks were drawn on the same bank, the bank I used for my business, K&L Real Estate.

The loan program used was one that allowed anyone to provide the down payment to the buyer. The fact the Feds said it was placed on the HUD incorrectly was not Julie's responsibility. Julie was responsible only for the seller's side of the HUD. In other words, Julie did not have a fiduciary duty to the buyer. She didn't represent the buyer, nor should she have given advice to them. She couldn't be held liable for any of the false statements on the loan application, since, as closing attorney, she was not involved in the loan process. Many of the buyers came with lawyers who sat there, allowing the loan to close.

But, we remembered that despite exculpatory evidence, 98% of the people who are federally indicted go to prison.

During jury deliberations, my two older sons were at work and our two girls were staying with Julie's mother. Waiting all day for a verdict was a nightmare, but no matter what happened, Julie was true to herself—what she thought was right and went to trial against the powerful Feds. I was proud of her, even though if she went to prison, I would never forgive myself. I would never be able to sleep again. Every time I saw my daughters, I'd be laden with the guilt of putting their mother in prison.

After about two hours the jury came back to the courtroom and said they couldn't reach a verdict. Eleven jurors had one verdict, the twelfth did not.

Later, Julie told me she was so angry with this juror she could have screamed out loud in the courtroom—until she learned the rest of the story. We understood then that the majority of jurors believed Julie was guilty, and one dissenting juror held out for not guilty. We couldn't believe what we heard. What persuaded the jurors to vote against Julie? Certainly, they could not base this opinion on the evidence presented in her trial. We were in shock.

The judge also looked surprised and directed the one juror not to succumb to the pressure of the other eleven. He gave the jury another three hours to deliberate. We stood in the outside hall room for another three hours. It felt like three weeks!

When the law promises a trial decided by a jury of one's peers, the outcome is not what most expect. First, the jury consists of people, most of whom don't want to be there. They are required to serve on a jury as part of their civic duty. The longer the trial, the more frustrated the jurors become. A trial might be so lengthy and tiresome that jurors mentally drift far away from the courtroom. Or, a juror could be hostile to a defendant simply because the juror is missing work and blames the defendant.

If a case is quite complex, there's a risk a juror could make an irrational decision simply out of frustration. Jurors have convicted defendants based on their shoes or suit, facial expressions, financial condition, or race.

Pretend for a second that you had a heated argument with a person because you accidently bumped their car. Now pretend that same person is sitting on a jury that is going to decide if you go to prison. Sitting on a jury and deciding the truth is difficult. Sitting on a jury when hungry, tired, and frustrated because the case you are there to try is impossible to understand is extremely difficult.

Julie's trial turned out to be complex.

At first, even Dan needed a long time to get a feel for it. Issues, such as a buyer not having to prove assets and liabilities, were new concepts adopted by banks to create no-asset programs for high credit borrowers.

Not listing or proving income was also a new and risky concept. However, a juror could get the wrong idea about lax practices banks created and put the blame on the defendant. In Julie's case, this was exactly the Fed's position.

Finally, the jury returned to the courtroom. The judge again asked if the jury had reached a unanimous verdict. Angry, the foreman said, "No, your honor. This one juror won't follow the directions we were given."

The judge immediately called this a hung jury.

Ruttles looked at Julie and hissed, "There will be a second trial!" He was very upset with the outcome.

I don't blame him. The percentage of wins for the prosecution is 98%. Ruttles just lost a conviction and the case fell into the 2%. Ruttles and his entourage stormed out of the courtroom. He was coming after me next, and that didn't sit well with me. I couldn't keep from turning to Julie, and quoting the wicked witch from *The Wizard of Oz*.

Dan was glad for a hung jury but upset the jury hadn't returned with a not guilty verdict. The trial had gone perfectly, and he still didn't get the good news he wanted.

Julie and I drove home in shock. We had to tell the kids what happened and that was not easy. I couldn't understand why the prosecution wanted to go to trial with Julie all over again. Apparently, Dan had told them she would be difficult to convict but they didn't listen. With a 98% batting average, they don't have to listen. They just keep winning and if they have a hung jury, they go to trial again with the next time the odds being even higher than 98%.

But now the Feds knew the defense strategy Dan would use in court. It would be impossible to win.

For the whole two weeks between the trials, I pestered Julie with my questions about what average citizens do and don't understand. Do people really know how close they are to a prison sentence? Our family was so upset. Julie's parents didn't know what to say to her.

Most of the time, Julie had a blank look on her face. It hurt me that she was finding out the hard way that it was not about the truth. Like most lawyers, she believed in the system and the system had bitten her right on the ass.

The hung jury was a miracle, but now we had to go back to court with the same defense and worse odds. It was scary.

Julie's Uncle Manny was freaking out. He felt so bad for Julie and the kids, and for his brother Freddy, Julie's dad. At night, when we went to bed, Julie stared at the ceiling, but I was on so much hydrocodone acetaminophen I fell right to sleep.


**"Julie gets benched"**


After a few weeks went by, Dan decided to ask Ruttles if he would allow a bench trial, meaning having a judge rather than a jury decide a defendant's fate. At this point, Ruttles might have outfoxed himself. His assistant had been Judge Conner's legal clerk, which likely had something to do with Ruttles agreeing to Julie's request. He probably figured the judge would show him favor because of their relationship.

On the first day of the second trial, Conners was candid about his former position being Ruttles' clerk. I believe Ruttles still assumed the judge would show him favor. But Conners was a no-nonsense guy. He'd written books on the defense side of government cases, so he also knew the strategies the government played to Fin a conviction.

Dan wanted a bench trial because he feared no jury would understand the case. We now knew Conners understood the case. Otherwise, why would he urge the one juror to stick to his beliefs? He could have given the rest of the jury much more time to strong-arm this one juror. As it turned out, the fact that the prosecutor's assistant once had been the judge's law clerk for the judge probably pushed the judge further away from siding with the prosecution, as if proving he was being fair.

## A miracle!

According to the rules of the bench trial, the attorneys could use only the boundaries of the previous trial, meaning no new witnesses could be called. So, it was just like the last trial, but without the jury. Again, friends and family were in the courtroom but Julie decided not to bring the girls. Although our four sons, David, Mike, Gary, and Barry did attend.

The trial took place in a smaller courtroom. I was more relaxed, confident the judge understood the case. The judge began by saying Ruttles had handed him a plea agreement signed by the vice president of the title company saying she was aware Julie was doing wrong in each of the closings. But, because it was obtained at the last minute, Conners said he wouldn't allow it to influence him. Apparently, the Feds made a last ditch second deal with the V.P. of the closing company. If she signed a statement saying she knew Julie was fraudulent at the closings, they would let this VP off with a misdemeanor and not have a costly trial.

Julie's Uncle Manny was nervous. He told me Julie was in big trouble. "She'll be taken out the back door," he said, "and they'll hold her in a cell until she is transferred to Federal prison."

Shocked, I asked Manny why he would say such a thing.

"Because it's one chance out of a million that the judge lets her off," he said.

As if I hadn't been nervous enough before, Manny managed to make me even more afraid and stressed.

The judge began reading through all the charges the prosecutor threw at Julie, including HUD transactions, down payments, and bank loan closings. He read that my taped conversation described how worried Julie was about actions of the appraiser, Jim Hayman. He read there was no evidence of her being privy to any of the broker's information and no evidence of any wrongdoings between Julie and the title company.

The judge spoke for what felt like a week, but was just over forty minutes. In the courtroom itself, the only sound was the judge's voice; no one seemed to be breathing.

At one point, Uncle Manny grabbed my hand and squeezed so tight it hurt. My hand felt like putty. "He's going to let her go," he said. "I can't believe it. It's a miracle."

I had to mentally dissect every word the judge read to be ready for what came next. I'd never felt this anxious in my life. Could Uncle Manny be right? He was a criminal attorney after all, but how could he tell so early in the proceedings. The judge read with a no-nonsense, matter-of-fact voice. No apparent emotion.

The judge explained that Julie was not responsible to read each point on the HUD, since she only represented the seller. "We all are guilty of not reading the fine print on loan documents," he said. "I believe these banks were all fully aware of what part they played in the banking disaster that punched this country in the gut.

They were fully aware of what these predatory lending programs would do to the state of the economy!"

This judge got it. He knew this accusation was a masquerade. It made no sense that Julie could close 250 loans in which the HUDs were all falsified. Julie never hid the down payment from the title company.

Finally, Judge Conners said that there was a lack of evidence or proof beyond a reasonable doubt. He found Julie *not guilty.*

The courtroom filled with our family and friends erupted. People shot out of their seats laughing, screaming, tears flowing. Uncle Manny yelled, "It's a miracle!"

I quickly moved to embrace Julie, tears flowing of joy and immense relief. Such a ponderous weight had been lifted from my shoulders. I felt light and humbled, full of love for Julie and gratitude to God, who does miraculous things and provided an astute, honest judge.

Then, I ran to Dan and hugged the doggedly fatigued and radically relieved attorney. I could read on his face the heavy toll the previous verdict had taken, and now *he had won. He had beaten the odds.*

This verdict truly ranked as a miracle. Our attorney had done his job, explaining Julie's innocence. The judge was intelligent enough to understand the situation and put the blame squarely where it belonged—on greedy banks and loan officers.

Ruttles left in a huff with his team, again. Their expressions revealed their thinking: a terrible criminal had gotten away scot-free and would now go on to *further hurt innocent people.*

Now that the judge had declared Julie not guilty of any crime, I was fairly confident the same fate would be mine. After all, Julie is my wife and attorney. The judge would surely consider my situation with the same logic as he considered Julie's.

I thought about the time I'd spent at the computer, sending emails to Dan about the case. Dan would surely say he couldn't have done this without my help. I had read hundreds of articles referencing other cases and their outcomes. I had analyzed past bank programs, and the many predatory lending programs that took place under the subprime mortgage market. One of the banks programs, Stated Loans, got the nickname "Liar Loans" because of all the false information given to the banks after the borrowers learned they didn't have to substantiate their incomes. I'd worked hard to get across to Dan the greed the banks were exhibiting in the subprime marketplace. I had never been so determined to do something in my life. This was as important as life and death.

Next, it was my turn to learn my courtroom fate.

# Part II

# Chapter Six

## The Blind Plea

Relief about the outcome of Julie's trial was matched by the anxiety about my case. Despite Dan's negotiations with Ruttles for a plea agreement, the best deal he could get was dropping 23 of the 24 counts against me. I was elated—until I learned that this *single* count could still cost me 20 years imprisonment. In response to the offer, Dan demanded a blind plea, which is an agreement handed down directly from the judge. Dan believed this was my only option; it meant I'd appear before Judge Conners for sentencing.

Julie and I rode the train downtown for my hearing on a hot, sunny day. We took the train because the Black Hawks had won the Stanley Cup the night before, and we ran the risk of being caught up in the celebration traffic. But the train was delayed an hour, and Julie and I ended up racing to the courthouse and bursting inside. I was pretty much a wreck, breathing hard, with windblown hair, my suit wrinkled and tie undone.

Because we were so late, Judge Conners wasn't in the courtroom and we ended up waiting for him to come back, at which point he motioned for me to approach the bench.

He then read me the riot act, first about being late. If I was late again, he'd send out the U.S. Marshals to pick me up and throw me in jail. I didn't dare explain about the Black Hawks Fining the Stanley Cup and traffic was terrible.

Then, he began asking me questions that were blinded by the truth: did your attorney force you to enter into this plea? Are you aware you are waiving your right to a trial? Did anyone coerce you to plea? Do you understand if you believe you're not guilty and you plead guilty, you can go to prison? Are you aware you can't take back your plea? Do you understand I can give you probation or 20 years imprisonment?

These questions seemed ridiculous to me. Didn't the judge realize that if convicted by a jury of my peers, I'd get at least twice that number of years than if I pled and was found guilty? Why would the judge ask if my lawyer pushed me into this plea, when it was my lawyer who told me I'd be punished if I exercised my right to a trial. Even the one count of bank fraud could have put me away for the balance of my life.

Furthermore, I was still convinced a jury would have a hard time comprehending my case. The prosecutor had already sent my lawyer the written testimonies of witnesses he intended to call. I knew much of the testimony of Ruttles' witnesses amounted to perjury—they had lied. Some of these witnesses had already testified about issues not pertinent to the case. They'd say I advised buyers not to bring their lawyers to the closing, even though their lawyers had been there. The burden of proof is on the defendant. The more the Feds say, the more things you have to prove. They choke you with red tape.

One witness spent one hour talking about the poor workmanship of my contractor. That could have been true. It seems I was always arguing with my contractors about the quality of their workmanship. However, this had nothing to do with a Federal fraud case. (This testimony even had less to do with Julie's trial, but had been presented.) Besides, complaints about workmanship aren't Federal criminal matters, but are addressed in civil courts. If every time a buyer got into a fight with a contractor, someone was sent to prison, the prisons wouldn't have room for anyone else.

Standing in front of the judge and answering yes to his questions, I was given no opportunity to discuss these facts because I had felt forced to accept a blind plea. This is an example of our system not working, but rather, stacking the deck against the defendant. We are taught we're innocent until proven guilty, but that's not the reality today—as I'm sure you've heard. The burden of proof is on the defendant now, not the prosecution.


## This is serious


Eight months after Julie was found not guilty, it was time for me to go back to court again for sentencing. Given Julie's acquittal, I was certain that Judge Conners wouldn't give me any prison time. How could he? He told Julie there was no evidence of fraud in her case. Everyone in the courtroom had heard him say the banks were not innocent victims and had been aware of what they were doing to the real estate market with their predatory lending practices.

Nevertheless, my lawyer told me to be prepared to go to prison. I just couldn't bring myself to believe him and thought he was only preparing me for the worst. When the day came, my heart raced. I couldn't wait to get to the courthouse and be done with this nightmare. At 7:00 AM, we drove to the courthouse for a 9:30 court call. Those who had attended Julie's trial were there, along with all four of my kids. They were in good spirits and confident in a positive final result. After all, they knew Dad was no criminal and would not intentionally hurt anyone. They also saw me upstairs by the computer working until the wee hours of the night.

I had written a speech, approved by Dan, to recite to the judge. When Conners asked me to approach, I was in a fog as I attempted to walk to the bench. All the hard work staying up at night working at my computer, trying to educate Purdom and research bank fraud and how to prove my wife and I never tried to commit a scheme to defraud the banks flashed before my eyes.

The judge started out with this scary statement. "Mr. Keith, this is a very serious matter. You have not yet apologized to the people of the United States of America. I am sick and tired of everyone blaming the banks for the crisis that now exists in our country. You know what steps you took to fool the bank."

Was he serious? When was I supposed to apologize? I never got a chance to speak in the courtroom. Did the judge realize what he said is the opposite of what he said when my wife stood before him? This made no sense. Knees weak, I began to feel faint and in no condition to comment. Besides, this was the same person who threatened me with the Federal marshals for being late to his court. I wasn't about to argue with him right before he handed me his verdict.

I'd prepared a speech explaining that I'd never hurt anyone and the system itself was broken. I wanted it known Mr. Ruttles had been grossly unfair throughout this whole ordeal. I intended to state the facts proving I couldn't have known what the broker was doing when he created false documents. I also wanted the judge to know that when Mr. Ruttles found out I had four children he answered, "Boo hoo."

When I began reading my speech, I noticed the judge wasn't looking at me, apparently not interested in anything I said. That's when I decided to take a chance. I knew he wanted an apology, but I had absolutely nothing prepared. I went ahead anyway. I looked up from my paper and said, "If it would please the court, I'd like to read the speech I wrote without my lawyer's help."

That got the judge's attention. "I wish you would."

Instead of standing there with nothing to say, I began reciting words as they popped into my head. I have no idea where the words came from. I went on and on about how I hadn't meant to hurt anyone and that I should have stopped working in the Englewood area. I should have taken my losses and the losses of my best friends and gone home. I spoke very deliberately and slowly while Dan's mouth hung open. The judge didn't take his eyes off of me.

I had no idea what I was going to say next. Words just kept coming out of my mouth for 20 minutes. You could hear a dime drop in the courtroom. The things I said I should have done weren't possible to do, but from what I could see, the judge seemed to love hearing it. If I'd walked away, my friends would have lost everything they'd invested, not to mention the customers who had bought houses that were not finished yet. The banks would stop getting their mortgage payments and the city of Chicago would start condemning the rest of my properties.

I spoke of having no malicious intent but had hoped to profit from the homes' sales. I wanted to explain putting fixtures in after the closing because of theft, but I knew that would land on deaf ears. Finally, I told the court I was sorry I hurt the banks. Inside my head I knew the banks hurt the banks. On that point, I couldn't believe I managed to get that bullshit out of my mouth. But I did it in the spirit of a man's got to do what a man's got to do.

When I finished, the judge asked me to take my seat. I sensed he'd been moved by my talk. As I sat down, Dan's right-hand man whispered, "Why couldn't you speak this way before today?"

I wanted to answer, "Because today, I'm facing 20 years in prison," but instead I said nothing.

The judge stared into the courtroom for about 30 seconds, fiddling with his gavel and his papers before he spoke.

"It is obvious Mr. Keith is a good man," he said. "I have no doubt that he will never be in front of me again. So, Mr. Ruttles would you agree that Mr. Keith didn't mean to hurt anyone and found himself in the middle of a rock and a hard place?"

"Yes, your honor, I agree."

Then the judge again spoke to me. "Sometimes, good people do bad things. As a judge, I must punish these people to make an example to others. For the crime committed against the people of the United States of America, I sentence you to 40 months in Federal prison."

Shocked silence.

My four kids began to cry. That crushed me. I felt disembodied, somehow, as if I'd just died and was watching my own funeral.

Then, Conners looked at my children and said, "Forty months is not a long time. Your father will be fine." He got to his feet and left the courtroom.

I turned to look at Mrs. Wilkinson and she did not look happy. She was the one person responsible for this entire nightmare that my family had to endure and they didn't even know her. Many of the buyers knew I installed the fixtures past closing because of repeated, costly thieving. They also knew I had no knowledge of any fraud on the broker's part. If the broker wanted to falsify statements he was creating for the bank, how would I stop him? I'm not a cop. The Feds believe that not stopping a broker meant you were in on it. That means you're part of a conspiracy, which means you're screwed. If you ever get in trouble with the Feds, you, too, will learn to hate the word *conspiracy*.

I couldn't understand why the judge thought one way about Julie's involvement and another way about mine. Conners admitted he knew I would never come before him again. He also admitted he knew I was a good man. Maybe Ruttles acted too quickly on the information he received and couldn't turn back once he recognized the truth. On the other hand, maybe he believed I was intentionally trying to defraud the bank. I'll never know.

## The unspoken fix is in

Being a defendant in Federal Court is big trouble. Unbelievably, the judge told me during my sentencing that since I didn't help the Feds get whom they wanted, he couldn't show me mercy. *I remember thinking, even if I'd have to lie to help?*

I consider being a snitch negative at best; however, to snitch and lie about the incriminating information to help oneself? That is a real crime. How would anyone sleep at night knowing freedom came from lying for the FBI? Could I look myself in the mirror if I gave the Feds the story they wanted to hear in court?

I can understand rewarding a prosecutor for putting criminals behind bars, but not citizens who made a mistake with no intent to harm. Every citizen should be aware that the only reason the Feds hold a 98% conviction record is because so few individuals can afford to risk going to court!

Sad but true, defendants in a courtroom are paraded in front of a jury. They look guilty. The jury thinks of the FBI as the good guys. They look at those accused and wonder why they're sitting in the courtroom. What did the FBI catch them doing? Defendants aren't smiling. They may be minorities, or poor, or both. Or, if they appear affluent, how can they afford such expensive suits?

In the end, many lawyers scare defendants into pleading. They know the outcome before they meet with their clients.

Again, individuals serving on a jury probably have no experience in the topic at hand. Even the government witnesses are instructed about what to say on the stand. For example, the vice president of the same bank the brokers used in dealing with my customers had absolutely no idea about no-source, no-seasoning programs, although we proved his bank was offering them. When he learned he was wrong, he shrugged it off by saying he hadn't been involved in subprime lending.

I was given a date when my prison sentence would begin: March 3, 2012. Because I knew I wouldn't be able to concentrate on my job or really enjoy time with my family, I made the grim decision to start the sentence almost three months early. The prison system is very obliging.

The night before leaving, we invited some friends to our home to say good-bye. In the middle of everything, my one-and-a-half-year-old golden retriever inexplicably died in the middle of our foyer. That sent a dagger straight into my heart. Life's crises were completely overwhelming me.

# Chapter Seven

## We're Not in Chicago Anymore

When the day came, Julie and I left for the USP (United States Prison), or rather, the prison camp. Franklin Prison was a 5-hour drive from our house. The building is surrounded by a fence with tall guard towers overlooking it. I hugged Julie a long time, obviously not wanting to let her go. I was already feeling the agony of separation for what would be a 40-month good-bye.

The woman at the desk inside found me in her computer and said someone would be with me in a while. What did it matter how long it would take? My life was over anyway.

Eventually, a guard appeared to take me to another building. As we started walking, he held his hand out to me. I thought he wanted to shake my hand, so I gripped his hand in a friendly way. Turned out, he was reaching for the plastic bag of medicine I had brought with me.

"Why would I want to shake your hand?" he asked. "You're a piece of garbage."

Nice. It took two minutes in prison for me to feel like an idiot.

Later, I found out he did this to every inmate before me. What an asshole. This same guard strip-searched me and took my street clothes. In place, he gave me khaki pants two sizes too large for me and a green shirt. He watched me get dressed, all the time saying nothing. He started some small talk while he fingerprinted me, first asking if I was a football fan.

Sure, but I wasn't eager to talk to him. He considered me garbage, and had told me so. He could go to hell.

Another guard asked about my medication. He checked out each type of pill and told me what I could or couldn't keep. Anything from a pharmacy had to be given from the prison pharmacist.

Then, more waiting until I could be driven to the camp. At least I wouldn't be staying at the fortress-like building, cold and dark and surrounded by barbed wire. It was like the old, dreary prisons on TV.

I waited in a windowless room with only a toilet and a sink. I had to press a button to get water. Would I be spending two and a half years in a room like this? While waiting, another man came in and sat down. He was another self-surrendering inmate.

When he asked me how long I had, and I told him, he said that wasn't too bad. Forty months would go fast. That was not the last time I heard this in my prison camp stay. This man would be there eight years, so I could understand why 40 months didn't sound so bad.

I asked him if we'd have a toilet in our rooms, and that's when I first learned about "the hole," the place you went when you broke rules. The hole was an 8'x10' cell with a toilet and a sink, but no bed.

"You sleep on the floor with a towel," he explained.

I looked at him like he was crazy, but he insisted he was dead serious. A stint in the hole could mean sleeping on a cement slab for two months to a year. I *knew* he must be playing with me, a first-timer. No one could sleep on a cement slab for more than an evening or two.

I kept asking questions and he kept giving me answers. Inmates in the hole were fed through a small opening in the door. You're cuffed behind your back when you leave the room through a door. One shower a week, the water is cold, and you're allowed out an hour a day. What do you do in the hole? More or less nothing.

"If you're lucky, you can get hold of an old magazine and read it over and over again."

So, I decided I wouldn't be breaking any rules. At least, that's what I thought at that moment.

The commanding officer came back and escorted me to a car driven by a man dressed in a sweatshirt and sweatpants.

I got in the car and said, "Thanks for the lift, Sir."

He surprised me by saying, "Don't call me sir. I'm an inmate just like you."

He extended his hand and when I asked if he wanted to shake mine, we got into an exchange about the guard's words.

"Don't pay him any attention. He just wanted to be a prick!" Then, he introduced himself using a name I would never forget. "Hi, I'm the Wizard."

Shock and wonder. How could an inmate ever survive in prison with a name like the Wizard? It wouldn't take long for me to find out.

The Wizard dropped me off at the front door to a red building that looked much like a grammar school. He gave me a tour of the place where I'd live, from the laundry to gym to the visitor room and the educational building. I was surprised when I saw a baseball field, track, a volleyball net, miniature golf, and bocce ball. I expressed astonishment at seeing all these activities.

Wizard brought me to another inmate he introduced as Mr. Fin. Fin was black and soft spoken. "I am a man of the church and want to give you some free items that inmates put together." He handed me a toothbrush, toothpaste, dental floss, a pen, shower shoes, and a bar of soap. Taken for granted at home, these items were a Godsend here. In spite of the kindness of these two men, I was still deeply saddened and totally alone. Uneasy and anxious, I couldn't let go of the idea that I shouldn't even be here.

Wizard brought me to my cell in SO2. The room

had rows of four 2-men bunk beds. I had a top bunk. I put my toothbrush and shower shoes in my locker and went looking for the couple of inmates whose names I'd been given on the phone by a former inmate I met before I came to prison. Did anyone know a guy named Hollywood, I asked. He'd left the prison six months before. Another guy, Moon, was in Room 6 on S02, the room next to mine.

Moon turned out to be a bald guy about forty years old. He greeted my extended hand with a fist, saying, "This is how we shake hands in here."

I explained that a friend, Miles, gave me his name.

Moon's eyes lit up when he told me our mutual friend had helped him get his GED. "Whatever you need, you got it," he said.

Well, finally a bit of good fortune. A possible friend on my first day in prison.

Moon had been down for 20 years. He'd served ten in a medium-security prison and nine years here at "the camp."

"What are you in for?" I asked.

"Marijuana."

"Twenty years for pot?" I yelled in disbelief.

That's when I learned that about 75% of the inmates in that prison were doing time for drugs.

All I could say was, "That's crazy!"


## Count time


Around 3:30 PM, Moon told me to get ready for "the count." He explained it as the time the guards count inmates who stand against the wall or in their rooms. They do the count to make sure no one escaped, and the counts were timed, 4 PM and again at 9:30 PM, midnight, and twice during the night.

I wondered why they worried about escapes. No doors were locked and no fences kept the inmates inside the prison camp.

Moon explained the Federal Security Prisons all have locks and fences. When inmates in those prisons were counted, all prisoners in all types of facilities all over the country were also counted at the same time.

Our conversation was interrupted by an inmate yelling, "Rolling."

Every inmate stepped outside the room and lined up against the hall wall. It reminded me of scenes I'd seen of privates in the army being ordered to stand at attention.

About ten minutes later, two guards walked by us, counting. When the first guard got to me, he stopped, asking if I was new.

I said yes, and he continued down the hallway, counting. When the counting was over, we all went back into our rooms and waited.

I introduced myself to my cellmates and they all seemed pretty cool. Russ, who looked like Moon, but much taller. Pete looked like a forty-year-old hippy from the 60s, with his ponytail holding back shoulder length hair. Rhino stood about six-feet tall and wore glasses, and Hooper, who looked barely twenty-two, was chunky and spoke with a southern drawl. Gary, short and stocky, was in the back top bunk above Rhino. Ron's bunk was in the back, top right. Ron was a black guy with a large build and glasses. Beneath him, Pedro, a stocky man from Mexico with bad teeth, had black hair everywhere. Although he appeared tired, he had a stereotypical bandito look about him, which made me think I'd leave him alone.

I eventually learned that except for Hooper and me, the others were doing time for drugs. They had sentences ranging from three to 25 years. Hooper was doing time because he'd been a guard caught bringing contraband into the prison camp.

At one point, Rhino asked what drug I'd sold. It was an assumption. I began explaining my situation by repeating a version I'd been using for many months. This is how I put it.

*Brokers and appraisers were writing and closing loans based on bank programs promoting predatory lending practices. The Feds decided to leave the banks alone and come after the brokers, title companies, lawyers, appraisers, borrowers, and anyone else that had done business with the banks during this greedy sub-prime lending environment.*

*Even though I was the seller and had no license and had nothing to do with the banking side of the business, I was the one charged with fraud. Everyone who was in any way dealing with these loan programs was considered guilty, as if our actions were a conspiracy against the American public.*

My cellmates understood being charged and convicted on conspiracy charges. That's what had happened to them. Some had never been caught selling or possessing drugs. Yet, they were convicted of a crime. A light went on in my head: my case was not uniquely unjust.

Abruptly, the loudspeaker outside of our cell sprang to life, "Clear."

That meant we were allowed to walk freely around the prison camp. It was dinnertime and I walked with the others to the chow hall, where the line was very long.

I picked up my dinner about 20 minutes later. Dinner was a whitish slop that an inmate slapped onto my tray with a big oversized ladle, followed by a gob of spinach and an orange. When I tried to get ice for a drink out of a large container, I discovered there was no ice. The so-called salad bar offered only lettuce and a creamy dressing.

About 400 inmates sat in the chow hall. I needed to find a place to sit, so I went up to a table of guys and sat down. I nonchalantly nodded a hello, and two guys acknowledged me by nodding back. I ate the salad, but I wasn't hungry enough to eat the slop.

## Looking for Alfonzo

After dinner, I went in search of Alfonzo, an inmate the Feds interviewed about my case. Prior to being sentenced, I read Alfonzo's written interview and learned his explanations were accurate. He admitted the houses were not finished by the loan closings, and the quality of workmanship wasn't good. He was candid and stated to the Feds that he told his buyers to exaggerate their incomes so they could buy my houses.

I'd hired Alfonzo as a salesman/contractor. He acquired buyers and then turned them over to Michael, the broker who processed the loans. Since Alfonzo dealt with the brokers, he was thrown into the overall scheme. He also worked with another builder, Larry, who was also in trouble with the Feds. My understanding is that Larry deposited cash into his buyers' accounts to make it appear the buyers paid their own down payments.

Alfonzo said the Feds asked him to testify that Richard Keith was working with the broker and appraisers to defraud the banks. But Alfonzo refused to lie, so he ended up in the same prison camp as me. When I arrived, he'd already been there fifteen months.

As I asked around, I mentioned Alfonzo was from the Philippines, and one inmate told me about a guy who hit tennis balls against the wall every day. That sounded like Alfonzo. I'd played tennis with him myself. And so, I found him hitting tennis balls against one of the gym walls.

I approached, noting how thin he'd become and that he'd grown a moustache. I yelled to him, but he must not have heard me coming. When he spotted me, he just stared. Then his eyes lit up as he realized it was me.

We shook hands heartily, but then he said that in the camp, we "knock fists." And so we did. He led me to his cell room and offered me some fried chicken.

"Where did you get fried chicken?" I asked. "I just

had dinner and it was a bunch of slop."

"You can get all kinds of food from inmates. It's underground."

Later, we shot some pool and talked. I admitted I was like a fish out of water and it was all too much to take in. But Al was happy to see me and pointed out we could play tennis together just like we did on the outside.

We also talked about our cases. Larry, involved in his court case, was going to prison in a different state, and I told him about Julie's two trials. Alfonzo declared this was next to impossible. I said that's what Uncle Manny had told me, but I hadn't quite believed it then. I'd not understood what had occurred for Julie ranked as a true-to-life miracle.

Soon it was time for count. "If there is anything you do right in this camp, it's count," Alfonzo said. "Don't mess with it."

When the guards finished their count, I grabbed my prison-issued white towel and toiletries, and headed to the shower at the other end of the hall wearing my boxers. I quickly showered and headed back to my cell room, but was stopped by three inmates.

"Hi," one said. "What's your name?"

I told him and another inmate said he liked my underwear, but not as much as Denny did. I looked at the inmate next to this guy and saw he was extending his hand out to convey he was gay. Then he asked if I'd like to join him in the shower!

I immediately realized no inmate walked to the shower in his underwear—boxers or briefs. I thought fast and asked, "Which one of you guys is interested in having sex?"

All three looked shocked and embarrassed, exclaiming in protest, "We're not gay!"

With a serious, angry face I asked, "Then, why are you looking at me in my underwear leaving the shower?"

They turned and walked away.

I'd never walk through the hall like that again. At

the tennis club, I could walk naked from the shower, but this was *prison,* and the same "rules" didn't apply.


## Withdrawal


Sleep didn't come easily that night. I stared at the ceiling and tried to drift off. The bed was very uncomfortable, and although I turned over several times trying to find a comfortable spot, I never did.

The steel bed was not the only problem. Buprenorphine-naloxone, an anti-anxiety drug, had been helping me stay calm for the past year. A doctor suggested I use the drug to wean myself off of the hydrocodone acetaminophen I'd been popping like aspirin under the extreme stress of my business, and then in my dealings with the Feds. My doctor assured me withdrawal would be mild. However, as I lay in this uncomfortable steel bunk bed, it became clear I hadn't left myself enough time. The effects of the withdrawal made my legs and arms tingle to the point I couldn't sleep.

After hours of trying, I finally gave up and left the room to walk the downstairs hall. I walked the hallway a few times back and forth until I spotted a guard in the Central Camp Office, known as the bubble, who motioned me to the window.

He looked surprised to see me and asked, "What are you doing in *my* hall at 3 AM?"

I started delivering a dissertation on Buprenorphine-naloxone, explaining how the withdrawal was keeping me energetically awake. I explained I'd recently stopped taking the drug, prescribed for me by my psychiatrist, and though the withdrawals were supposed to be mild, I just could *not* fall asleep. I thought I'd been logical and had fully explained why I was walking his halls at 3 AM.

The guard looked at me the way the sergeant looked at Gomer Pile. "I could give a fuck about your problems! Now, get back to your cell or you're going to the hole."

I ran back to my room looking like I was in an old Jerry Lewis movie, the one where he was running after the old lady who was falling down a steep hill in a wheelchair with Lewis running behind her. (The Disorderly Orderly.) I prayed the withdrawal symptoms would diminish quickly. I had no idea that the pernicious persistence of Buprenorphine-naloxone withdrawal would make sleep difficult for the next two weeks.

## Sweet dreams

For most people, a deep, restful sleep seems like a gift from the gods. But in prison, steel beds were one of the major prison hardships, making sleep a battle against thin, worn mattresses barely covering steel strips running between the sturdy steel frames. My back hurt so bad, I couldn't fall asleep. Legally, sleep deprivation is considered torture, allowed in some circumstances, but torture nonetheless. And the BOP covertly uses it.

Early on, I knew I had to figure out what to do in order to get some sleep. I kept somehow breaking the rules in the process, but in trying to sleep or eat better, I was ready to break the rules. I approached an inmate named Kevin, the one person in the hall who sewed well. He was a miracle worker with a needle and thread. I asked if he could make a cushion to put under my back at night.

"No problem," he said with a smile. "It'll cost six stamps." (Stamps were currency in prison.)

Thankful, I thought this was a small price to pay for sound sleep.

The next day Kevin brought me a handmade cushion that I placed under my mattress that night. Worked perfectly. Ahh.

Then, just about a week later, an official named Teller did a walk-through examination of our rooms—a "shake down." She came into each room to check for any cushions under the mattresses, a place inmates might hide contraband. Teller's shakedowns were primarily for finding cell phones and tobacco, but she also removed items meant for basic comfort. Even now, I can't get past how mean she was to remove cushions that were not used to harbor some illegal item. I was fifty-nine-years-old and there were inmates in their seventies and eighties left to sleep on the steel beds. I consider that cruel and unusual punishment, like the hole.

While Teller searched our room, I approached her and told her how I got the cushion and why.

Teller regarded me with obvious disdain. "So, you ruined government property? You could go to the hole for this."

I later learned even using a pillowcase or sheet to make a cushion could be considered *destroying* government property. She took my cushion and left the room.

On another of Teller's searches, her goal was to ensure no inmate had more than three pairs of undershorts, undershirts, and socks. If an inmate had more than that, she forced him to throw the "extras" in the garbage. Doing my best to avoid this, I hid my extra underwear under the drums in the music room.

In addition to hunting for cell phones and tobacco, Teller was on the lookout for any other contraband she could confiscate, including food like eggs, bread, Red Sauce, cookies, and fruit. Coolers or extra bowls were contraband and confiscated. To the inmates, this confiscation was a joke. Everything she took was replaced the next day.

On another morning, the Camp Administrator, Antonio Rain, aroused me from sleep to ask why the area behind my lockers was dirty.

I wasn't wearing my shirt, and since an inmate can be sent to the hole (more on that later) for that, I jumped up out of bed and grabbed a T-shirt from my footlocker.

He asked what the hell I was doing.

Then I remembered it was okay that I was still in bed, so I asked what he wanted.

"I want the back of the lockers in this room *clean*. If not, you're going to the *hole*."

*Why is everything an inmate is asked to do accompanied by a threat?*

I told him I would handle it, and he left my room.


## Prison monotony and finding a job


The first morning I woke up in prison I started what would be a regular morning routine—a shower, shaving, and going to chow. That first full day there, I walked around the camp by myself to take in my surroundings. It already seemed that every inmate developed his own routine. Each had some sort of assigned job. I talked with the others about available jobs, but none appealed to me.

An inmate could work in the kitchen washing dishes and floors and wiping off tables, or he could sweep hallways or work in the laundry. Some took advantage of the possibility to teach courses in the Education Building, but there was no guarantee that work would be considered a job itself or the inmate would have to get another job, too. An inmate wouldn't know until he showed up to teach if it counted as a job—too late. I had no trade skills to fill jobs for plumbers and electricians. Inmates could cut the grass using a tractor lawnmower, and orderlies cleaned rooms and closets.

Whether I liked it or not, many jobs meant getting up earlier than some of the other jobs. If I didn't pick my own job, the Camp Administrator, Rain, would pick one for me.

At that point, I hadn't met Rain yet, but I'd heard he was a bear to deal with, always threatening to put inmates in the hole for walking the hall, or being slow to count, or for an untucked shirttail. Rain never actually talked, he just yelled. Originally from South America, his grasp of the English language was not all that good.

That night, my second at the camp, I passed the bathroom after chow and noticed Gus and a few guys smoking pot. I stopped and asked Gus how he got hold of pot in here.

"This isn't pot, it's tobacco. It just looks like a joint. We roll it ourselves." He offered me a drag of his cigarette, but I refused, explaining I didn't smoke cigarettes. I was a cigar smoker and loved to have a smoke right after dinner.

"Smoking kills time," he said.

But was smoking illegal? Apparently, but Gus said the guards never came up to this floor.

*What the hell?*

It sounded safe. I took a drag and as soon as it hit my lips, a CO came from around the corner. Gus and the others had a look of disbelief, while I stood there with the cigarette still lit in my hand.

"What do we have here?" the CO said.

I said nothing.

"Are we smoking a cigarette?"

I managed to say, "I don't smoke."

The guard motioned me to follow him, so I did.

As we walked down the stairs, I asked, "Are you going to send me to the hole?"

He stopped. "I've never seen you before. Who are you?"

"Richard Keith."

"When did you get here?"

"Yesterday," I said quietly.

"And I already caught you for smoking?"

"I don't smoke, Sir."

"Are you telling me I didn't catch you smoking just now?" he asked.

"No. You caught me, but it was my first time."

Smiling, he warned, "If you got caught smoking this quickly, you'd better be really careful the rest of your time here." He handed me a squeegee and told me to clean the windows in the bubble office. Since I'd feared he would send me to the hole for sure, I was happy just to get extra duty.

After I finished cleaning the windows, I returned to my room. Gus was there, laughing so hard, he was crying.

I asked him what was funny, but he was laughing so hard he could barely talk. He knew this guard well, and knew I'd only get extra duty. On the other hand, Gus had never been caught smoking in all the time he'd been at the camp.

I was just happy the ordeal was over and needed to shower since I was sweating profusely. I undressed and flipped my underwear on my bed, put on a pair of camp shorts, and headed for the shower.

When I got back to the room, Rhino was standing by his bed holding up a pair of underwear that looked just like mine, only they appeared to be soiled. Rhino demanded to know who put dirty soiled underwear on his bed.

Without paying him any attention, I went ahead and started getting dressed.

"Hey, where's my underwear? I put it right here." At least I thought I had. *Oh, shit!* The underwear Rhino was holding *was* mine. And the embarrassing brown spot must have resulted from my nervousness during the smoking fiasco and my fear of the hole.

I grabbed my underwear from Rhino. "I don't know how they ended up over on your bed. Sorry about that." I threw them in the garbage.

I must have become confused after coming back from the bubble and had tossed my underwear on Rhino's bed. Thankfully, Rhino had heard I'd been caught smoking, and thought it was funny. Otherwise, I would have been dead meat. He was big and had been pumping iron for years. He could have smashed me with his bare hands. He still needed to stare at me with a mean face, but he let it go. In prison, you have to look tough when someone puts his dirty underwear on your bed, especially if it's soiled.

## The job issue

I took my time choosing a job since inmates told me I had three weeks before Rain would assign me a job. I still had no inclination to take on any of the dreary list of jobs. One afternoon, I went looking for Alfonzo and found him hitting a tennis ball against the gym wall. I asked if he wanted to play tennis outside. He agreed, but when we got to the court, I saw the surface damaged with major cracks, as if it had been blown up by a land mind. Despite that, we played a few sets anyway.

Before either of us had gone to prison, Al and I had played tennis twice in the street. I'd beaten him both times. But now, I could see that practicing every day in the prison had greatly improved his game.

It occurred to me how strange it was to be playing tennis in a prison camp. Is this what the judge had in mind? Then it dawned on me that punishment was not only intended to punish *me*, but to punish *my family.* It was disheartening on so many levels. I missed my family while playing tennis. Meanwhile, my wife was left to pay all the bills, to raise our girls, and I was playing tennis. Absurd. The entire system was absurd.

When we were done, I'd won six games to Al's four—a good match. Walking back to the gym, he looked straight at me and said, "The Feds wanted me to say things that were not true concerning you and Julie, but I wouldn't."

This didn't surprise me.

During Julie's trial, one of my contractors who became a government witness claimed Julie knew everything that was going on in the business—he blurted it out without even being questioned by my lawyer. The Feds had asked me to help them convict someone from the title company, but Julie and I explained we had no knowledge of any wrongdoing. The prosecutor told us that if we didn't want to help, plenty of other defendants would. If we didn't help him, we would be the number one and two defendants in the scheme. That's what happened: Julie and I were placed at the top of the indictment list. Even at my plea hearing, the judge said, "If you don't help the Feds, you are punished severely."

In other words, a defendant is awarded for being a snitch.

I thanked Alfonzo for having dignity and integrity.

His response was, "How could I sleep?"


**Early connections**


As I tried to get into some type of prison camp routine, staying out of trouble was the priority, or I would surely end up in the hole or beaten up. I heard there was an Alcoholics Anonymous (AA) group that met every other Wednesday. Since I was going to try and get the RDAP program (a drug program), joining the AA group would be a prudent step. Getting into the program would take one year off my sentence, so if taking this AA program would help my chances, I was all in.

At the first meeting, six inmates sat in a circle. Since I'd smoked some pot and taken pills in the past, I thought I'd likely feel at home discussing my problems with this group. One inmate in particular struck me as someone I could relate to. He was around fifty, and had been involved in real estate in a low income area of St. Louis. He'd flipped houses with Section 8 tenants living in them.

We met after the meeting and immediately hit it off. Seems Richard's real crime was paying taxes with a bad check, a check drawn from a bank that had told him the check was good. He'd mailed the check in good faith, but the bank allowed the check to bounce. If done *intentionally*, the transaction would constitute fraud. Like me, Richard had no intent to commit fraud, but was convicted and sentenced to eighteen months in Franklin Prison Camp.

Richard had begun his prison term in a county jail. Everyone agreed they were the worst, even the food was worse than in Franklin. Richard was then shipped to a camp in Leavenworth, and from there, he was shipped by "Diesel Therapy" to Franklin. Diesel Therapy describes inmates sent to other camps by bus, with their legs chained and hands cuffed. This assuredly is *not* the ideal way to travel.

Many inmates had to spend their time awaiting trial, incarcerated in a jail cell at MCC. This was a holding cell in a prison attached to the courthouse.

Richard knew a lot about the United States prison system and had taken an accredited course to acquire a license to counsel soon-to-be inmates. He was knowledgeable about RDAP, the drug program everyone wanted. He also understood the 100, 200 & 300 series shots given by the guards if an inmate did anything wrong. The lower the number of the shot or demerit, the worse the punishment. A 100 series shot would mean the dreaded hole.

He knew how to hunt for food and buy it for reasonable prices from the prisoners in the camp. He had a job working recreation that entailed keeping a TV room clean. He knew the rec CO and promised to get me the same job.

I'd not liked the idea of getting up at 5:30 AM to work a job for $2.00 a month, legal only if you're a slave-labor inmate, obviously.

As it turned out, a rec job had no set hours and I wouldn't need to start work so early. There was nothing to do on the job, and I'd still make the $2.00 per month.

Richard went to Jewish services every Friday night, the start of the Sabbath. Sharing a common background helped us form a more personal bond.

At one point, I mentioned another inmate, Ronald, from a suburb of Chicago, who Julie's aunt knew.

Richard thought he might work in the basement of the building where they keep tools, so I went off to find him.

# Chapter Eight

## Trying to Adjust

As I went in search of Ronald, another inmate on the floor pointed him out to me. When I saw him, I guessed him to be about sixty-five. Although he had a worn-out look, his salt and pepper hair hung over his ears and made him look older.

I introduced myself, but Ronald had no idea who Julie's aunt and I were.

He was in prison for art fraud. As he explained it, he bought expensive fake artwork overseas and sold it to galleries and private collectors. The fake art was done with precision, so expertly that even appraisers couldn't distinguish them from originals. Ronald would purchase fake art purported to be the work of Salvador Dali, Picasso, or Andy Warhol. He bought them for a minimum price and sold them 20% under retail price.

According to Ronald, it was a good racket while it lasted. When I met him, the TV magazine program "20/20" had asked him to be part of a segment on one of their reports, but he'd declined. Later, the story aired on TV and the whole prison camp watched. Although Ronald wasn't named in the program, everyone who knew about the story could tell the narrator was describing him.

Starting with my first days at the camp, I asked many inmates what they'd done to end up in prison camp. Based on what I was told, I began to believe most of them were not incarcerated for serious crimes or any kind of crime at all. In case after case, it seemed to me the inmates should've been home living their regular lives with their families.

Ronald was an example of an inmate that didn't look or act as if he'd purposely hurt a flea, physically or financially. On one occasion I said, "I bet you didn't even realize the art you were selling were fake pieces."

He refuted this immediately. "No, I was aware it was fake."

Not convinced he should be in prison, I said, "But I'm sure you didn't mark up the price much more than you paid."

He stared at his shoes and said, "Yeah, I marked it up, sometimes twenty to thirty times what I paid!"

Still not convinced he was a total crook, I asked, "But, I bet you were ashamed of yourself and couldn't sleep at night."

With his head lowered, he said, "Well, I kind of liked the money and slept fine."

Looking for a shred of hope, I finally said, "Well, I'm sure you will agree, everyone makes mistakes and you learned your lesson."

"This is the fourth time I've been in prison for art fraud."

I gave up. I picked the wrong guy to make an example of. "Well, maybe you *should* be in here," I admitted, "but many inmates shouldn't." This guy was a friken crook and hurt people on purpose.

I ended up sharing this story about ten times to other inmates, who, as you can guess, *all* broke out in fits of laughter.

When I first met him, Ronald asked if I had figured out how to get stamps yet. I asked what he meant and quickly learned that U.S. postage stamps were the currency of the prison. You could buy a maximum of two books (20 stamps per book) from the commissary for $8.00/book or as many as you need from inmates for $6.00/book.

Inmates traded stamp books, so if you had cash, you could buy stamps for $5.00/book. But Ronald warned me that cash isn't allowed in the compound. If I got caught with cash, I'd go to the hole and eventually I could get shipped out, meaning being shipped to a higher security prison.

"If you receive a 100 or 200 series shot, you get shipped out," Ronald said. "You can lose the good time you get, which is 13.5% of your sentence, plus visiting privileges."

I thanked him and took heed of his advice, although this warning didn't stop me from breaking the rules. You needed cash to buy stamps.

**"Hello, good-bye"**

A week after I arrived, I had my first visit with my family. It was exciting, even thrilling that Julie, Danni, and Jackie were coming to visit. I dressed in my full uniform, which was worn just for visits. On TV, prison uniforms are usually orange, but ours were dark green. I'd ironed it and also shined my prison-issued black shoes. My name was on the shirt pocket—spelled wrong.

I stood at a window in the hall overlooking the parking lot and watched for Julie's car. Anticipation welled up inside me. Then, I heard the loudspeaker go live saying the words every inmate *longs* to hear, *"Keith, you have a visitor."*

I entered the visitors' room, and there they were, the three of them, standing by the seats. I hurried to embrace and kiss Julie, then Danni, and finally Jackie. After we sat, I told them what had happened since I'd arrived and how I'd spent my time. All three noticed how much weight I'd already lost but also commented that I looked rested. It was true. I'd finally slept better after the buprenorphine-naloxone withdrawals mercifully ended.

Oddly, it's possible my restfulness also resulted from a sort of freedom from stress that occurred in these early days of imprisonment. For the first time in a long time, I wasn't worried about payroll or payments or any of the financial burdens I'd carried. Not that this was fair to Julie, who was forced to carry all the financial burdens. (Are judges aware of the real hardships placed on families during the absence of adults who may be bread winners? My absence meant loss of income for my family, and Julie had to continue doing her own job and make up for the losses my absence caused.)

I was so proud of my daughters and sons for handling this whole nightmare the way they did. My sons had jobs that they had to work hard in and my daughters needed to keep their grades up in school. I needed to be strong and not give them anything to worry about while they were going thru their lives' pressures. They had enough to deal with. I was so happy they came to visit me.

Many of the inmates weren't so lucky. They would watch at the window as other inmates' visitors walked into the prison. I was one of the lucky ones. I knew I had great kids.

We enjoyed the pleasant give and take of family small talk, but the time flew by. All of a sudden—and shockingly too soon—we had to say our good-byes. I was thrown back twenty years earlier when my first marriage ended in a divorce, and I had to say a brokenhearted good-bye to my two sons, David and Mikey, after my visits with them. Saying good-bye to Julie and the girls was so hurtful I began to wonder if the visit was worth it. But I killed that thought as soon as it hit.

Of course, it was worth it to see, hear, and touch my loved ones. Thankfully, in the camp there was no window or barrier. Naturally, I wanted to leave the prison and go home with them. In my mind, it would be so easy, so normal to just walk out the door, hand in hand with Julie as we left with our girls. Coming back to reality with a heavy sigh, I forced my thoughts to focus on the words, "This too shall pass."

The visit over and back in my room, I began changing into a normal white tee shirt and green shorts. Then it occurred to me. I could wave good-bye to my family from the grounds outside my unit.

I ran out and waved to them as they were getting into our family's black Toyota. They stopped, and I had a sudden idea. I told Julie to get the camera.

I leaned up against a tree and made a muscle, then did all kinds of silly poses just for laughs. A few minutes later, they drove away.

Out of nowhere, a prison police car drove up to me. He rolled down his window and said, "You know you can't do that."

"Sorry," I said.

"The next time I see you do that," he warned, "you're going to the hole."

I'm still not sure what I'd done wrong. I was standing far enough away from my family and just clowning around. But I distinctly remember my relief that the officer gave me a second chance.

# Chapter Nine

## The RDAP Ghost Program

The RDAP (Residential Drug Abuse Program) mentioned earlier is a drug program within the prison system. You had to have an abuse problem with drugs or alcohol within one year of your arrest, and the issue had to be noted on your prison papers, and a judge had to recommend the program. Taking part in it meant the sentence could be reduced by up to one year. But it was nearly impossible to get into, and insidious game playing went on over it. The psychologist in charge at the camp played with inmates' emotions in awarding and refusing entry, but there was no rhyme or reason to her decision. For example, she called me a liar because I couldn't remember when I started taking buprenorphine-naloxone.

My lawyer had told me about RDAP, because I'd been taking hydrocodone acetaminophen to relieve the stress of the real estate business and then continued to take it to relieve the stress of my case. I'd been getting hydrocodone acetaminophen from street dealers, not from a medical doctor. But I'd also begun seeing a psychiatrist because of the case and to get off the hydrocodone acetaminophen. My psychiatrist, who happened to be familiar with the tactics the Feds use to win a case, prescribed buprenorphine-naloxone, a drug used to wean people off hydrocodone acetaminophen without withdrawal symptoms. The first time I took it, the withdrawal symptoms were gone after ten minutes. I'd been taking buprenorphine-naloxone ever since.

Later, when it came time to visit my parole officer, who I had to meet with before entering prison, I explained my hydrocodone acetaminophen problem in response to questions about past drug use or prior legal troubles. He asked when I'd started taking the drug, but since I didn't know an exact date, he told me to guess.

I did guess, but later I'd pay the price for that. I had no idea how important these questions would be to get into the program.

Because of my issue with buprenorphine-naloxone and hydrocodone acetaminophen, I wanted to check into enrolling in RDAP right away. Whenever an inmate wanted to make a request, he wrote a "Cop Out," a form that's then delivered to the relevant department.

I completed a form requesting an interview with someone in the psychology department. A month went by without an answer, so I filled out a second form. Then another month went by, so I completed a third Cop Out.

Finally, my name came up on the Call Outs—the list of messages sent to inmates in response to a request. I was scheduled to see one of the psychologists and showed up at the appointed time.

After I greeted the psychologist, she asked if I was Mr. Keith. When I said yes, she said, "So you're the one who sent three Cop Outs to my department."

Oh boy, I thought, this can't be good. I apologized and sat down.

She began by asking when I first used hydrocodone acetaminophen and the date of my arrest. That was that.

About two weeks later, I was again on the Call Out list to see a psychologist. This time, I was met by a different woman, Dr. Friendly, who immediately quipped, "So you're the one who sent all the Cop Outs!"

Here we go again. I understood I was on their schedule. If they didn't respond in a timely manner, it was tough shit for me.

One of the questions went like this: "One of the chief stipulations of the RDAP Program has to do with the period of time you abused your drug. Did you use your drug hydrocodone acetaminophen within twelve months of your arrest?"

"I'm not certain. May I consult my doctor?"

Dr Friendly got very angry. *"Don't lie to me, Mr. Keith!"*

What? Is this doctor really yelling at me because I couldn't remember when I had begun using hydrocodone acetaminophen?

Then she yelled, "You will *not* be admitted to RDAP!" in a firm tone. The length of my incarceration actually depended on this quack!

Once again, I apologized, but didn't mean it. Dr. Friendly repeated I would not be able to enter the RDAP Program, but I would be able to attend some of the other drug programs offered by the prison.

I asked about these programs and was told by her that there would be no time taken off my sentence for taking these other programs. Who the hell wanted that, I thought?

I explained the situation all over again, and pointed out I didn't provide a date because I was unsure of it. However, my doctor probably had the date in my medical records. Telling me there was no need to contact the doctor, she told me to take the other classes, which I now knew didn't offer the 12 months off like RDAP did.

This episode meant I had to get to work on a BP-8, a review procedure used when an inmate thinks he is being treated unfairly. I sent the BP-8 to Dr. Raven who was the head of the department. She explained I would need to produce my doctor's records to prove the true and correct dates of hydrocodone acetaminophen use. This seemed foolish, since I was prescribed buprenorphine-naloxone to get off hydrocodone acetaminophen. This exchange evolved into a situation in which I had no choice but to file another form, a BP-9, which is submitted to the warden. Since Julie had sent me my doctor's records, I enclosed a copy with the form.

Unbelievably, two weeks later an answer came. I was asked to send the medical records, as if I hadn't already done that. So, off the forms went again.

"Please send us your doctor's records."

Now I had to send my doctor's records again, along with another form, a BP-10 to the Regional Office.

Two weeks later, I received another request for the doctor's records.

Since I had no one to talk to about this nonsensical cluster of red-tape, I sent yet *another* copy of my doctor's records up the chain with still another prepared BP-11, which went to the Legal Department in Washington, D.C. Each time I sent an appeal letter, I had to enclose four copies and drop the envelope at the post office as certified mail.

Fulfilling these requests was not easy, since I had to obtain a copy card to work the copy machine that was often broken, and I had a two-week deadline to respond. This meant running all over the prison, getting the forms, pens, typewriters, paper, stamps, and anything else I needed. It was all very difficult.

The legal department responded that they were entitled to another four weeks to consider the request, but I never received a response from them until six months before I went home. Start to finish, it took a year to get their answer—a denial.

During this time, I received orders to start taking one of the non-residential drug classes offered at the camp, but attending these classes brought no reward of time off.

When I entered the first class, I was surprised to see the teacher was Dr. Friendly. Now, it made sense. She had put me in this drug class to keep her job. If she didn't have any students, she would have no job. I had approached her for help to get into the RDAP Program, even giving her my doctor's records, asking if she would give them to her boss, Dr. Raven. She'd promised to deliver them that very afternoon.

Two weeks later, after class, I asked Dr. Friendly if she'd heard anything from Dr. Raven about the RDAP Program.

She was a completely different person, looking at me with contempt in her eyes. "You're a liar and have no drug problem. Don't bother me anymore."

Her mind game was working. I was confused. In the real world, I would have fought for what I believed in, but in prison it was hurting me.

I approached an inmate, Mike, who was known as Wizard the Magic Man to learn if he could help me with this absurd dilemma. He took me to the Camp Administrator, Rain, who said he'd talk to the psychology department.

After a couple more months, Dr. Raven put in a Call Out to me. This doctor explained she'd received my doctor's records, but found no mention in them about a drug problem.

So, I had to produce the records again.

She insinuated I could have typed this up and given it to her. In other words, now I was accused of cheating. I told her to call my doctor and verify his records and she said she would.

At the next drug class, I had to take an easy 10 question test about personal experiences. I didn't need a notebook to take it, but when Dr. Friendly asked me where my notebook was, she was upset when I said I'd let an inmate use it to study. Apparently, she thought an inmate was copying my workbook, but that made no sense.

She said, "If this inmate's book has your handwriting in it, you're both going to the hole!"

The entire episode was absurd.

The inmate Abdul was Serbian and didn't speak English very well. When he came into the classroom with my notebook, Dr. Friendly told him to leave and expelled him.

So much for helping him.

I ended up taking the test again, in a seat next to her desk which she pulled over next to her (with me still in the seat) so I couldn't cheat. I had to be the last person to leave the class so I wouldn't give the answers to the other inmates coming in to take the test. I needed to pass this test because without passing this drug class I couldn't get into the RDAP Program. I felt like I was seven years old again.

I'm not a quitter. I really wanted to be in the RDAP Program and receive the benefit of a full year off my prison sentence. This led me to continue my efforts, and both my lawyer and my psychiatrist assured me I was entitled to the RDAP Program. My family became distraught over how badly my requests were being handled.

Even with all this, I was still optimistic about the drug program.

A couple of days after taking this test that a ten-year-old could pass, I was again summoned to Dr. Raven's office and told I wasn't approved. Was she in touch with my doctor? Yes, and the dates she was looking for were supplied, but I still wasn't approved.

When I left her office, I went to find my team leader, a guy named Lloyd Pew, intending to let him know how I was being jerked around by Dr. Raven. However, Rain entered my team leader's office, and apparently having heard what happened, expressed how sorry he was that I hadn't been approved for the program. He seemed truly compassionate.

This entire ordeal over RDAP went on for almost a year, but to no avail. I'd gone through so many ups and downs during the time that I tried to get into the program, motivated by going home a full year sooner. Mentally, I'd already deducted the year from my 40-month sentence.

Now, I had to give Julie the bad news.

I learned other inmates were denied entry into the

RDAP as well. It was difficult to believe the rejection was due to writing too many Cop Outs too soon. It was also highly unprofessional for a psychiatrist to call me a liar. Whatever motivated that slander remained a mystery…until a few months later when *USA Today* ran a story about the Bureau of Prisons (BOP) being short of money and unable to support all the inmates in the Federal prisons who wanted to enter the RDAP program.

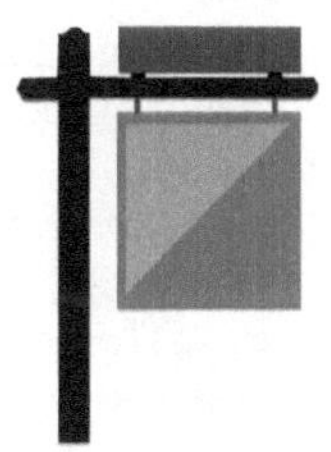

# Chapter Ten

## Getting Along—How Not to Become a Marked Man

My corridor, SO2, was the noisiest in the camp. Inmates were often up talking into the wee hours. I found it impossible to sleep and wondered why no one on the floor bitched about the noise. One night, the guys were especially loud, smoking and playing cards just outside my room. Around 2:45 AM, aroused out of a sound sleep by their noise, I yelled, "Would everyone just shut the hell up!"

The floor got real quiet. You could hear a pin drop.

I went back to sleep, but my roommate Gus woke me up.

"You shouldn't have done that," he said. "Now you're going to have to leave the floor."

"I give him credit," Rhino whispered. "He said what everyone wanted to say, but didn't have the balls."

"Yeah, but we just lost a good roommate," Gus replied.

Whoa, I hadn't realized speaking out would make me a marked man. But I couldn't change what I'd done.

The next morning, with bright sunlight shining into our room, I went to my counselor's office and asked to be transferred to S07. That floor housed inmates aged forty-five and older, and I should have been assigned to this floor in the first place. No sooner than I arrived in S07, inmates asked me where I got the guts to demand some quiet. As I'd learn many times over, in Franklin Prison, news travels at the speed of light!

I had six new cellmates. The first was Randall Gore, a grumpy seventy-five-year-old, who looked like an old-time farmer. He didn't glance up at me when I came in.

Another was Doc, who was impressive at over six feet tall. He seemed about my age—fifty-nine. He was a chiropractor, in prison for selling cocaine, but he used his skills to work on inmates' backs and necks.

Denny was next. He took one look at me and asked, "Are you rich?"

"No, are you?" I said.

Denny winked. "You're rich. I know that look."

Compared to the other white collar criminals in this prison I was definitely not rich.

To the right of Denny, there was Rory, a tall, muscular black guy too busy selling stuff from his locker to be bothered with introductions. Studying his face, he looked young, about thirty-five years old, but I couldn't be sure.

Next to these guys, I felt small at 5'10" and 175 pounds.

Art Fist, a little taller than me, he had straight hair hanging down his back. He was a southern boy who sold a legal drug easily found at any pharmacy, but he sold a heap of it at a store he owned. Art was attached to his Confederate flag, or so he told me later.

Leroy Sisk was a black man standing at a whopping 6'6" and carried 330 pounds. I had met him in AA and found him to have a quick and mean temper. I befriended him quickly.

Leroy asked me if I played chess and when I said I'd played years ago, he suggested we play sometime. That suited me.

My new roommates also included Tom Walters, a former U.S. senator. Life was full of ironies. He had been in Oxford Prison first, and then shipped to Franklin a couple years prior to my arrival. I'd met Tom the first time while having dinner at the Ritz Carlton with my brother about a year before I went to Franklin Prison Camp. That night in the restaurant, the senator stopped at our table and greeted my brother by asking about his steak. They exchanged some pleasantries—they weren't close friends, more like professional acquaintances.

When the senator was out of earshot, my brother whispered, "He's on his way to prison. I hope he handles it okay."

At the time, my legal case was nearing the end, but I still didn't believe I would do any prison time. How crazy it was that a former U.S. senator had just greeted my brother by name, only to be heading to prison soon, just like any ordinary citizen in legal trouble.

When I first saw the senator at the camp, he was sitting in an undershirt and shorts, which is what inmates wore when out of uniform. His face looked pale like he hadn't seen much sunlight in a while and his snow white hair was thinning. What a contrast with my last view of him in a designer black suit.

I walked over to him and introduced myself as Matthew's brother. Matt worked for a TV station in Chicago, and had interviewed Tom many times.

Tom invited me to sit down and asked how I was handling the camp.

I told him I was fine. He said he compared it to being in the army. He seemed to be liked by the inmates in his room, and he had a way of taking command of a room. When he told jokes, everyone laughed.

I figured being friends with Tom would probably be the prudent thing to do. Once a man of stature and power, Tom was sitting on a bunk in the prison camp surrounded by drug dealers and criminals. As the saying goes, the bigger they are, the harder they fall. Tom was serving a 10-year sentence after his conviction on corruption charges.

Later, after dinner with Tom and the others, I arrived back to my room and I saw an old man, about seventy or so, lying on a sleeping bag at the end of the hall. He had long white hair and a beard, like a Santa Claus without the big belly. I asked him why he was there.

"I have a heart condition," he murmured, "and they won't assign me a bottom bunk. I could kill myself trying to climb up to the top bunk."

"But you can't just lay there in the hall," I warned.

"Why not?"

"Because they might put you in the hole."

"I'm not afraid of the damn hole," he yelled with more force than I'd expected. "Let them take me there, kicking and screaming!"

Day after day, he stayed in the hall. He'd go to chow, read in a chair, and other inmates brought him soap, towels, cookies, blankets, a pillow, and anything else he needed.

One day, I sat beside him and introduced myself. I asked how long he expected to sit in the hall.

In a firm voice Ben said, "As long as it takes these assholes to give me a lower bunk."

Another two weeks he lived in the cold hallway. What a determined guy. He displayed a kind of charisma and most everyone admired his "don't back down" spirit. He was not going to sleep in a top bunk, and that was that. He called the CO's bluff and eventually won. They didn't take him to the hole because he wasn't afraid to go there.

I was so taken by his spirited stubbornness I wrote a poem about him.


**The Man in the Hallway**


A man sits quietly
Alone in the hall
I ask him the question
From where did you fall?

*Prison Clown*

His hair hangs down sloppy
On his shoulders it sits
His beard looks like cotton
With grey whiskers it's mixed

His eyes, they are weary
They just stare into space
No one takes notice
He just takes up some space

A man with no castle
No, not even a room
He sits in the hallway
Outside with the brooms

He sits there for hours
He never gets up
I pass him at midnight
As he sits with his cup

I decide to approach him
To ask him, why here?
He glances up towards me
His voice sounds so dear

The senator sees him
And offers his hand
But the man in the hallway
Just doesn't understand

The government's got me
And stay here I must
But they do not own me
So, I'll put up a fuss

The man in the hallway
Does not notice time
For the moment he'll sit here
For the moment, he's fine.

One morning, Senator Walters had coffee with Ben, and I soon joined them. Before long, more than ten other inmates were sitting on the floor with Ben. The very next day, Ben was sleeping in a bottom bunk in a room.

Over time, I became good friends with Ben. He was a good conversationalist and had a solid knowledge of politics. He taught me the lesson, one I thought I'd learned, that we can't judge people by physical appearance.

## The fundraiser and the health club

Former politicians (and their friends) were not rare in prison. In fact, another politician learned a good friend of his, a Republican fundraiser named Lou, would be imprisoned at Franklin Prison Camp. The politician was leaving in a couple of weeks and asked if I'd give up my lower bunk for his friend, now seventy-nine-years old. I agreed, because I knew the politician wanted someone to look out for his friend.

On my way to my room one afternoon I saw the politician and Lou talking, so I introduced myself and we all went to chow together. I knew this guy had to be somebody special because the senator was waiting on him hand and foot.

Lou looked every bit his age. He was thin and had only a bit of hair left on his head. He seemed to be a talkative, pleasant guy, and not too nervous about coming to prison. I guess if you have someone like the ex-pol making you feel at home, it's easier.

Lou put a photo of an eight-year-old girl on the wall,

his granddaughter. "Isn't she something?"

She obviously meant the world to him, so I said she was beautiful. Then I asked how long his sentence was.

"One year and a day."

"You'll probably only have to do about eight months," I responded. "What exactly are you in for?"

"Conspiracy for extortion. The Feds said I extorted money from a movie guy, but I never did."

I told Lou I had just read an article in the newspaper about a guy who raised money for politicians. The Feds said they got a big shot politician who extorted $11,000,000 from a big movie mogul who produced the movie, *Baby, You're a Rich Man.*

Lou quickly told me he "never extorted *nobody*," and especially not this guy. He had business dealings with a man trying to raise money from another guy, Johnny, who was having a hard time getting the deal done and he'd asked Lou for a favor. Lou then asked the pol to help. It seemed there was no one Lou didn't know.

Because Lou got in between Johnny and the new guy, he became embroiled in the investigation, and that's how he ended up at the camp. Lou and I quickly became friends. He'd tell me stories about all the people with whom he had business dealing with.

One evening, Lou was reading a newspaper in our room completely naked. I guess he thought prison was like a health club. Anyway, one of the inmates pulled me aside and told me I had better tell him to get dressed before he got hurt.

I did just that, and Lou looked shocked. He quickly got dressed, and that was the last time this old man showed up naked anywhere in the prison.

**The blessing of visitors**

It was always a joy to head to the visiting room to see Julie and my children. Jackie came along most frequently, since David and Mikey worked and Danni was away at college. Jackie would sleep all the way down to the camp and wake up in the camp parking lot. She would put her head on my shoulder and really start waking up once she sat next to me. Jackie would jump in front of Julie so she could sit next to me.

Julie and Jackie had to learn the rules, too. It was okay to hold hands and kiss briefly. You could only eat the food that was in the vending machine, but after eating in the chow hall, vending machine snacks tasted like gourmet foods.

Anything brought in or out of the visiting room was considered illegal contraband and strictly forbidden. Having chewing gum, books, candy, sandwiches, cookies, aspirin, or anything else not from the BOP is a Federal crime, punishable by five years in Federal prison.

On one occasion, Julie brought me a kosher corned beef sandwich and chips. I couldn't bear to tell her that this was illegal and would be considered contraband. I quickly gobbled down the sandwich and enjoyed it like it had fallen from heaven. Each bite was incredible. I felt like I was back home and a free man.

The next time Julie came, she brought a Super Dog with crispy French fries. This was an all-beef dog that was really thick. Again, I should have told Julie she had to stop this, but the smell of the food was too much for me. Again, I ate the food quickly and felt like I had died and gone to heaven with my family with me. I knew Julie liked watching my joyful and thankful face while I was eating.

The next time Julie and Jackie came to visit, she brought me a breakfast sandwich from McDonald's, which we heated in the microwave. This time, I had to tell her that what she was doing was against the rules—against Federal law. She had to stop bringing food—contraband. She could even get in trouble for it. No more outside food for me.

Julie had other ideas, though. She knew it was

against the rules, but she wanted me to be careful and not let the guard see me. She didn't want me to be deprived of delicious food. She continued bringing food in and somehow, we managed to get away with it. It seemed ridiculous we had to be so careful. Julie brought me nasal spray, which was also against the rules, and I held my breath in fear while taking it from her.

## Jackie's premonition

The prison camp was a five-hour drive from home and Jackie usually fell asleep on the way down. On one occasion, she woke from a deep sleep and said to Julie, "Don't bring any food to Dad today."

Julie asked why, but Jackie couldn't explain. She just repeated, "Don't bring food to Dad today."

Julie thought nothing of it and brought in my food like she always did.

As they got closer to the guard window, the visitor in front of her was asked to open her purse and the guard found a sandwich inside of it.

The guard yelled at the visitor and told her to go home and not to visit again for six months.

Another warning. This time, Julie slipped my food from her purse into the trash outside the camp. They got in just fine.

Julie told me the story, but we never found out why or how Jackie had that premonition, but we sure were lucky she did.

## Hidden gifts

Like nearly every inmate I met when I was in prison, my heart ached for my family and friends. Incarcerated, without freedom of movement or communication, I painfully realized I had taken people I loved for granted. I wished I'd spent more time with them. One "gift" prison gave me was a second chance to appreciate my family. Like everyone else, I'd focused, too. I had focused too much on my business and not on my family.

My teenage daughter, Jackie, had wanted time with me to talk about her day, but even if I sat with her, my mind was focused elsewhere. I didn't *really* listen to what she was sharing. This hit home in prison.

Looking back, my selfishness shocked me. That changed, and during Jackie's visits, I focused on *her*, hanging on her every word about her boyfriend, school, friendships, her relationship with Mom or whatever she wanted to share. I cherished our time together and prayed that she knew I valued her—and thought she was beautiful.

I wrote about this newfound gratitude, and while I wasn't especially religious, I'd begun listening to late night radio.

I couldn't sleep anyway, because of the steel bed. The show I tuned in to had a host who lectured on marriage, family, ego, love, business, and life, and of course, Jesus. One lecture focused on personal trials and why God puts us through them or allows them. The host said that if we want to know why God has us going through a trial, to just ask Him.

So, I did. I asked why I was sent to prison. I wasn't being punished, was I? I never intended to commit a crime, but even if the Feds didn't believe me, I thought for sure, God did.

One of the most important things I learned in prison is how incredibly blessed I've been to have Julie, a loyal and dedicated partner. I always valued my wife, but I came to value her even more when we were forced to be apart.

Not everyone was so lucky.

Another inmate, a guy named Heck, had a wonderful family, including three grandchildren. But then his daughter and son-in-law ran off and left the children with Heck and his wife. He told me stories about horseback riding on his land with all of his "children," including a little girl about five years old who had her very own horse. She could ride like the wind and wasn't at all scared.

Unfortunately, Heck and his wife cooked meth, which is why he ended up in prison. His sentence was five years, not long considering he was involved with methamphetamines.

One day, he was sitting in the prison hall looking depressed, a look I came to recognize. Sometimes when I'd walk down the hall, an inmate would approach me and say, "Are you alright?"

I felt warmed by this show of concern. I would answer, "Yes, how about you?"

This would go on for a month until I heard one inmate say it a few times in one day. I finally realized this was not a real show of concern, but just a greeting to say hello.

Anyway, I asked Heck if he was okay, but I could see he had been crying and tried to pretend I hadn't noticed.

He explained he called his wife every day at 5:30 PM. Today was no exception, only he heard a man's voice on the phone.

When he asked his wife what was going on, she explained she had met the man the previous night at a bar, and they were talking about life until 4 AM. She qualified her story by telling Heck she did not have sex with this guy. I would have been livid knowing a strange man was in my house, even if no sexual activity occurred.

Heck learned that when the phone rang, the granddaughter tried to get his wife on the phone, but the bedroom door was locked. His wife made excuses about protecting the kids, but Heck likely believed his wife was covering up an affair.

I asked him if he believed her story, and he gave me a look that said, "Are you serious?"

Once I realized he knew what was really going on with his wife, we talked for a while, and then I left him alone to handle his situation. I sure felt lucky to have Julie.

About a week later, Heck gave me some of his belongings, mostly books and games. What was going on? Heck had often smoked cigarettes in prison, but he knew how to stay out of the hole.

However, I soon learned he got caught, and off to the hole he went. The cop who caught Heck told him to do some extra yard work to avoid the hole, but Heck said he couldn't because he had a broken finger. So, even though Heck was lucky to get a cop to offer a way out of the hole, he chose to go. I believed he was so depressed by his wife's unfaithfulness he wanted to be totally alone.

I heard many stories like this from inmates. I estimated about 90% of all married inmates who received a sentence of five years or more ended up divorced.

Another inmate, Pete, was locked up for six years without even a phone call, letter, or money from his wife. She had divorced him after 30 years of marriage and was now going to marry another man. She sent Pete a letter letting him know, and also hoped she and Pete could remain friends for the benefit of their adult children who now had children of their own. Whether or not a divorce is justified or makes sense, what a helpless, frustrated feeling to learn all this while imprisoned.

## Memories to live on

I had a lot of time to think in prison, and my family was always on my mind, especially as I anticipated another visit. One day, I was sitting on my bed doing nothing. I'd been reading and finished my book. It was only 3 PM, 90 minutes to go before we went to chow. I started thinking about a four-year-old blue and gold Macaw Julie and I had bought and named Chief. This bird's voice was loud! He'd wake us up in the morning with an ear-piercing shriek-yell. Since Chief's wings had been clipped and he couldn't fly, I thought it would be cool to build a tree perch for Chief to live on. He never flew off his perch to the ground, so our guests could admire him, marveling at his vibrant colors. Chief was dramatically beautiful.

One day while our housecleaner was in our home, the doorbell rang. An insurance estimator came to inspect our broken glass dining room table. We were away, and Chief got excited and flew down to the carpet. Chief stood two feet tall, had a sharp beak and talons. The housecleaner had never seen Chief come to ground, and afraid of him, ran upstairs, followed by the scared estimator.

They ran into the bathroom and slammed the door shut. As it happened, our cleaner spoke Polish and the estimator only spoke German. Although they could not communicate, they both were laughing hysterically while they were locked in the bathroom.

When the estimator dared open the door a crack and peered out, there was Chief waiting patiently for them to come out. After about a half hour, the estimator got brave. He rolled up a newspaper from a magazine rack, opened the door slightly, and swatted at Chief.

Of course, this guy did not know that I played this game with Chief, and he would tear the newspaper to shreds.

And that's what he did, which drove the estimator back inside the bathroom.

After another half hour, Chief left and went into our bedroom. That's when the pair took their chances and ran downstairs and out of our house.

When Julie and I got home, we heard the vacuum running and saw shredded newspaper all over the place. Chief was not on his tree perch.

We headed upstairs to find the bathroom light on.

When we looked in our bedroom, there was Chief sitting on our bed.

I offered my arm as a perch for him and carried him back downstairs to his tree perch. Our cleaner and the estimator admitted being scared—and embarrassed. From that point on, when we had our house cleaned, I had to lock Chief in his cage.

Sitting on my bed that day, the misadventure came back to me and helped me remember my life. I was grateful for memories because I saw guys in prison get lost without them. They forgot there is a life after. I was blessed with funny memories that filled me with hope and gave me the strength to keep going.

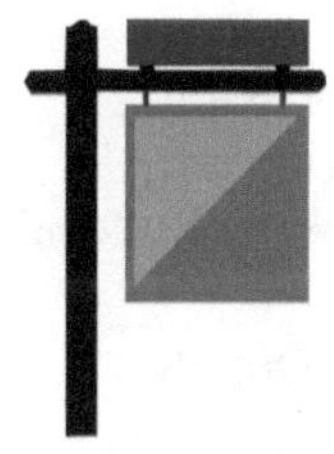

# Chapter Eleven

## Working for Peanuts—and Other Surprises

I had to find a job or eventually I'd be considered "unassigned" and Rain, the Camp Chief, would assign me one. Since I was sure I wouldn't like the job he'd choose, I set out to find one.

First, I sat with Richard, my closest friend then, (the guy who was also in for bank fraud whom I met at AA) and asked about my options. This is the list of jobs he showed me:

1. Hall Orderly
2. Kitchen Orderly
3. Bathroom Orderly
4. Chemical Room Attendant
5. Tool Room Attendant
6. Weld Shop
7. Green House Orderly
8. Bus Station
9. Pet Store
10. Bubble Orderly
11. Wood Shop

12. Fish Farm
13. Main Hall Orderly
14. Education Orderly
15. The Cup (Water Building)
16. Laundry
17. Recreation Orderly

I soon learned that jobs typically paid $2.00, not an hour, a day, or a week, but a month! Of course, this was disturbing. Richard told me the U.S. Constitution was amended to abolish slavery, but incarceration is different. Once again, I couldn't believe I was now a slave to the United States of America.

Richard told me the BOP was so broke, they can't even pay the inmates the money they owe for inmate labor. Since the pay was outrageously low, I saw no reason to take a job that meant working really hard. As for the easiest job, Richard mentioned either the fish farm or recreation.

On the way to have a look at the farm, Richard explained the BOP planned to have the fish farm produce tilapia for inmate meals in all three prisons, so that meant fish for 3000 inmates. At that time, the fish farm had a stock of about 3,000 fish, and tilapia grows to be about a foot long. We watched the keeper feed the fish, a process I found interesting. It was peaceful at the fish farm and I enjoyed the couple of hours we spent there.

When I got back, I saw another guy, Tommy, who lived one cell to the left of mine. I asked Tommy about a job and he said if I wanted something easy, he'd get me a job in Recreation. He knew the CO of Rec and she'd give me a job based on Tommy mentioning me. The pay was a little higher, if you can believe it, at $2.50 a month. But according to Tommy, no work was involved.

I told him I wanted the job and thanked him for his help and suggestion. I went to Recreation and spoke to Allie, the woman who ran the department, and mentioned Tommy's name. I asked if she had a job opening in Recreation.

After studying a list, Allie told me she had an opening for someone to clean the outdoor bocce ball court.

I told her that I'd do a fine job at this task.

Then she asked, "What are you going to do to an outside bocce ball court?"

"Now that you mention it, I don't really know," I said.

She smiled and said, "Okay, now you've got my drift."

She was pretty cool. For almost two years, I never touched the bocce ball court, and that was just fine with her.

It turned out Allie was a kind person who showed compassion for the inmates. She knew what the inmates were up against and let them coast.

Sometimes at Franklin Prison Camp, an inmate got a CO who hated the inmates in general, but other times you got a CO who was a decent person, like Allie. The inmates figured the hateful COs probably hated their lives, most likely hated their jobs. When you think about it, a lifelong career in the prison meant these guards and others would work at the prison for 25 years. We felt that was kind of like a "prison" sentence.


## Quack medical unit


I'd always assumed one thing you count on at Federal prison was fairly good medical care. The camp to which I was assigned supposedly served as an expert medical facility. In fact, inmates from all over the country came to the Franklin Camp for medical procedures since it was located by a hospital. That aside, treatment at the prison camp was hardly a model for good care.

Two months before I arrived, an incident highlighting

the medical care had taken place. An inmate about age seventy complained to another inmate about shooting pains in his side. The other inmate advised him to go to the bubble where he would at the very least be checked out by a physician's assistant. However, the CO at the bubble sent him back to this room.

"Don't bother me now. Sick days are Monday, Wednesday, and Friday."

It was Tuesday, so he was out of luck. The inmate went back to his room, but two hours later the pain worsened.

He went back and begged the CO at the bubble to let him see the PA. This time, the CO got angry and threatened the inmate with being sent to the hole.

On his way back to his room, the inmate collapsed in the middle of the hallway and other inmates clustered around him. Witnesses heard the CO screaming at the sick inmate. "Get back to your room or go to the hole!" The CO even *kicked* the man, who by now lay motionless.

When the guard went to pick him up, the man didn't move.

Within minutes, a screaming ambulance pulled up and took the inmate away on a stretcher.

Later, inmates learned the man was DOA—dead on arrival. The man died from complications of a ruptured appendix. His death likely could have been prevented with timely surgery.

Another inmate complained about chest pains, but the CO refused treatment more than once. The inmate kept showing up asking for help, but the CO working the bubble eventually sent the complaining inmate to the hole. Word got out that two days later this inmate also died on the way to the hospital.

It seemed inmates who end up dead always seemed to die "on the way to the hospital," and never at the prison itself. *Sure.*

This didn't surprise me too much, because before entering prison I wanted to learn about life as an inmate and contacted a few people, including a woman living in North Dakota. Her diabetic husband had been sentenced to prison for a white collar crime, but didn't receive his insulin at the proper times, which led to complications and improper treatment of diabetes. He died in prison, or as the Prison Camp Administration put it, "on the way to the hospital."

Word of these incidents constantly circulated among inmates. They had a genuine sense that the BOP did not consider inmates as human beings, let alone U.S. citizens.

During my first year in prison, I met a guy, Calvin, who complained to me about pain in his side, but the doctor told him to come back only if he was bleeding.

A few days later, I saw him walking through the halls back and forth, back and forth. He looked terrible, and I asked him if he was okay.

"I have some blood in my urine, but the doctor said there's nothing he could do for me."

After that, I didn't see him in the hall for several days.

Then a week later, there he was walking down the hall again, still looking like he was in pain. I found out he'd been in the hospital handcuffed to the bed for four days. Apparently, it's policy to handcuff an inmate to the hospital bed, even if he's a "camper." He had kidney stones and was not given pain pills after he left the hospital.

While I was there, another situation came up. A man on my floor was admitted to the hospital for triple bypass surgery. The operation was successful, and he was given a list of specific drugs he needed to take going forward. But he was never given any of the required medications. The prison doctor told him he didn't need them.

Hearing these allegations left me uneasy and feeling helpless. Naturally, after sharing these incidents with Julie, she more or less ordered me *not* to get sick. Most of all, it bothered me that the U.S. BOP would consider me or *any* inmate less than human. I already knew inmates had lost all our constitutional rights. We were under their thumb without a vote and considered less than fully human, not worth medical treatment allowed to animals.

## Chow: this is where they get you

To visitors, the chow hall looks clean and the menu appealing—BOP publicity in action. Just like German concentration camps, when Red Cross visitors showed up, the camp had been made to look good. Likewise, the BOP camp is also ready when the warden and visitors showed up. I realize the U.S. BOPs do not gas the inmates. I'm speaking of the food.

The menu is posted on the chow hall door. For example, Monday's lunch is chili cheese hot dogs. The hot dogs are the size of a popsicle stick and not fully cooked. Sometimes, they were served with buns and sometimes not. Tuesday's lunch is tuna fish sandwiches, which I hated, so I was given two cold hardboiled eggs. We had hamburgers on Wednesday— at least they were called hamburgers. The inside of the burger was red and the meat looked dried out and old. The fries with the burger weren't so bad. Thursday was chicken day, one piece of chicken the size of one finger.

One time, I was really hungry and tried to get another piece of chicken by getting into line twice. No such luck.

The guard yelled, "Hey, isn't this your second time?"

I owned up, and he hollered for me to get out of line.

This guard was a real jerk. When everyone finished going through the line, he took all the extra chicken pieces and threw them in the garbage. I couldn't believe he'd done something so nasty.

Friday was fish day. If you liked breaded rubbery fish, you were okay.

Our evening meals followed a similar routine from Monday's chicken in cream sauce. I couldn't stomach it, so on Mondays, I ordered pizza from an inmate who cooked them in the basement using a makeshift oven he put together by steeling the heating coil from the dryer and some aluminum sheet he cut from the shop. Pizza in the microwave was gross, but this guy knew how to cook the crust crispy. Tuesday night was pulled pork. Again, I ordered pizza.

Wednesday night was pork chops. This was by far the worst dinner all week. They gave us a small piece of cold pork the size of a silver dollar.

Thursday night was beef stew that looked suspiciously like canned dog food. Friday night, pulled pork again. I wasn't interested in the Saturday chow hall menus because Julie snuck me in an egg and cheese muffin.

All in all, the food ranged from more than disappointing to just plain awful. Thankfully, I could purchase from resourceful, camp-food-frustrated inmates, who cooked pizza, real hamburgers, burritos, nachos, and fried rice and eggs that were served on these occasions. We all knew this was against camp rules, but everyone was willing to take the risk because they, too, had to eat. Without access to this food, I'd not have made it.

## The warden is coming! The warden is coming!

When the warden planned a trip to the camp, Rain's feathers got ruffled. First, an announcement roared out, "Everyone get to their workstation to *clean*!"

So, we all cleaned our cells.

I can understand clearing off lockers for an inspection, but we were told nothing could hang on the walls. I thought that was going too far. Our lockers were so small our dirty clothing got mixed with our clean clothing. We had to hide coats and boots, nothing could hang on hooks, and no pictures could be out. The warden wanted every belonging stashed away in our lockers, but that was impossible, which is why I took my stuff and hid it in the music room inside the big bass drum.

I believe all this was more about punishing inmates with frivolous chores than concern about where a photo was displayed. Besides, it wasn't as if we were in the military and training to be combat ready.

The warden's inspections involved all kinds of trivial things. He'd drag his finger on the sprinkler pipes, and on the windows and lockers. If he found nothing wrong, then he'd demand the hooks pulled off the wall. Just to be pissy. As for the inmates, they only hoped he'd leave without condemning their rooms to extra detail.

## Tucked in shirts and missing screwdrivers

Logically, you'd think a prison dungeon like the infamous hole would be reserved for hardened criminals guilty of heinous crimes. Wrong. Take the case of the untucked shirt.

During a period of time in the camp, prison counselors wanted inmates' shirts tucked in. It took a few days to get used to it, but finally we all complied and reminded other inmates to tuck in their shirts.

On one very hot day, Freddy was helping another inmate carry a bed to the laundry. As he worked, his shirt came untucked. Teller (second in charge of the camp under Rains) walked by and gave him a warning about it.

Freddy quickly tucked it in and explained how it happened. The next day Freddy helped another inmate, who was changing rooms, carry a mattress. Oops, that shirt again came untucked. Teller saw it, and this time sent Freddy straight to the hole.

At that time, Freddy was supposed to have been

shipped out to attend the RDAP Program but ended up sitting in the hole because of his accidentally untucked shirt. This was so beyond ridiculous it was nearly a crime in itself.

But then, something close to miraculous happened.

Two days later, Freddy was released because the lieutenant at the USP (United States Prison) was angry with the petty reasons inmates were being sent to the hole. So, a week later, Freddy left for the RDAP program.

Around this time, another inmate signed a screwdriver out of the bus depot, which is one of the places inmates worked. That night, the screwdriver went missing. The eight inmates working that shift were given four hours to find and return the screwdriver, or (you guessed it), they would all be sent to the hole.

The inmate who had checked out the screwdriver remained anonymous since his fellow workers didn't want to snitch on him, so all eight went to the hole. Being a snitch in prison is far worse than being a snitch outside. I estimate approximately 75% of inmates who get sent to a camp snitched on someone, and once they arrived at camp, they might continue to snitch.

One reason a convicted felon goes to a prison camp is that the FBI uses snitches to get their targeted convict. The first man to snitch usually gets the best deal. Even if the snitch was actually a bigger actor in the crime, he may be credited for time served and less overall time, along with being sent to a prison camp.

About three months after the screwdriver disappeared, a bus broke down on the road. When an inmate opened the hood, there it was, the missing screwdriver.

The reason I was even more scared of the hole than the average inmate is that I suffered from a severe case of claustrophobia. I dreaded going in elevators or the back seat of a two-door car, or the middle seats in a theater or sporting event. Thank God the prison had no locked doors. The thought of being locked up in a small cell for 23 hours a day for months was enough to petrify me. I believe if I did not suffer from claustrophobia, I might have been able to handle the hole. So far, I hadn't found out.

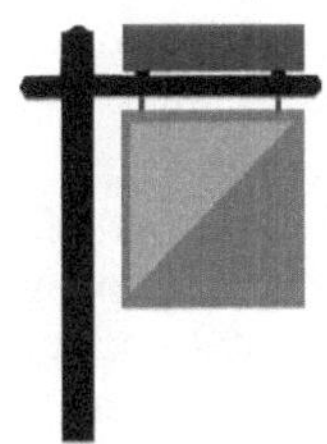

# Chapter Twelve

## Every Inmate was Unique

When I first walked into the camp "bubble," I saw a man standing in the hall. He introduced himself as Irving Gold. His white undershirt had food stains all over it, and with his scraggly beard he looked to be at least eighty-five years old.

"You probably think me a kook," he said, "but I want to tell you how naïve and oblivious the American people are about the taxation of this nation."

What had I walked into? The guy is a kook. I was concerned about being cornered.

"Did you know there is nothing in the U.S. Constitution about us having to pay *income tax*? Did you know American citizens don't have to sign any document that could later incriminate them? When we sign our IRS tax return, we are violating our constitutional rights."

I listened, impatiently and wanting to move on, but I was stuck like a rat in a trap. Finally, after twenty minutes of this, I cut myself loose. I concluded Irving shouldn't be in prison, but in a loony bin.

My best friend Richard had told me about the Sabbath service when I'd arrived, so on Friday, I walked down to the temple to observe the Sabbath and sat in the back of the room. There was a total of six

Jews in the whole camp and as I learned that evening, one of them was none other than Irving. He put on his yarmulke and tallis and sat beside me. Once again, he started talking about taxes, picking up right where he left off. He began telling me about books he'd had written on the unconstitutional taxation we subjected ourselves to. Meanwhile, I was politely listening, but in reality, he was driving me crazy.

We started services and to my relief, he stopped talking. The rabbi was a tall black man whose name was Lang. He apparently had studied to be a rabbi. He ran thru the prayers and did a great job.

I can't read Hebrew, but it made me think of when I was younger and went to Jewish services with my uncle. The rabbi's brother was one of the guys in the band, The OJ's. When services concluded, I saw Ronald (the fake art dealer) take Irving's arm and walk him back to the bubble. That was touching to me.

When the pill line formed, another inmate took Irving to the line where inmates got their medications. Everyone let him cut in line. This old guy was respected by the inmates.

The following day, I saw another inmate taking Irving. Everyone seemed to cater to the needs of this guy we dubbed the "Taxman," who I considered a nut. I was taken in by it, though. Who'd expected such caring from the inmates at a prison?

During the first Sabbath service I attended in the chapel, there were only six of us, including the rabbi, who chanted the prayers and the rest of us would answer back as the congregation. When the rabbi said the prayers, he would always beat a drumbeat on the desk, which sounded foreign to me. Nonetheless, it was still Jewish Sabbath and I enjoyed leaving the inmate population for an hour to pray.

Suddenly, Irving sang the prayer called "The Shmah." It sounded like what the rabbi had sung back in Lincolnwood, Illinois when I was a kid preparing for my bar mitzvah. Surreal.

He belted the prayer from his seat. I couldn't believe that haunting, powerful voice came from such an old man! Irving knew he could sing and went on for twenty minutes. This was the closest to home I ever felt while in prison.

I decided to get to know Irving. I knew better than to judge by appearances, but I kept making these judgmental mistakes. Irving was eager to find someone to help him read his mail or the information he received on his appeal. I decided this would be a good way to gain his friendship, so I sat down to help with his reading.

His trial and appeal were extremely difficult. He believed the Federal judges were all in cahoots with the government, against him, and his philosophy on taxation. He was one of those citizens that thought it was unconstitutional to pay taxes. He also told me the U.S. government considered him a terrorist. *Come on.*

We shared stories about our lives and families. He was very proud of his son, Stephan, who paid his taxes so he wouldn't end up in prison like his dad. (Come to find out Irving's son was a big news and precious metals guy.) Irving understood Stephan's reasoning, but Irving himself lived and breathed his cause, consumed with proving his point that the U.S. government is abrogating the Constitutional rights of the American people by making them file income taxes.

Irving was proud of the fact that during his trial, the judge asked for "order in the court," and Irving answered, "I'll have ham on rye." Irving believed the courts and their judges were stupid.

I was amazed to learn Irving was a comic genius. He'd rubbed elbows with many famous comedians, from Jackie Gleason and Shecky Green. And he'd done *The Howard Stern Show* and said that Stern was polite to him. He'd grown up doing stand-up comedy routines.

As I listened to his stories, I couldn't help wondering

how and why a judge would put an eighty-five-year-old man in prison for writing a book on taxation. It was true that thousands of people who read his book also didn't pay their taxes. Still, isn't it his right of freedom of speech?

On the other hand, maybe Irving was in prison for tax evasion, for not filing taxes. But why register him as a terrorist? It just seemed ridiculous to me to have a person who can barely see or walk in prison spending the rest of his life here. It's actually a terrible feeling to look at an inmate and know he will die in prison.


## Henny Youngman


After knowing Irving a couple of months, I decided to bring him into a public speaking class I was taking. Like all the classes, it was taught by an inmate and comedy was the topic. Who better to bring as a guest speaker than Irving? He accepted my invitation and seemed honored that an inmate would invite him to do standup comedy.

I introduced him to the class as Irving Youngman. And he knocked them dead. Everyone laughed hysterically as he told one joke after another. They were the same old jokes Henny Youngman and Rodney Dangerfield were famous for.

"Take my wife, please."

"My wife told me to take her somewhere she had never been before, so I took her into the kitchen!"

"What does my wife make for dinner? Reservations."

One joke he shared was about a man who underwent a penis enlargement operation by using an elephant trunk. About two days after the operation, he was at a dinner party and was sitting next to a beautiful lady. Having eaten too much, he loosened his belt, and his "trunk" came up and grabbed a potato and pulled it underneath the table. The man apologized and told her about the operation.

The woman exclaimed, "Actually I thought that was incredible! Can you do it again?"

The man answered, "Yes, I think so, but I don't think I could get another potato up my ass."

With this joke, the whole room went crazy laughing, both with and about Irving.

A few months went by, and the inmates heard a rumor that Irving's family had complained to the BOP that he wasn't receiving enough medical attention. This was true; but then none of the inmates were receiving satisfactory medical treatment.

Irving was shipped to another camp and had to start over again to acclimate to his new surroundings and make new friends. His family had to adjust to a new facility, too. I think the family was trying to get the old man home. Instead, the Feds sent him to another camp.


## The "Ghetto"


One night as I was just falling asleep, around 12:30 AM, my celly Denny woke me up and asked if I wanted to go to The Ghetto.

"Where?" I asked.

"The *Ghetto*," he whispered fiercely. "That's where the brothers hang out late at night. Would you like to come?"

I wasn't aware of any such place in the camp, so, up for an adventure I said, "Okay."

I'd never even heard inmates talk about the Ghetto, so I had no idea where I was going or what I would do there. We crawled out of our bunks and he told me to meet him in the chow hall in ten minutes, which I did. Then we both walked to Unit S01.

"Stay here and don't go anywhere," Denny whispered.

"No problem." I stood outside in the hall wondering what I was getting myself into, a thousand thoughts running through my mind. What's so secret about this place? Why have I never heard anything about it? Do these guys do drugs there?

About five minutes later, Denny came back out into the hall saying, "Okay, they know you're here." He led the way down the hall, and I followed until we arrived at Range, Floor S01.

The unit looked different than it did during the day. Now, at night, something seemed unusual. Under six black lights, the only light in the unit, inmates' white T-shirts glowed. In the daylight, the four card tables were checked in red and black; now they looked magical. A cherry fragrance permeated the unit.

When I looked for the source of the fragrance, I noticed incense sticks burning inside plastic drinking cups taken from the chow hall. Four inmates per table were playing Spades.

Another six guys were smoking cigarettes in the bathroom, but the two shower curtains were closed.

Out of curiosity, I pulled back one of the shower curtains and saw three guys smoking a skinny cigarette. When I asked what it was, they explained it was K-2, legal on the streets before it was outlawed. The street manufacturers kept changing its chemical makeup to avoid being caught.

I knew K-2 was illegal inside prison, so I got uncomfortable just being there. The BOP occasionally tested inmates for marijuana and cocaine, and a test had been developed for K-2, but at $100 a test, the cost was apparently prohibitive. That meant the BOP seldom tested for the drug. In any case, I knew to stay away from the drug—any drug.

I walked out of the bathroom, but then I smelled pizza. Ahhh. I grabbed a couple of pieces and a soda stored in a cooler loaded with ice. At the end of the unit, I saw guys boogying to radio music. Others were using their cell phones. Quickly, I realized I was the only white guy on the unit. It was cool to be invited to the Ghetto, since this was definitely *the* happenin' place in the camp. I was honored Denny invited me to

130

a party completely made up of black brothers.

I soon grasped the reason for my invitation: humor. I made these guys laugh. I took a drag of a cigarette while drinking more pop. All the brothers were struttin' their stuff in the unit, so I joined them. But my strut was a bit too white, and we all enjoyed a laugh over that.

Denny and I stayed until 2:15 AM and then we headed back to our cell by lights out time. I was told to keep my mouth shut and not tell the white inmates about the so-called ghetto. I did as I was told.

## The SS

Being Jewish, I was aware of anti-Semitism within the camp, and at times, had those negative attitudes directed to me, including "Jewish jokes" on the baseball field and on the tennis court. I learned it was often wiser to take the high road and let some comments roll off my back rather than confront people. As long as the jokes didn't come too often, my sense of humor went a long way to avoid arguments. As Shakespeare wrote, "Discretion is the better part of valor." To me, that meant choosing my battles.

The men in the room next to mine seemed decent enough. They gave me food or a snack, and I reciprocated. Although I enjoyed many good conversations with inmates about my Jewish religion, one inmate couldn't believe I never celebrated Christmas. Another wanted to know about Chanukah. They learned about my faith, and I learned about theirs.

The room I lived in was about 50% black. I liked everyone except Rory. He was down longer than me and running a store, which was against regulations. But if no one snitched, then he could likely run his store without problems. Rory purchased items from the commissary and stocked up on candy, cookies, chips, and any other supplies he could sell at a 40%

markup. Some of the inmates had no source of income, except their camp jobs, so an enterprising soul could increase his earnings $50-$100 a week by running an inside "store."

Rory had stashed his inventory all over our room, and customers came and went at all hours of the day and night. Rory had so much inventory he started using my space and my hooks. When I told him to take his stuff off my hooks, he told me to go fuck myself. That was the last straw.

I became so angry, Leroy, a black Native American and former U.S. Navy guy, who was also huge, had to pick me up and put me outside so I wouldn't get into a fight with Rory. Everyone in the room laughed as Leroy carried me out like a bag of peanuts over his shoulder. I kicked and yelled the whole time. Leroy just kept lighting cigarettes and handing them to me until I finally calmed down. This time the argument passed.

Another time, I was changing my shorts in our room, and Rory came in screaming that he didn't want to see my white ass in the room.

"Are you serious?" I asked.

"Fuck ya, I'm serious. Go to the bathroom and change in there!"

"Go to hell," I screamed back.

Rory stormed out of the room.

I later asked around to learn if this had happened to any others. Sure enough, I met at least three white guys who'd had a problem with Rory about changing in the room.

While Leroy helped me avoid fighting Rory, he had a seriously bad temper himself. After serving 15 years as a U.S. Marine, sadly, he'd ended up in prison for selling meth. He didn't like people in general, but he hated inmates. Had no use for them. He'd been sentenced to 20 years and finally worked his way down to the prison camp where he was trying very hard not to get into fights. As cellmates, we became friends primarily because I made him laugh.

To watch this big bear laugh was a trip. He and I would go outside by the back door and smoke a cigarette a few times a day.

Leroy's temper was his downfall. He taught history in the education program, and I took his class to help fill it. He was extremely intelligent and an articulate speaker who was also street smart—nobody's fool. But, if an inmate rubbed him the wrong way, *whoa,* he'd better get out of Leroy's way and fast!

One guy kept stealing Leroy's candy from his locker at the cup. (Electric meters were in the place called "the cup," and the inmates could work there.) One day while standing in the medicine line, Leroy filled a plastic bag full of ice and began whacking this guy on the head with it over and over.

In an attempt to alleviate the situation, I asked Leroy if I could have some ice from the bag before the bag broke, since the prison had run out of ice again, something that happened all the time.

I thought that would break up the fight, but I was wrong. One of the COs spotted this and sent both men to the hole. I was lucky Leroy didn't kill me with his bare hands. I never saw Leroy again, because he was shipped out to another facility.

With all of the dissension in our room, Alex, one of the guys in the room next to us, asked me to move into his room. He'd heard my arguments with Rory and knew Leroy would no longer be there to stop things before they got too heated. I considered this for about a week, and then decided to move.

Occupants of this room included Tank, a guy I had been staying away from because he was a hard ass who worked his way down from a high prison. He was skinny, but man, he was mean. This guy couldn't stop riding me—riding me to no end—about being Jewish. This was the closest I ever got to taking shit about my religion. I thought being his roommate would help the situation.

It was strange, but once I got to know Tank, he wasn't such a hard ass after all and we actually gambled together. He was a good handball and softball player, too.

Many inmates were afraid of him because of how mean he looked. He would bump an inmate in the hall, and I'd tell the guy Tank didn't mean it. He got all the college football scores correct on a ticket where he didn't have to worry about the spread—and he actually paid me my half.

Then there was Tommy, the guy who helped me get my recreation job. He was one of those people who didn't believe the Holocaust ever happened. I spent night after night talking until I was blue in the face proving its reality.

Tom, another guy in my new room, kept to himself. He loved sports, and as a strong athlete, he participated in all the camp had to offer.

Pasqual was a Mexican who seemed like a good guy but nobody in the room talked to him.

Then there was Alex, only 5'6" and covered with tattoos from his head to his toes. He reminded me of a nice Charles Manson. Alex was living proof that an inmate will be institutionalized if his stay in prison is long enough. He'd been normal coming in, but prison made him quiet and withdrawn. Only after he'd been incarcerated for 15 years had he placed tattoos on every square inch of his body.

One day, he asked me if I thought girls would be turned off by so many tattoos. I was honest and told him some would. So, he suggested having sex in the dark until the girl got to know him better.

Alex was in for the manufacturing of meth, which he didn't deny. Still, he didn't believe he deserved his sixteen-year sentence. When he began his prison sentence, Alex's daughter was too young to remember him. They spoke every week by phone, but, as usual in inmate-family relations, his ex-wife wouldn't allow their daughter to visit.

I heard many stories about the life that led to prison. Alex would make a batch of meth with a profit of $32,000. Then he and his wife would fly to Las Vegas and party with friends. To get some cash, all he had to do was make another batch of meth. Like everyone in the camp from meth, one of his buyers got caught and ratted on everyone else.

Alex started at the medium security prisons and worked his way down to a prison camp. He always compared the life in the camp to USP, United States Prison.

"At the USP, you couldn't eat food other than from the chow hall," he'd say. "At the USP, one cigarette costs one book of stamps instead of one stamp. At the USP, you can't cut in line. There are gangs there, and the gang leaders solve all the problems and disagreements the inmates may have."

Whenever, I'd consider transferring to another camp, he would tell me how lax our camp was compared to the other camps he's been to and that I should stay put.

Alex was getting close to the end of his sentence. He was scared about getting out and making the transition back into society. He didn't remember how to live in the outside world. I could tell Alex had some good common sense, but he'd become institutionalized.

The thought of being sent away from my family for sixteen years was impossible to comprehend. I wondered if I'd have the strength to do the time. Or, would I be tempted to take the easy way out? Suicide would certainly have crossed my mind. If I'd been sentenced to twenty-five years, that would make me eighty-seven years old when I left prison. Although inmates say they do what they have to do because of their kids, it seemed to me, it would be hard on the kids to see their father behind bars for so many years. I am thankful I didn't have to consider the consequences.

One afternoon, Alex said he wanted to show me his art project. We went upstairs and to my disbelief, he showed me a bead pattern of the Nazi SS insignia!

Of course, I confronted him. "Do you know what this insignia means?"

"Yes," he said. "It's the Nazi symbol from World War II."

"Do you know who the Nazis hated?"

"Yes, Jews and blacks."

"So why would you take me up here and show me this?" I demanded.

He stared at me and said, "I have nothing against you being Jewish. *Hitler* did. I just wanted you to see my project."

So, I asked Alex straight out, "Are you a Nazi?"

"No," he answered. "I just wanted to show you my project. I'm sorry if I offended you."

This felt very strange to me. Was I living with a bunch of Nazis or a bunch of idiots? I asked myself if I should transfer out of the room. But judging from the way I was treated, I decided to stay, but kept my eyes open. Maybe these guys didn't like Jews, but they thought I, as an individual, was okay. Of course, that prejudice is behind that ridiculous remark, usually made in self-defense: "Some of my best friends are Jewish." (Or, black or Hispanic or women or gay or whatever!)

About a week later, as I chatted with Tommy in our room, he decided to change his shirt. My heart almost dropped when I saw a swastika tattooed in red and black on his upper arm. It looked exactly like the swastika on WWII Nazi SS uniforms. *Unbelievable.* I'd had unknowingly roomed with a bunch of Nazis. *Why* did they want *me* in their room? What were they planning on doing to me? I immediately called Tommy out on it.

"I was held in a high security prison when I started out," Tommy explained, "so getting tattooed was something I did to prove I was a tough guy. I didn't realize the ramifications of what I was doing. Now, I wish I didn't have this stupid thing."

Again, who knows what to believe? I knew I wasn't

going to have anybody over for dinner until I learned the truth. Tommy was the guy who treated me with the most friendship. He even covered me with a second blanket when I was freezing because Alex turned his fan on me when I snored.

Because I'd been welcomed, and both men had apologized, I stayed. But I couldn't help laughing at what Julie and my friends would think when they learned I was living in a cell with Nazis. What a weird predicament. It was insane.


## And then there was...


It's no surprise that lots of haters exist and Jews usually are included among the groups these haters hate. To be humorous about it, Richard would say "the Jews are supposed to be the Chosen People, but just once let there be someone else chosen!"

Anyway, I always had to be careful in my dealings. For instance, one night, dinner consisted of green bean soup and a spoonful of salad—by spoonful, I mean teaspoon. Thankfully, I found Jaime who makes kickass fajitas, like what we'd buy on the streets in Mexico. Without the food inmates cook, I would surely have died a slow, hungry death.

One night, Jaime and I ate his fajitas. Afterward, he wanted to share a cigarette, but when he checked his pockets, he realized he was out. He came back with Don, who lives on his floor, and was the president of the KKK.

Don came into the back stairway, where I was sitting and lit one up. Just that second it hit me who he was.

Jaime must not have known I was Jewish when he invited Don to smoke. Don was bald and tattooed with Nazi crosses. There was a lightning bolt tattoo, which I remember seeing on the Nazi uniforms at Nuremburg rallies I had seen on documentaries.

Rather than leaving, I decided to stay and see how

Don would act towards me. I wasn't sure if he knew I was Jewish, since he didn't get around camp much and we seldom saw each other.

I saw him on a TV program called *Notorious Gangsters*. I think they changed his voice, but I'm not certain. I remembered hearing that when he entered camp, rumor was that he had a tattoo of a black man hanging from a tree. I never saw it, so I couldn't say one way or another.

Don kept smoking and never made eye contact with me. Finally, after a couple of minutes, he asked me where I was from.

I told him, and I filled him in how long I'd be at the camp. One thing led to another and he invited me to his store, which he ran out of his room. (Many inmates do this to earn extra money.)

I explained that I didn't come up on his floor much, since the younger guys smoke K-2, a drug the inmates smoked like pot. They have phones, too, and they didn't like the older inmates on the range.

Then he yelled, "Fuck those N—s. You come up here and if you get a problem, tell them to see Don."

So, the President of the KKK was going to vouch for a Jew? He began talking about blacks and how much he hated them.

"I don't judge people on their skin color," I said, "just as I don't want to be judged as a Jew."

He opened his mouth and it just stayed open. His face color paled to a greenish hue. That was my cue to bump fists and say good-bye.

The next time I saw him in the camp, Don was polite but very quiet. I wanted to think I had embarrassed him, but likely not.

Don made hamburgers on a grill he hid in the camp. After that, I was always careful when I ordered food from Don. Timmy, my roommate, and I ordered a hamburger from him a couple times a week. I believed my burger would be safe because we always ordered two burgers and Don wouldn't know which I'd eat.

Then one day Timmy asked me why I trusted the

president of the KKK to make me a hamburger. I told Timmy that Don would never do anything funky to my burger since Timmy was not Jewish, and Don would not take the chance to hurt him.

Timmy told me something very disturbing. He pointed out that when he ordered the burgers from Don he told him to "make mine with cheese."

"So, he knows you get the burger with no cheese, right?" Timmy fell over laughing. That was the last time I ordered any food from Don. OMG! I turned pale.


## Lunch with Eli


Some people are afraid of Muslims simply because the current state of things in the world. For a period of time, it seemed that news channels only reported on beheadings and bombings.

The prison camp had quite a few Muslim inmates. During the month of Ramadan, a holy holiday, the Muslims held their prayer service in the chow hall. Since it went on for 30 days, some of the guys were upset because they couldn't watch their TV programs. Some inmates also wondered why more good and peaceful Muslims weren't standing up and condemning their brothers for the senseless murders happening around the world?

I didn't have a problem with the Muslims in the camp since they treated me with respect, even though I'm Jewish. Of course, I'd known that supposedly Muslims hate Jews, but I never had a problem and a couple of them became friends.

Once, when I was walking through the hall going to the Wizard's rec room, an Arab inmate, Eli, stopped me. He was extraordinarily gregarious. He would go out of his way to say "Hello, my dear Jewish friend." He'd invite me to the Muslim prayer service, and feeling pressured, I went.

The prayer service was quite interesting. Eli spoke about the relationship between Jews and the Arabs in the Middle East. He introduced me as his guest, and since he was the Muslim leader at the camp, he probably saved me a lot of problems with his group by doing so. He spoke about peace and how we are all brothers. He seemed very convincing, but I was always careful to keep an eye out. Eli knew so much about Jewish culture; I finally realized he knew more than I did.

I found this out one day when he invited me to lunch outside his room. I arrived at 10:30 AM to see one of the game tables set with napkins, cups, and the tops of Tupperware bowls set out to use as plates. Eli was proud I showed up for lunch, especially because I'd become good at sidestepping his invitations.

To my dismay, lunch consisted of hummus, eggs, and bread. I'd never tried hummus and was not eager to try it now.

Eli had obtained a special kosher butter for the matzo bread. I explained I didn't like butter and wasn't eager to try the hummus. Eli buttered my bread and dipped it into the hummus, entreating me, "Go ahead and try some."

As if it weren't bad enough, he offered me food in his bare hands. Eli's table was set right outside the bathroom and all three stalls were being used. The newness of hummus mixed with the bathroom stench didn't help the experience.

While I tried to get the hummus down, Eli began talking to me about the Torah and the Koran.

He explained the Torah was lost after Moses had written it on Mount Sinai, and was rewritten in Arabic many years later. Eli continued to explain that Abraham was also the Father of Islam, as well as Christianity and Judaism. He explained who Mohamed was and how the Israelites saved him when he was being chased by some other tribe. They gave him refuge and protected him against these other people. I learned there were similarities between our two religions and started to get comfortable.

Then out of nowhere Eli asked the million-dollar question, "Why is it okay for the Jews to move in and take over Palestine?" He went on to say this was the Arabs' home and the Jews just bullied their way in. "I have family there and Israeli soldiers stop them to look at their IDs before they go into the Temple Mount when they go to pray."

Oh no. Now I was getting nervous.

Gracious as he was, Eli directed the conversation toward a very difficult issue. I decided to bow out as graciously as possible and excused myself by saying I needed to get to an inmate tutoring session. Whew, I made a narrow, but successful, escape.


## Give me a hallelujah


One day, the temperature reached 100 degrees. Thankfully, one of the few air-conditioned places was the chapel. I was so hot, I went to the chapel and sat down in a chair. I eventually fell asleep because I hadn't been able to sleep at night. I would stand in the shower most of the night because of the heat.

I awakened hearing a live band playing. Forgetting I was in the church, I felt very out of sorts.

About 75 guys were happily, worshipfully dancing to the music of a live band—one guitar, a trumpet, piano, drums, and three singers. I was shocked.

I sat there watching everyone singing and dancing, but one inmate pulled me to my feet and started dancing with me. It was a dance I've seen before in movies—singing and dancing and shouting "Hallelujah" with hands raised.

After a few minutes, I got into it and was dancing and clapping my hands with everyone else. I lost myself in the music and joy and began singing "Hallelujah, Hallelujah, Hallelujah!"

I got carried away. I soon noticed many of the inmates staring at me and smiling. I believe they had thought I had been converted. True, I was enjoying myself, but born again, I don't think so.

It was strange, though, to be a Jew dancing to gospel music in a church with all these Christians. It was quite an experience—a good one. Little did they know my intention was only to find a cool spot to relax, not to find Jesus.


## The kosher pizza


I enjoyed attending Shabbat services with the other Jews in the camp, but Friday night was also the night Gregg, the best pizza maker in the camp, made me a pizza in a real steel box using one of the dryer coils from the laundry room. By the time I was finished with the services, the pizza would be sitting in my room cold. A hot pizza was to die for. I needed to figure something out to tell the guys at the service.

I told Gregg to make the pizza and then come and get me from the church when it was done. Then I told Rabbi (Levin) that I had something very important to tend to but I didn't want to discuss it with everyone in the room. It was personal and I needed to leave about a half hour early.

The rabbi asked what could be so important on a Friday night in prison. But I kept up the talk about it being something I didn't want to discuss even with the rabbi.

Completely forgetting that I told Gregg to get me if I wasn't back in time from church where we held the service, I heard a sudden knock at the door.

The rabbi opened the door and asked what Gregg wanted, pointing out we were in the middle of a service.

Greg yelled, "If Keith is in there, could you tell him his pizza is ready?"

I had that feeling all of us get when we're caught in a lie and we have nowhere to hide. I looked at the rabbi and said, "Wow! I guess someone made me a pizza. I better go eat it while it's still hot. Don't want to be rude."

## The sarcastic shrink

When any bowl, book, cup, or pair of glasses was found in the unit, an inmate could be sure it's mine. I tended to leave things behind, like my shampoo in the shower, along with my towel and clothing. It was common to hear an inmate on my floor say, "Keith, is this your lotion?" Or, "Keith, you left your shampoo in the shower again." A guy might say, "If your head were not attached, you'd leave it in the shower." I didn't know why I was so forgetful.

A psychiatrist showed up on the unit as a new inmate. I'd hit the jackpot, or so I thought. A psychologist would have been wonderful, but a psychiatrist was perfect. After everything I'd been through, I thought it would be a breath of fresh air to speak to a psychiatrist. Maybe he could give me some tips on handling the heat and how to keep from losing everything in my mind.

When I sat down with him to exchange small talk, he told me he was a doctor, so I took the opening. "Can I ask you a personal question?"

"Sure," he said.

"Why is it that I forget things in the shower and in the unit so often? Why am I so hot all the time? Why do I find myself in the middle of some crazy situation?"

I felt like I was asking the great and powerful Wizard of Oz for a brain. I knew this doctor would level with me and give his true perspective.

He paused for a minute and said, "I think you may be cuckoo."

Feeling ridiculous, I asked if he was serious.

"You'll get my bill in a month," he said.
Just my luck to find a sarcastic doctor.

# Chapter Thirteen

## The Wizard

Before I first walked out the USP door for the drive to Franklin Prison Camp, I met an inmate known as the Wizard. He was of medium height, a redhead with alert green eyes set in a pale freckled face. He asked me if I was okay and spoke to me in a peaceful tone. "Don't be nervous. This is the easiest part of your nightmare. All the courtroom drama is finished and so is the waiting, the not knowing—it's over."

I thanked him for his calming words.

"Where are you from?" he asked.

"A north suburb of Chicago."

"In case you haven't guessed, I'm an inmate just like you are."

"But," I countered, "you drive a car. What if you wanted to escape?"

He surprised me. "Anyone can escape. There are no fences. But, if you try it and get caught, you'll get an additional five years added to your sentence."

"I'm not going anywhere then," I vowed.

"Good," he said. "Just keep busy, do your time and get home to your family."

That was my plan.

I asked him why he was called Wizard and he told me it was a long story that I'd hear later. I also learned his real name was Mike Powers. I couldn't have guessed it then but not too far into my prison future, I would hear his name over the camp loudspeaker many times a day, not to mention he made prison bearable for me and a lot of inmates.

I began to ask myself, *who* is this guy? Why is he so *busy*? *What* is he doing *here*? A year later, I finally learned who Wizard really was.

He originally got his nickname when he first got sent to the hole because the camp warden let him become so powerful, he had to remind him who the boss was. Wizard survived that hole for 60 days and when he returned to the camp, he resumed running it.

This guy had his hand in everything. He even sat in the meetings with the camp administrators. If anyone had a problem or got in trouble, including the prison guards, Mike would get them out of it. He had such a hold on the camp, anyone but the High Prison Warden had to go through him. Soon, the nickname Wizard stuck.

I could see why that name would stick to a guy an inmate could go to if he needed a favor. If you were having trouble with a commanding officer, you could go to Wizard and he'd fix it. If you were being bullied, Mike would take care of it. He was able to retrieve the scoop on every single prisoner because he ran the bubble. Any information in the computer was at his fingertips. He knew all the codes and possessed all the keys to the prison.

If Wizard thought you were bad for the morale in the prison, he had the power to put you on the next bus and ship you to Minnesota. When the inmates wanted to play baseball on a field with manicured grass and a perfect diamond, Wizard made it happen. If you wanted a scoreboard with an announcer to call the game, see Wizard. He took training and received a license as a professional umpire to referee the games, and we even got statistics—hits, runs, and batting averages.

The answer applied to playing organized basketball, or to bringing medicine or cigars into the camp. Guys even went to Mike if they wanted a furlough to see their wife and their counselor said no. But how did Wizard get his power in the first place? Here is the story few inmates know.

When Wizard first entered the camp, he took a job driving inmates back and forth from the USP to the camp. One day, the camp warden, Mrs. Brown, needed a ride home.

They got so close that Mrs. Brown hired Mike as her personal driver. He would take her to the airport and dinner meetings. She watched over him and made sure he was safe.

After a couple of years, she got promoted and was sent to Washington. She never forgot Mike and stayed in touch with him. Mike had a cell phone she gave him so she could get ahold of him when she needed him for a ride.

Wizard became close with some of the guards since they saw how close he became to the warden.

Then one day he got his big break. Two guards were in trouble for not calling Count on time—they were in real hot water. Rains was about to fire them when Wizard contacted the past warden and saved the two guards' jobs. Mike told the guards not to worry and that their problem would be fine.

Sure enough, the problem just disappeared. These guards spread the word on what Mike did for them and that's how he became the Wizard.

From that time on, Wizard ran the bubble and the camp. If he needed something from the guards, he got it. He was included in the CO meetings as well as private meetings with Rains. When a new guard was hired, Mike would train him. He was even allowed to be placed on a list that gave him the authority to miss count. If Wizard were out of bounds, he was untouchable. Rains even gave him a cell phone that was prohibited in the camp.

On one occasion, the former senator, now at the camp, needed to contact his lawyer. Mike arranged the meeting.

The senator asked Wizard if he would let him use his cell phone, and Mike obliged, telling him to use the phone on the QT so he wouldn't have to rescue him from the hole for using a cell phone.

Using a cell phone was one of the worst offenses in the camp. Having or using a cell phone is worse than getting in a fistfight. To hear the senator trying to speak quietly into a cell phone was like hearing God call to Moses on Mt. Sinai! When the senator finished talking, he *yelled* down the hall to Mike, "How do you turn this friking thing off?"

The entire unit heard him, and you could hear laughing all down our unit and into others. Mike told him to be quiet or he'd get in trouble. The senator simply said, "Okay, Wizard, who do I need to talk to?" He forgot there was nobody to fix things for him anymore, not like when he was an elected official.

To command this respect and power as an inmate is amazing within a Federal prison camp. I began wondering how in the hell the Wizard got all this influence and power.

The Franklin Prison Camp consisted of Camp Administrator, Rain; Case Managers, Teller, Pew, and Squirrel; and Counselors, Street and Wayne.

I'd heard rumors about Mike gaining his influence and power, one of which suggested he'd made a deal to get things done in the camp for the Camp Administer Rain. He would have his friends throughout the camp take care of some chores, then report back to Rain when they were finished. It was like a communication chain for Rain and all he had to do was talk to one inmate, Mike.

One rumor maintained that Mike worked for Rains and not the inmates. I can say with certainty that rumor wasn't true. In all the time Wizard held the reins in camp, not one inmate was sent to the hole because of information supplied by Wizard. In fact, countless inmates escaped the hole or avoided it altogether because of Mike's successful negotiations with guards or Teller.

Once, I was going to the hole over a cigarette incident, but Mike talked to the guards and got me out of it.

Another time, an inmate was caught drinking beer and was certainly going to be shipped to another camp far away from his loved ones. Mike spoke to the commanding officer and resolved the issue.

It was also rumored Wizard split his poker profits with Rain. Because he is the house, thousands of dollars pass through the poker table every day, and Mike got a cut on every transaction. That rumor would explain all the legalized gambling going on, but that rumor also wasn't true.

Mike could bring food back to the camp, at first for his own consumption, but later for his friends in the camp. Mike enjoyed his newfound clout and power to unofficially run the camp. Soon, all the case managers and counselors would bring Mike into meetings to confer with him. Together, Rain and Mike called the shots, but Mike carried them out.

Mike even built a second commissary for the inmates that he put in his casino. He made pizza from a toaster oven and sold slices for stamps. He had all kind of chips, pops, and candy all for sale in the casino. The poker table was even made of the same felt used in the real casinos. He had employees selling soda, waiting on the inmates as they played poker. At one time, there were so many televisions in the room it was like going into a sports bar.

It didn't take long for Mike to begin increasing the range of activities and facilities available to inmates at the camp, which is how the organized sports teams got equipment—uniforms and the scoreboard and such, and leagues based on skill levels labeled A, B, and C. We had a league that fit the skill level of every inmate. Turned out Mike was also a BEMI Pro-Licensed Referee (Bemi being the name of a legendary referee), so he'd ref the games himself.

Mike did the same thing for the baseball league, even arranging to use tractors from other prison facilities in the camp to improve the dirt on the infield. The field looked like a major league baseball field. Wizard even posted the statistics for each player, who then would strive to improve game to game, which boosted self-confidence. The best part was being treated like valuable human beings after having been treated like criminals with the mental capacity equivalent to grammar school students.

Wizard's activities offered a contrast to the negative brain washing carried out daily at the camp. Guards talked down to inmates, calling them dirt or a piece of shit when they gave orders, usually foolish orders in the first place. For example, they ordered inmates to leave a leave a floor they didn't live on just to harass the guys because they could. One time a guard came into my room after I took a shower. He asked if I had a cell phone on my body. I was naked when he asked me. We could be playing cards and minding our own business, but a guard would come by and order everybody out of the room for no reason. It applied to everything, even forming a line against a wall. Be a little out of the line and the guards would go nuts.

Because of the way he managed so much of the camp, he also had the power to ship inmates out of state if they pissed him off. An inmate who got into an argument with Mike was on a bus to the camp in Minnesota the next week. Mike also made out the list when inmates had to go to the USP and serve lunches to the inmates when they were on lock down. He had that kind of power.

He could also get inmates anything they wanted—dental floss and aftershave, and if you needed food, he had it. He had pizza, and the oven. His Super Bowl party had everything from drinks to cake. And the warden knew about it. What prison camp in the US has a casino?

According to conventional wisdom, inmates are in prison to be *rehabilitated.*

Not really. I still believe the only rehabilitation in Franklin Prison was a result of what Wizard did for inmates. He even invested his own money to arrange tournaments with prizes for tennis, ping-pong, chess, various card games, and so on. He even organized Super Bowl parties and provided the food. (His Super Bowl parties were better than those I've hosted in my own home!)

Mike also threw going away parties for inmates who had been instrumental in facilitating the camp activities but were finally going home. Everyone would celebrate, which gave others hope. Their day would come.

Almost single-handedly, Wizard helped inmates develop a sense of self-respect and pride, often replacing the prison-related depressive feelings of failure and remorse. When an individual's spirits are high, the chances are strong this positive attitude will spread to the rest of the inmates. Mike sold this idea to Rain.

In any group, the higher the morale the better life becomes. This is especially true when living an incarcerated life. Prisoners lose income while in prison, but they also lost family and friends. When an inmate serving a 10-year sentence can keep himself occupied by sports and recreational activities, it occupies the mind and keeps the inmate in good spirits. Mike made this miracle possible. Without him, some inmates would have slept most of the time and given up on life.

I knew one inmate who lost his father while in prison. He went through all the correct channels to get a furlough to attend his father's funeral but was denied each time. The man then found Mike to ask him if there were anything he could do.

Mike jumped on it immediately, and he *succeeded* in getting the inmate a furlough so he could attend his father's funeral.


**Hundreds of rules**


Mike knew all the rules and how to get around them.

There are hundreds of prison rules that inmates tend to break just because it's almost impossible not to make simple mistakes. Here are just a few infractions:

1. Talking during count
2. Being late to count
3. Not standing during count
4. Walking thru the parking lot
5. Being out of bounds
6. Being late to work
7. Not following orders
8. Not returning a tool you checked out
9. Smoking tobacco or having tobacco
10. Loitering
11. Bringing food out of the chow hall
12. Keeping non-commissary food in your room
13. Using vending machines
14. Bringing contraband into the camp. (Contraband is anything not originating from the camp itself.)
15. Having cushions under the mattress
16. An untucked shirt
17. Not being in your complete uniform during daytime hours
18. Sitting in a visitor's car
19. Having movies from outside of camp
20. Having pots or pans in the room
21. Having a cell phone
22. Having a picture or name on a shirt—not allowed
23. Wearing a hat in the hall
24. Taking pictures in the camp
25. Having more than the allowed 3 books of postage stamps
26. Being caught with money
27. Possessing illegal drugs

28. Being caught cooking
29. Possessing naked pictures

Inmates who broke any of these rules and were unlucky enough to get sent to the hole would know Wizard was on the case. Mike had a visceral aversion to the hole, having spent two months there, so he had compassion for anyone who was sent there. Mike made every effort to save a prisoner from the hole—that mean and cold punishing environment.

Mike also got involved in fights between inmates, and inmates had plenty of their own rules to abide by. Here are just a few:

1. Do not look into a room while passing by
2. Always knock before entering
3. Do not reach over an inmate while eating at the table
4. Absolutely no snitching inside the camp
5. Be dressed going to shower
6. Take fast showers
7. Keep the shower curtain closed
8. Use your own hooks and keep your space clean
9. Eat your own food
10. Be respectful of other inmates
11. Do not sit on your roommates' bed
12. Do not wear shoes in your bed
13. Do not steal
14. Lights out at 9:00 pm
15. Do not change TV channel without asking first
16. Do not sit in another inmate's seat
17. Keep your word
18. Pay your debts on time
19. Do not butt into others' discussions

20.  Mind your own business
21.  If you borrow something, return it


**On the other hand...**


Rules aside, Mike knew how to throw a party. Someone had asked Mike to hold a Bulls basketball party in the gymnasium, with only inmates from Chicago invited. In typical Mike style, he set up a big screen color TV and about 100 chairs. He served us dinner—pizza, nachos, and cherry pie for desert—taken from the chow hall kitchen.

This party was against the rules, but the guard that night was Sergeant Schultz, so Mike had no worries. What Mike didn't realize is that inmates from the party began walking through the halls carrying food and wearing brightly colored red Bull shirts, also against the rules. The inmates decided to hook up a stereo system and blast loud music in the gym. It looked like a bachelor party without the liquor.

As I was walking through the hall with Mike, Sgt. Schultz ran up to us in a panic. "You said you were going to have some pizza and watch the Chicago Bulls," the guard said. "Now it's all this!"

Mike would never stand for Schultz getting into trouble because the guard was too valuable to the inmates in the camp. Schultz had begun giving Mike a heads up before any searches, as well as other important information. He helped to keep us out of trouble.

So, Mike immediately did away with any Bulls shirts and inmates were then directed to stay in the confines of the gym. The music volume was lowered, a relief to Schultz. But the party continued for a couple more hours, and the inmates cleaned up everything before heading back to their units.

For the most part, Mike used his power for the benefit of inmates and nothing more. For example, when an inmate got hurt or really sick, the prison medical staff generally did absolutely nothing. They might prescribe aspirin for pain, but that was all. Even for a broken bone in a leg. The staff justified it with, "There's nothing I can do."

Wizard felt responsible for accidents on the field, since he had arranged for most of the physical activities. When an inmate was in unbearable pain, Mike would stop at a drug store when he was driving on his errands and pick up stronger pain medication. He did this knowing he was at risk of being sent to the hole and then possibly shipped out of the prison camp. Even the Wizard had to obey some of the camp rules.

But he helped the inmate anyway. He was just like that—helpful in any way he could be.

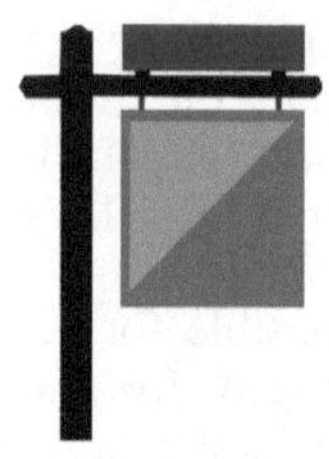

# Chapter Fourteen

## Another Near Miss

At some point, nearly every inmate realizes he's coming in contact with people he likely wouldn't have met on the outside. It was like the notion of diversity on steroids. Some of these individuals will remain in my memory for all kinds of reasons.

When it came to staff and inmates, Lieutenant Soup had authority over all other lieutenants, and he acted like he ran a prisoner of war camp. He ran the maximum security or USP prison in the complex, which has a death row, with an iron fist. The Franklin Camp, where I was, had only nonviolent prisoners.

As I understand it, at one time this prison camp only held white-collar criminals and no drug dealers. However, when Ronald Reagan was president, drug dealers started being allowed to do their time in a prison camp.

Soup didn't care for camp inmates because he thought we were "weak." So, if Soup caught an inmate doing something wrong, it was a frightening experience. Soup issued no warnings and gave no second chances. He treated inmates like serial killers who should never get out.

Before an inmate headed to the hole, Soup read them the riot act. As we stood erect at attention, Soup let us

156

have it just like a drill sergeant would in the military. Problem was, at that camp, we got the third degree in-your-face for things like untucked shirts, smoking, food in our lockers, and so on. It didn't matter that we never had violent crimes in the camp like they had in maximum security prisons. In his eyes, we were *all* mangy criminals, so he had no problem screaming and cursing, and tearing an inmate down until an inmate wanted to go to the hole just to be left alone!

The camp inmates dreaded when Soup came to conduct count at the camp. One day, as I stood for count, I noticed Soup was the guard assigned to handle it. That was scary, so no one spoke as all eyes looked forward.

As Soup walked down the hall, counting, he threatened the hole to anyone using the public phone before count was cleared. When he reached the end of the unit, he discovered he had one inmate unaccounted for. He turned and began walking the other direction, recounting. This time he got a correct count; everyone was there. But Soup called for the late arrival to step forward. He never considered he might have miscounted the first time.

When no one came forward, Soup grabbed the arms of a white inmate, a Hispanic inmate, and a black inmate and sent them to the hole. Everyone knew the lieutenant had miscounted and was taking it out on innocent inmates, but we said nothing. He had to be right and that was that. So unjust. I resolved to steer clear of this guy.

One night I felt like smoking a cigarette, something I'd never done before coming to prison. After the 9 PM count, I stepped outside the fire door to smoke, even though it was illegal. Lieutenant Soup loved to catch smokers and put them in the hole.

Nevertheless, I took a chance and smoked for about five minutes.

Suddenly, a powerful flashlight beam coming from a moving car nearly blinded me and a loud voice commanded, "Don't move!"

In shock, I leapt higher than I thought possible and instinctively ran back inside to my room and bed. The door opened behind me and there stood Soup. He asked if anyone noticed an inmate run through the emergency exit.

Everyone shook their heads.

Meanwhile, I was hiding in my bed unable to take a breath. When I heard the unmistakable voice of Soup, I knew I was dead meat. All I could think about was the hole and him *screaming* at me for stepping outside to smoke, although I'd claim I was getting a breath of fresh air.

Usually, the lieutenant would lock down the unit until the poor culprit surrendered. This time, though, God was with me and he went back to his car.

When I came out of my room, everyone stared at me.

One inmate said, "Hey, Keith, you must have a horseshoe up your ass."

Thankfully, that was my only dangerously close exposure to Lieutenant Soup.

A guy named Pete Strand also had an experience with Soup. Pete sat down in another inmate's seat in the TV room, ready to watch the football game. The guy rudely asked him to get up, but Pete stood his ground, saying, "Your name isn't on it."

The guy who wanted his seat was 250 pounds of solid muscle, even at age sixty-five. He wasn't someone you wanted to fight with. But no one told Pete that.

This guy punched Pete in the face, and the next thing you know both of these guys were on the way to the hole.

When they got there, Pete got to meet Soup. Not a pleasant experience. Soup screamed at him and called him every name under the sun. Pete told me Soup yelled so loud he couldn't understand him.

Finally, one day, the guys came back to the camp. As Pete said, it was not a place you wanted to spend any time in.

## The secretary

A lower bunk pass was the single most important comfort perk in prison. The pass allowed an inmate to easily sit on his bed during the day instead of on a plastic hard chair. It was supposed to be reserved for the elderly and sick. However, this was never the case. Many disabled inmates, even those who had lost a leg or were older were not given a lower bunk pass, while healthy young guys could enjoy the bottom bunk. The strongest inmates got the lower bunks. The exact opposite of the rule.

Fortunately for me, I was healthy and well, so I could climb into the top bunk without too much trouble. When I was in my second room with Rory and Leroy, one of the cell members was moving out, so I approached forty-five-year-old Rory and asked if he'd mind if I asked my counselor, Street, for the lower bunk. I asked Rory because he'd been in the room for two years before me and would have made my life miserable had I just gone and taken it.

Rory agreed to let me have the bunk because he didn't want to take it only to lose it to an older inmate who took my place when I left. I made the request for the bunk pass and got it.

When I returned to my room, Rory told me he'd changed his mind and would take the bunk pass himself. Then, I had to go with him to visit Street to let him know I was okay with it. So, Rory got the lower bunk.

About two weeks later, Rory was told he was to be sent to the hole and shipped out to another prison, which usually meant going to a prison with a higher security level. Ms. Teller had reprimanded Rory because another guy was changing clothes in the room and Rory flipped out, which led to an altercation.

Teller stepped in and shipped out Rory for being a bully. Forcing an inmate not to change his pants in his room and sending him into the bathroom was considered bullying. It turned out I got the lower bunk after all.


## Hogan's Heroes

Given all the negative situations and attitudes prisoners faced daily, we often found humor in unlikely situations. One night when Wizard, Bob, Pete, and I were enjoying our now-regular "500" card game, one of the COs showed up and joined in. Officially, guards weren't allowed to fraternize with the inmates, but this guard seemed not to care. He turned out to be a decent guy and we all got close over time—as close as an inmate can be to a guard. We even dubbed him "Sergeant Schultz," like the character from the *Hogan's Heroes* television series and gradually became friends. You never know when a friendship like this could be useful.

One afternoon during count, I was in the bathroom and not against the wall with my unit. When I walked out of the bathroom, I sensed everyone was afraid for me. We couldn't miss count. Talking to anyone or not being present for count—for *any* reason—meant being sent to the hole. I don't know how I mistook the time when I headed to use the restroom. I quickly joined the line, relieved to see the guard on duty was Schultz. I apologized for being tardy, and he said, "Next time you sit out, and I play cards." What a huge save. I would have been a goner—headed to the hole.

Another time, Schultz let us know that a certain unit (507) would be shaken down that night.

Immediately, I ran to my unit, notifying everyone, and made certain I hid my stamps in a safe place. You were only allowed three books of stamps and I'd amassed 20. I hid the surplus in a little slot I'd cut into the broom handle. It turned out Schultz was right, and our entire unit was shaken down that evening. Everyone thanked me for the heads up.

On another occasion, Schultz told us he was going

to patrol for smokers. I carried out my own patrol, alerting inmates to hide their tobacco products and not smoke that evening. Again, I was thanked. I had begun to get the type of respect Wizard enjoyed. Someone who can obtain information beneficial to the inmates rises to the top quickly. Inmates began asking me if the coast was clear for certain elicit activities like smoking, cooking, using phones, transferring goods back and forth, and so on.

One evening, the warden told Rain to put the camp on lockdown. No inmate could leave his unit. No laundry, shopping, or even warning intended visitors. A visitor flying in from another state was turned away during lockdown.

I'd been playing cards with Schultz when he let us know there would be a lockdown in two days. I managed to get the word out, so inmates could do their laundry, call home, and shop at the commissary, which drove up my popularity at the camp. Some inmates asked if I were going to run for mayor of the camp, but of course, there was no such position.

Another guard at the camp was like Radar, the character on the TV show *M.A.S.H.* He was the voice on the sitcom's public address system. This guard stood over six feet tall and I could see he'd weigh in at around 300 pounds. His bald head shone like the moon, and his shirt was always halfway tucked in. He was always smoking one of those fake vapor cigarettes. But he chirped like a bird over the microphone. When he announced chow time, he'd say, "The time for the meal of the day served at your elegant diner." Or he said, "Today, we are having rib eye steak. Please tell your server how you would like it prepared."

Sometimes, he would open the door to the chow hall like he was the maître d'. When he called an inmate to the bubble, he would ask, "Will Inmate Bill Smith please come to the bubble when you are free or at your earliest convenience? I hope you can find the time sometime this afternoon."

One morning, an inmate didn't report to work, so he

announced on the PA system, "Mr. Smith, it's time to wake up and get to work. Please have your coffee and shower and shave at your earliest opportunity, then report to Education. By the way, if someone knows where Mr. Smith's room is, please gently wake him up and tell him to get to Education."

It wasn't unusual to hear him chime, "It's time to get your free drugs at the pill line. Please don't push in line. There are plenty of drugs for everyone."

He used humor at every opportunity. Another of his pages was, "Alley 7 is open for the next bowling group. Don't forget to pick up your bowling shoes before you check in." Another time we heard, "Free swim for one hour. No running into the pool!"

Rain was our Colonel Klink. When Rain wanted something done, Wizard did it. Once, Rain ordered all the recreation orderlies to the recreation room for a meeting. He reamed us out for not cleaning our departments well enough and explained to each of us how to clean our areas. He gave us each a number 1, 2, or 3 and put us in groups. He spent an *hour* teaching us a teamwork method he believed would help us do our jobs in an organized fashion.

Unfortunately, Rain's command of the English language left a lot to be desired, so we had no idea what he was telling us to do. (He was from Cuba and spoke heavily accented English.) When he ended his speech and turned to go, we went directly to find Wizard. We figured Mike would understand, but we still ended up cleaning our areas like we always did.

Richard, my fellow bank fraud inmate and best friend at the camp, worked with me in Recreation taking care of the bocce ball court. It was the middle of winter, and no one played bocce ball in the snow. So, Richard and I watched movies and played indoor sports all day long. One day, out of nowhere, we were called to the Rec Office to review our work positions. We had no idea how we'd explain our jobs to the Rec "COP" with a serious face.

Richard spoke first, the brave soul. When the COP

asked Richard if we really did any work at all, he answered honestly and said no. But the COP let him stay on the job because he'd been honest. I responded to the COP's question the same way.

We were thrilled to keep our jobs. The fact that it paid $2.50 a month didn't bother us. We just wanted to be left alone.

The next month, however, Richard was not so lucky. He'd passed Rain in the hall and Rain asked Richard about his job. Richard told him he worked in Recreation.

"Not any more you don't," Rain said. "Now you work at the Cup."

The Cup was the place the boilers ran. When the temperature outside was 95 degrees, the Cup reached 105 degrees. Richard had to work an 8-hour shift starting at 6 AM. Richard was miserable there, and his attitude was never the same again. I learned that when you saw Rain in the halls you turned around and walked the other way.

## Jerry Lewis does count

I was always talking and acting like Jerry Lewis, my favorite comedian. The inmates laughed at me and I loved screaming "LADY" when I was in the casino. One evening right before count, Wizard asked me to talk like Jerry on the camp loudspeaker. But that would surely put me in the hole. A regular inmate couldn't even go into the bubble, let alone talk on the address system.

But Wizard persisted and assured me I wouldn't get into trouble. But it still sounded crazy to me. Nobody would have the nerve to do something like this in prison. But Wizard took me to the bubble and told the guard to let me do Jerry Lewis on the loudspeaker for the night bed count. The guard told us to come back in 30 minutes and we did.

The guard showed me how to work the microphone.

As I pushed the button in and out, I was acting like Jerry asking stupid questions like, "When do I let the button go?"

Meanwhile, the inmates in the camp were congregating in the halls and laughing their asses off. Then I did my Jerry impression, yelling, "LADY, it's time for all you nice inmate people to go to sleep so you can wake up early and work for our wonderful government."

I never heard such loud laughter in my life. When I returned to the casino, Wizard was red and out of breath from laughing.

## Good Fellas

The general public has never shown much compassion toward criminals. For the most part, I went along with the attitude that if you did the crime, you have to do the time. I used to think that if you were sent to prison it meant being guilty of hurting someone. When Al Capone was sent to prison, he deserved to go. When Bonnie and Clyde, Dillinger, Pretty Boy Floyd, and Bugsy Segal were shipped off to prison, they were crooks that knew what the consequences were. On the TV series *The Untouchables,* I knew the FBI's Elliot Ness was the good guy and the mob were the bad guys.

Still, like many people, I sensed there was something exciting about being a gangster. That's the trouble with romanticizing the bad guys, like the old western fighters. They were wrong to break the law, but they were portrayed as tough. The power and respect they held seemed breathtaking. They constantly lived in danger, but it seemed they had no fear of the law or even fear of going to prison.

*Good Fellas* is one of my favorite movies. It's based on a true story about a group of guys who all trusted one another like family in a group of tight friends. They planned a heist and pulled it off. It was an exciting movie.

About six months into my sentence I met an inmate named Louie, an Italian, who was convicted of stealing truckloads of merchandise from shipping docks. A big guy, Louie weighed around 350 pounds and loved food, especially pasta. He invited me to dinner, to sit, and to help him cook.

Of course, the food served in prison was disgusting, scooped onto a plate like mush, whether cottage cheese, pork, chicken, chili, peas, soup, or whatever it was.

Louie was in the prison five years before I arrived. In that time he'd acquired all the utensils, pots, pans, spoons, bowls, and spices needed to cook. Not allowed to have anything sharp, certainly not a knife, Louie made do by creating some of his own utensils. For example, his pasta strainer had been the vent of a dryer. A coiled wire would heat up and melt the oil he would steal from the chow hall or kitchen. Sometimes, the inmates would go into the BOP warehouse to get food not served at the camp.

In *Good Fellas*, some of the gang buddies were sent to prison. Like Louie, these guys managed to fashion or procure pots and pans and pasta and all the ingredients needed to cook a fine Italian meal. Watching Louie cut onions or garlic with a stolen razor blade, I couldn't help but think of the movie. In my wildest dreams, I would never have imagined I would ever live like that.

I gave Louie the nickname Pauly, after the boss in the movie, who also cooked. Because of Louie, I was lucky to be eating a robust Italian meal while the other inmates were downstairs in the chow hall eating slop. The table where Pauly cooked was in the hallway right outside the inmate cells. My job was to be the lookout and make sure no COs were coming. Garlic bread. Spaghetti. Salad with onions, mushrooms, green peppers, and Italian dressing were to die for.

The climax of these Italian meal experiences came one night as Pauly and I stood in the chow line. The prison servers were serving up mush for dinner, and I said, "Let's have one of those famous meals you cook tonight."

Pauly agreed, and as we were leaving I heard one inmate say to another, "Did you hear that? They're good fellas. They don't have to eat this shit. They eat what they want."

What a joke. I was being compared to a good fella by a fellow inmate.


## Another kind of big shot


The Feds can steal time from your life, but for many of us, exercise maintained or restored our vitality. We might even live longer. Despite the despair of being in the prison camp, I ran the track three times daily, six laps equaled 2.5 miles. I also got on the stationary bicycle three times a week. But weightlifting was the most fulfilling exercise for me. I grew stronger and my body became more defined, which increased my self-esteem.

All around me, guys were lifting 200 to 300 pounds. Being a beginner and sixty years old, I'd been lifting 145 pounds. The personal trainer said these stronger guys had started at the bottom, but they stuck with their exercise programs and achieved their goals.

One day as we were picking up our weights, I saw a new inmate I'd met only three hours before. Tim had been sent to Franklin Prison Camp from the medium security prison across the way. He wanted to fit in and make friends, and he'd been sentenced to 25 years for drug trafficking. Tim had owned a corporate jet and made his money from picking up pot and cocaine in Colombia, then distributing it in the United States.

Tim swaggered to the weight pile and began gathering weights to place on his workout bar. He grabbed the 45-pound weight plates, placing three plates on each side of the bar. Tim stood only 5'8" and weighed about 165 pounds. As he gathered his weights, he noticed me watching him from my workout station. He swaggered over to me and we exchanged a few words about how he'd lifted weights for the past five years.

Lonnie, my trainer, made money training inmates. He gave Tim a hard look and said, "I think you have too much weight on the bar, Tim. I'd prefer you didn't hurt yourself."

Tim quipped, "Are you kidding? This is a walk in the park."

Now Tim had something to prove. This was his chance to make a name for himself while everyone in the weight station was watching him.

As Tim walked to his station, he pulled up his shorts high on his waist, as if to say, "Wait till they see this."

"Let's wait until Tim finishes lifting before we start," Lonnie said to me, "because I have a feeling he's going to need help."

Tim didn't have a spotter, so I walked over to spot for him. Tim swiveled his arms around and then flexed his hands. He sat up and got comfortable. He took three deep breaths and said, "Okay, give me the bar."

I lifted the bar down to Tim gently.

He immediately yelled, *"My weight!"*

It took three seconds of Tim holding the bar at arm's length before the bar and weights came down heavy on his chest. "Quick! Get it off," he screamed. *"Get it off*! Get this fucking thing off me."

Fortunately, Lonnie was still watching and ran over to help us. He lifted the bar quickly and Tim took in a big breath. "I told you there's too much weight on that bar!" Lonnie yelled.

Tim got to his feet. "Give me a minute and I'll try again."

Lonnie spent the next fifteen minutes scolding Tim, telling him to just let it be and try another day after he worked up to it.

But Tim wouldn't listen to the trainer's wisdom and sat down again on the bench to try again. He took five deep breaths this time, and the whole scene repeated, only this time Lonnie let the weight sit for a bit on

Tim's chest before lifting it off.

The entire weight pile began laughing, but I felt sorry for Tim. I knew how badly the guy wanted to make a good first impression on the camp guys.

Tim got up from the weight bench, brushed off his gym pants and tried to make the incident seem lighter than it was. "Well, I guess it's been awhile since I lifted." With this, he grabbed some lower weight dumbbells and everyone noisily cracked up again, filling the area with their laughter.

## Please Mister, can I have some more?

Louie was cooking spaghetti when he discovered he was missing garlic bread. It just so happened buns were being served at dinner in the chow hall. The chow CO usually passed out extra bread to the inmates who wanted it, so Louie asked me to run down to chow and try to get four pieces of bread for garlic bread.

When I got to the chow hall, I scored six pieces and headed towards the door of the chow hall. That's when I heard a voice from behind me ask, "Hey you, get over here. Where do you think you're going with that bread?" It was against the rules to take any food out of the chow hall.

I turned and saw a CO wearing a white shirt. When I approached him, he asked, "Where did you get that bread?"

"From the chow line," I said.

"Did you steal it?"

"No, Mr. Hail gave them to me and many other inmates."

He took me to Hail and asked, "Did you give permission to this inmate to take bread out of here and up to his room?"

"I never told you he gave me permission to take the bread to my room," I blurted.

Just then, Hail said, "Yes, I gave him the okay to bring this bread to his room."

He really hadn't. On the other hand, it was implied, because who could eat six buns at one sitting in the chow hall. It was sure good of him to come to my rescue.

The CO who'd stopped me ordered me to throw the bread in the garbage. Perfectly good bread. While I was in the midst of this conversation, I saw inmates walking past us carrying buns and ice cream bars. They were taking all this to their rooms. I didn't dare say anything because I could be looked at as a snitch. This CO was just being a jerk. He walked away from me back to the service line.

Instead of throwing out the bread, I decided to sneak it up to Louie's room so we could enjoy some garlic bread. As I made my way to the door, an inmate rose up and quietly encouraged me. "Go ahead. He's not looking."

Another inmate also got up and said, "Hurry up and you can make it."

Then another and another. Before long, almost everyone in the chow hall had gotten up and started yelling.

I had caused such a commotion, I decided not to chance it and gave the buns away to other inmates. A low groan came over the chow hall.

When I got upstairs to tell Louie what had happened, he already knew. News travelled like crazy in prison. He told me the CO in the white shirt was a lieutenant, which scared the hell out of me.

Back in the chow hall, inmates were throwing out oranges, apples, pears, bread, cake, bananas, and everything else the guards would not let them take out. I wonder how the American people would react if they ever got word on how their dollars were being thrown into the trash.

I don't know how many people care about the conditions of prison, but I do know that about 100% care about how their dollars are being spent. I'd like to see the expression on the faces of a group touring the prison if they saw so much food tossed in the garbage.

Many times, the kitchen cop is an asshole and when inmates ask for another helping of food he says no, then adds a dirty look for emphasis. But the amount of food being thrown into the large garbage bin in the back of the building is horrendous.

## Lock down

When I learned I might go to prison, my first concern was claustrophobia. However, I learned the Franklin Prison Camp wasn't set up with small cells, the exception being the dreaded hole. I hadn't heard about "lock down," where inmates' movements were confined for days or weeks to their hallways.

About two months after arriving at prison camp, the CO came on the loudspeaker and announced that all inmates were to go back to their halls and lockdown. Apparently, two inmates were caught fishing down by the river, which was approximately 500 yards from the grounds. Someone in the camp notified the press, who called it an attempted escape. Local media ran with the story and the BOP got pissed.

Inmates aren't allowed to have cell phones, so calling the press using an unauthorized cell phone didn't help. Besides turning the fishing expedition into an escape attempt made it all worse. Rain called for the lockdown, and that meant we were confined to our units, which consisted of about 20 rooms on each hallway.

This caused me extreme claustrophobia. It wasn't terribly hot yet, which was good, because being locked up in the heat would have made the claustrophobia worse. Kind of like getting stuck in an elevator.

I was used to a bunch of inmates cooking meals for me, so how would I survive eating in the chow hall? As luck would have it, while we were locked up, Richard would sneak down the stairs over my unit and throw a bag containing a piece of fried chicken out the window. It landed right outside my window and I ran outside to get it with the whole unit watching. If I'd been caught, I'd have been thrown in the hole. But boy, did that chicken taste good.

During lock down, we couldn't do laundry, which gave me something else to worry about. Only having two pairs of clean underwear and undershirts freaked me out. I certainly didn't like wearing the same clothes to sleep in that I wore when up. Especially the same underwear.

However, right before the lockdown, Wizard told a couple of inmates that it was going to happen, so I had time to wash clothes.

I could also call Julie and let her know what was happening. I was fortunate. Many other inmates were not able to let their families know they were locked down, so spouses and kids were left to wonder and worry what the hell happened to them. That was a fun little punishment for the inmate's families. These COs and guards had hearts made of tin.

During lockdown, lunches and dinners were served in sacks. Each inmate received an apple, a bologna sandwich, chips, and a cookie. (The bologna had been frozen.)

Fortunately, I'd grabbed a book before being herded into the containment area, so ironically, I spent my time reading *The Hunger Games,* whose theme involves a controlled society in a post-nuclear situation. The government ruled from a centrally located and entirely separated position in which the luxuries of life were plentiful. Those in the outlying colonies faced starvation.

I drew a strong connection between the government of our present times and the novel's plot of pushing and forcing people to spy on and betray innocent neighbors to save their own lives and the lives of their families.

Experiencing lockdown also gave me a sense of how it would feel to be sent to the hole, where there are no windows, but the light is on constantly. There is no mattress, and you sleep naked. You don't have a change of clothes and can only take one shower a week. No reading or listening to music in the hole, and of course, you are confined to an 8 x 8 room. A normal inmate did not like the thought of the hole and could end up talking to themselves after months of nothing to do to occupy their time.

I, on the other hand, would not have made it out alive because of my claustrophobia. The hole was my personal nightmare.

Lockdown lasted for four days. Afterwards, inmates were released and free to go outside into the amazingly fresh air. It seemed so unfair to punish all the inmates for what only two did, but that's the rule in prison. One inmate can cause a lock down for the entire prison.


## My brother, the TV star


One afternoon, my brother, Matthew, sent an email letting me know he was going to be on a Chicago TV station to discuss presidential candidates. I couldn't wait to tell the other inmates since I was proud of my brother and all of his accomplishments.

Later that night, I got situated in the chow hall with the TV tuned into WGN, the Chicago station. Everyone began piling in to see my brother, including a guy named Bruce Walters, a politician.

We waited and waited for 7 PM, and the program came…and went. We waited until 7:30 PM, and then the guys began leaving. A couple of inmates said in low voices, "He doesn't have a brother on TV!" I couldn't figure out what happened, other than a scheduling change.

Fortunately, Walters was still sitting in the room and spoke up. "His brother *is* on TV and he has his own show. I watch him all the time and am proud to say I am personal friends with Mathew." Bruce helped everything turn out fine that night.

The next day, Mathew emailed and explained the problem. He said he would be on that night. I got everyone together again to watch, but this time we sat in the visitors' room. Mathew came on, and as usual, looked great in his dark suit and royal blue tie.

The room went silent, and finally my brother began talking about the pros and cons of each presidential candidate. He knew his stuff. I couldn't have been more proud. Seeing him gave me a sense of family pride and renewed *hope* that I would once again have a life and see my family soon.

# Chapter Fifteen

## The Prison Clown

When I first got in trouble with the Feds, I remember telling a joke about being in a cell and when someone asked me what I was in for, I would reply, "I put the fixtures of the house in after the closing." My friends would laugh and agree it was a ridiculous reason to go to prison. Still, the FBI didn't think it was one bit funny. It turned out they thought Julie and I did a lot of worse things than that. They thought Julie, who wouldn't hurt a fly and was the most fair lawyer I have ever met, perpetuated a scheme to defraud the bank by laundering money by secretly putting the down payment down for the buyers. The Feds thought I did something so evil I deserved 10 years.

At one time, a Fed said to me that I taught the broker how to commit fraud on the banks. The broker owned a family brokering business that the father started when I was still in college. I ended up making jokes about getting caught and thrown in the hole and being sent on to a higher security prison. Imagine how foolish it would sound if Al Capone asked, "Hey pal, what are you in for?" and I'd answer, "I ate a sandwich my wife brought in the visitor's room."

That joke turned out to be not so funny. It became one more ridiculous quip about the absurdity of being at that camp. I'd spent my entire life making people laugh. I had a very calm temperament. I believed myself to be a loving father and husband. If my parents needed something from me, I was always there. My brother and I had always been close. If a friend needed help, I'd always been there for them. If I did something I knew was wrong, I couldn't fall asleep. The corny lessons that TV shows like *Leave It to Beaver* and *The Andy Griffith Show* tried to teach were my favorite shows. I'm not saying that I'm a saint or a man of God or whatever, but for the Feds to put me in prison makes the entire judicial system look like a bunch of prison clowns.

## Speaking of clowns, the camp doc is a serial killer

One night I was in the TV room watching the news with Bruce Walters. Out of the blue, the reporter on the TV showed a photo of a serial killer on the loose. Suddenly, Bruce yelled, "That's the camp doctor."

Oh my God, he was right. They showed the doctor's Ferrari, and his Lotus that was always parked at the prison.

I hadn't spent much time with the doc since I didn't trust any of the BOP staff. But this guy had apparently murdered *seven people* after he was fired from the medical department of a local college. The inmates thought it just like the BOP to hire a serial killer to care for its prisoners. This was indicative of the competence of professionals hired by the Bureau of Prisons and integrity of its background checks.

## Swapping stories

Early on, I learned inmates enjoy swapping stories. One of my favorite topics was *how* the FBI arrested them. Since this was a Federal prison camp, the Federal agencies were always involved. I remain thankful for the way they "came" for me and Julie indirectly, when they called my wife on her cell phone while I was, literally, up among the clouds in a 4-seater prop plane with my friend Cliff.

Until we arrived at the office, we had no idea what they wanted. Their mission was to close down our company and seize our records. We weren't arrested until a year later when we were indicted for fraud and we showed up at the Federal building to "self-surrender." Scary. Surprising, too, because I hadn't expected to see many of our customers and all of my appraisers. It was uncomfortable, probably just what the Feds wanted.

No one we saw was angry with me since they all knew I wasn't a crook. Sure, some customers were unhappy with my quality of work, but that's not a Federal crime. They also knew I had nothing to do with the loans, but that was a bit of information the Feds told them not to admit. All those individuals knew Julie and I were being set up for a fall. Someone had to pay for what the banks had done and there we were. I understand technicality of violating a rule, but the prosecutor talked to Julie and me like we were the most terrible people on the planet. It made me wonder what he thought we did. Where did the anger come from?

I admit my contractors sure left a lot to be desired as far as the quality of the rehab, but that's not what this indictment was about. Problems like that are handled in a civil suit. I'd had only three of those during my time in business.

The marshals took us one by one for mug shots and finger printing. It was so degrading. All in all though, the marshals were nice to us. They said the FBI is nothing like they appear on television. In fact, these marshals showed distaste for the FBI.

When it was over, Julie and I went home feeling judged to be "white trash," which I know is one of those insulting terms I shouldn't use, but it was the truth. I felt especially sorry for Julie. She was an attorney, so I can only imagine how she must have felt.

Other inmates were not as fortunate as we were. I became good friends with another inmate, Pete Strand, a guy about fifty-five with a full head of silver white hair. I met him playing cards—a game called "500" that I wasn't familiar with until I got to the camp.

But it caught my interest, and I ended up playing cards with Pete during my entire prison term. Pete was a registered nurse who owned his own company. He set up appointments and administered allergy shots to insurance company clients in their homes. Pete made it convenient for clients to receive their allergy shots, and almost everyone insured by this company was able to get their needed shots.

Surprising to me, Pete explained that the insurance company didn't like the allergy shots becoming so readily available and eventually wanted to *shut down* Pete's company. When he wouldn't do so, the state of Illinois investigated him for foul play. Lisa Madigan's office, according to Pete, (Madigan was Attorney General of Illinois at the time) released a statement in the newspaper stating that Pete had broken no laws.

I don't know how the Feds got involved and picked up the case, but after three times presenting "evidence" in front of a grand jury, they finally indicted him. The charges were related to:

A) Shots consisting only of a saline solution. *Saline is only the first step in making the allergy shot serum.* When the Federal agents investigated his office/laboratory they found only syringes in this preliminary stage of saline solution.

B) The Feds declared that Pete's office/lab environment was not sufficiently sterile for preparing shot serums, due to [non-sterile] carpet flooring.

C) The Feds found vials of frozen blood in the medical freezer in his office. *When the insurance company client's claim had not been accepted or the allergy shot was not yet covered under the client's policy, Pete would freeze the blood until he got the okay from the insurance company to make an appointment and administer the allergy shot. Apparently, Pete had to send a sample of the client's blood to the insurance company.*

In spite of the truth, Pete was indicted and sentenced to nine years. When the Feds came to arrest Pete, he was at home with his dog. The agents burst through his front door, guns up and ready.

Pete had the presence of mind to snatch up his small dog and gently toss him into the bathroom and shut the door. He was that afraid the dog would be shot.

I've since learned the protocol for FBI agents encountering a dog—no matter how large or small—is to shoot it. Pete was read his rights, handcuffed, and driven to jail.

**Another bank error**

Richard, the builder/rehabber from St. Louis, was indicted for bank fraud. He owed the IRS money, but one of his checks bounced, and it was noted NSF. It happened because his bank had promised to deposit the necessary funds, so in good faith, Richard mailed his check, only to learn afterwards that the bank reneged on their promise. None of this agreement had been put into writing.

Richard was asleep when the Feds came for him at 6 AM. In a helicopter! He heard his name through a loudspeaker. "This is the FBI. Come out with your hands up!"

And now, he was at the prison camp, and all because of a bank error.

## A costly impulse

Charles was playing craps on a riverboat in Kentucky. He was distraught over losing $5,000. When he headed to his truck to drive home, he spotted a car with its windows open but with no one inside. He saw a laptop on the passenger seat. Desperately trying to come away with something for his lost money, he reached in and took the laptop.

When he got it home, he turned the laptop on and was totally freaked out at the words, "FBI Agent" staring him in the face. Charles ran to the bathroom and lost his dinner.

While he cleaned up, he determined to return the laptop to the FBI office in town the next morning. He built a story about finding the laptop in the parking lot of the riverboat and wanted to make sure it got back to the Feds safely. When he returned the laptop, the FBI agent receiving it thanked him, and Charles went on his merry way.

Six months later, the FBI contacted Charles and indicted him for stolen Federal goods. He was sentenced to six months in prison camp.

## Age means nothing

Sandy Gore lived in my room. He owned a warehouse, and the Feds claimed they found 20 pounds of marijuana there. Gore knew nothing about it and had never seen it in his warehouse. But for six months, the government accused him of having the pot there. Finally, one day, the marijuana showed up in the warehouse. Gore believes it was planted there. When I met Gore, he was seventy-two-years old and had never smoked a joint in his life.

If there was ever a man who looked innocent, it was Gore. He had no reason to lie to me and I believed him. But even if he lied, he should have never received a sentence of *30 years!* This is more time than many *murderers* get. Even if he did have the pot, why the hell was he in prison for so long?

This man got up at 5:30 AM every morning, went to work in the greenhouse where he picks vegetables, and then drove them back to the unit to share with everyone. When I met him, he'd been in prison for 24 years already. What an outrage.

## Cigarettes for cheap

Every time I talked to new inmates about their cases, my distrust of the Federal judiciary system worsened. One day, I was in chow line and talked to an inmate who owned one of those "Cigarettes for Less" stores. A cigarette sales representative visited him twice monthly, and he'd purchased 600 cartons of cigarettes from this salesman over a three-year period.

When the storeowner was approached by Federal agents, they told him there were no authenticated stickers on any of the cigarette cartons. The owner learned this was illegal, and there were sixteen other co-defendants involved in the sale. Turns out, this inmate was assigned the same judge who worked on my case. This guy was sentenced to one year and one day.

I told him this seemed like a lot of time for his mistake. He shook his head. He said he felt very fortunate. The prosecutor asked the judge for a three-year sentence. Seems the government added up the total of all the cartons of cigarettes sold, also adding the amount of money spent by the government while prosecuting the case. *Each* of the sixteen defendants was charged a restitution of $4 million! But this man had just turned fifty-five, his store was closed, and he had no way to pay this restitution.

## The Gun Club

During one of the softball games, I met an inmate who looked to be about thirty years old. He was soft spoken and had a very nice demeanor. His story was even crazier than the cigarette store owner's. This guy collected antique rifles and was a member of an antique gun and rifle club. One of the members bought one of his rifles, and the collector completed all the required paperwork and provided the bill of sale.

When Federal agents approached the collector, they asked if he knew that the buyer was involved in running/selling drugs. The collector said he had no idea!

This same collector was indicted, and then coerced into a plea bargain. He pleaded guilty to gun conspiracy involving drugs and received a five-year sentence.

## Here today, gone tomorrow

Eric Snyder was one of the guys I hung around with. He was thirty-one, engaged to be married, and had a young boy from a previous marriage. Like me, he was accused of bank fraud. He'd been a mortgage broker, who completed the loans for his buyers and gave them up to $10,000 as a gift if they purchased his houses. He never listed this gift on the HUD properties, so Eric really had committed bank fraud.

Seemed the government finally incarcerated someone who actually committed the crime they were convicted of. In a sad way, this was refreshing. But Eric was a faithful family man and father and we got along well as we became close friends. He possessed a keen sense of humor and he made me laugh a dozen times a day.

When we played the card game "500" and I won the hand, I got in a habit of singing the James Bond

"Goldfinger" song. Eric was too young to know the song, but absolutely cracked up when he heard me sing it. He laughed hysterically at the song's lyrics. Also, I sang it loud and with a deep voice, so he thought it was hilarious.

Late one afternoon, I came in after running track and saw about ten inmates standing in the hall. One of the guys said the FBI had come to the prison to take away an inmate. It was Eric!

The two FBI agents had entered his room wearing black suits and then escorted him out of the camp and took him over to the hole. Later, I learned this was the first time in many years the FBI came into the prison and took an inmate out.

You can't get too attached with anyone in prison. One day they're here and the next day they're gone. I didn't know if I would ever see Eric again.

Some days later, I headed out to the main corridor and was surprised to pass Eric. We touched fists (the prison hello) and I asked, "What the hell are you doing back?"

"They let me out of the hole," he said.

The rumor spread around on "inmate.com" which was inmates talking in the halls, was that Eric and his fiancée ran a credit card scam. She'd been indicted along with Eric.

After talking to Eric, it turns out "inmate.com" got it all wrong. It's incredible how fabricated rumors are started by inmates—sometimes they'd spread misinformation for fun.

The truth is an inmate in the hole began inventing accusations on others so he could get out of the hole, as though he were an informant. The inmate landed in the hole because he had been caught with a cell phone and was about to be shipped to a higher prison. That's scary stuff. You get convicted on a non-violent crime and after making some careless mistakes, you find yourself in a cell surrounded by gangs. That's when he got scared and began lying about other inmates. One of his false stories implicated Eric. Based on a lie, the hole inmate told camp officers that Eric brought contraband into the prison with the help of a guard. This is why the FBI picked up Eric.

The FBI first approached Eric's fiancée and forbid her to accept any more of his calls. Eric knew something was wrong when he couldn't get in touch with her.

It took the Feds a full three weeks to uncover the lie. Meanwhile, Eric had to sit in the hole while the Feds sorted things out. These guys work like snails.

While in the hole, Eric was released for an hour each morning to exercise in a 15' x 15' room. The rest of the time he sat in a 10' x10' concrete cell with no windows. Once a month, he could use the telephone for fifteen minutes.

The fluorescent lighting in the hole remained bright 24 hours a day. Eric described how bizarre it felt not knowing if it were day or night. Of course, that disturbed his sleep and threw his body rhythms out of whack.

Eric went through this punishment all because an inmate lied to benefit himself—to avoid being shipped out. And this turned out to be only part of the story.

The storytelling inmate invented lies about fifty inmates. The Feds began reviewing each story, and when they found a road map of lies, they finally stopped questioning inmates. Eric just happened to be among the first this guy lied about.

This lying inmate got his punishment, though. The inmate who shared this guy's cell intercepted a Cop Out and learned about the liar's accusations and ended up beating the living daylights out of the guy. He beat on him for ten minutes before guards finally heard it and pulled the guy off the perpetrator. But the damage had been done, and the lying inmate was sent to the hospital with two broken ribs and a punctured lung.

Eric was exuberant to be back at the camp. He's a bright guy and I knew my instincts were correct when I didn't buy into the scheme on "inmate.com."

## Don't judge a book by its head

Moe, one of the inmates, was crazy about softball. When I first met him, I thought he looked like a kook, because his entire baldhead was filled with tattoos. Why would a guy tattoo his entire head? But kooky looking or not, as time went on, I came to think of him as a decent guy. When my daughter Jackie came to visit, he'd call out "I love the Beatles." He knew Jackie was like me and loved the Beatles. He wanted to say something nice and friendly to her.

While we were having lunch at the chow hall one day, Moe asked me to organize a team so he could challenge me to a softball game. I accepted, and got 10 players to join my team. I based my team name on my passion for the Beatles. The first game was between my team, The Beatles, and Moe's team, The Wild Cats. I planned the line up and assigned myself to cover first base and bat third.

When I got up to the plate, the loudspeaker blared the Beatles recording of "Twist and Shout." I was stunned, and all the spectators and players clapped! I felt the best I'd ever felt since coming to the camp 18 months before.

I got a hit and as I rounded first base, the Lennon-McCartney song "I Saw Her Standing There" blasted over the loudspeaker. I started doing the twist on second base, and everyone cracked up.

I went 3 for 5 that game, hitting two singles and a double. It was pretty cool that these guys, knowing my love for the Beatles, would go to the trouble of setting up the music. For the first time in a long time, I felt good. I won't ever forget that game.

## Fathers and sons

One day a new inmate introduced himself as Kirk, shortened from Kirkowitz. He was in prison for bank fraud, based on a scheme his father concocted to receive money by falsifying income tax returns. When a refund was received, it went to Kirk's dad. Kirk, by this time, was thirty years old, and said he and his brother were runners for his father but had nothing to do with the scheme. He delivered sealed envelopes to people for his father, so he said he never knew what he was delivering. I can see why the Feds were suspicious. It was hard to believe he was not aware of the scheme. I think if I was delivering a package for someone and they didn't tell me what was inside, I probably wouldn't feel good about delivering it. With the justice system the way it is, he was dead meat.

Kirk was sentenced to 68 months, the first 61 were spent at MCC (Metropolitan Correctional Center). Until recently, his attorney hadn't even tried to get him transferred to the camp, the reason Kirk was extremely angry with his attorney. He had to rot in the MCC because his attorney was too busy to get him to a camp. Kirk's restitution was $4 million, the same as mine. He looked lost, since he'd come from the MCC and not directly from home. MCC was a real jail. You could get killed there.

I told Wizard about Kirk's case and remarked that he didn't seem like a guy who should be in prison. He probably got dragged into a scheme, with his father leading the way. He looked so young and was very respectful.

Mike's pupils opened wide. "Are you crazy? Do you know who his father is? The guy was falsifying tax returns and getting their refunds. Refunds from prisoners and dead people!"

Apparently, Mike knew everything about Kirk and his dad. Until then, I wasn't aware that Mike did a search on every inmate that entered the prison camp. That way, if the inmate gave him or any other inmate a problem, Mike used this information to straighten him out. While ratting was usually a grave sin, taking information to Wizard was not considered ratting. Going to Wizard gave you some hope of fair play rather than being treated badly. If one guy started the fight and the other guy got beat bloody, Mike would send the culprit to the hole instead of sending both inmates like the COs or guards would do.

On one occasion, a fight started during a basketball game, and one teammate called another teammate a bitch, which led to a full force fist fight lasting for a full three minutes. One inmate had a hole in his lip that needed stitches, and Mike went with him to see the nurse.

This inmate went to the hole since the nurse was required to make a report of the incident. The other fighter stayed out of the hole because Mike made sure that the lip-stitched inmate never gave him up to the camp administrator.

Mike learned the Feds had indicted Kirk's father around 1985. To get his evidence back, he posed as a Fed and went to the courthouse, gathered all the evidence on his case, and walked back out. His actions severely hurt the prosecutor's case. Apparently, Kirk's dad was a professional criminal mastermind. Today, there's a rule that a defendant can't look at the evidence without a representative of the prosecution watching. This rule actually came about because of Kirk's father.

## Timmy, my roommate

Timmy was one of those guys I'd run into with a long record. I met him when he was about sixty, gray-haired, and a bit overweight. He'd gone to prison at age twenty-eight and received the 10-year mandatory minimum sentence for drug trafficking. After serving his time, he went into auto financing, but soon started selling drugs again, got caught, and was sentenced for 18 years.

I thought Timmy was a smart guy, in spite of making the same mistake twice. Other than Wizard, no one maintained a more positive attitude while in prison than Timmy. Had I been sentenced 18 years in prison,

I don't know how I would have survived, but Timmy said the mind conforms to the punishment. Maybe for some people, but I couldn't imagine accepting life in Federal prison for such a long period of time. Timmy listened to me complaining about my 40-month sentence, and somehow, that settled me down. It's a cardinal sin to complain about your sentence when the inmate you are complaining to will serve longer.

Some days, he and I lifted weights after dinner. We were the same age; I benched 180 pounds, Jimmy benched 240. I curled 100 pounds, Jimmy curled 135. Of course, he lifted six days a week to my three.

After the weight room, I showered and he ran the track. Finally, he relaxed with the radio, usually tuned to news and politics. I soon realized Timmy lived each day in prison as if it were his last. He constantly told me not to waste a day.

"Get busy with something positive," he'd say. People like him made it possible for people like me to persevere.

The saying, "Watch the pennies and the dollars will take care of themselves," applied to Timmy. When he first entered prison, he asked for a job paying $200 a month—and there weren't many. He saved every penny he earned and began investing in stocks—purchasing a stock here, a stock there, and before long, his portfolio exceeded $20,000 and kept growing!

Timmy put in a seven-hour day as the Finance Controlling Officer of UNICOR Corporation (one of the companies the Federal prisons operate and use inmate labor to run). He eventually was put in charge of UNICOR hiring. He was fair, too, and not only hired good guys, he made sure they received the raises they deserved.

## Old McDonald had a farm

After dinner one evening as I headed up to the floor S02, I saw a new face, an older man, maybe sixty-five years old or so. He looked befuddled so I asked him if he was okay. He smiled and gruffly greeted me, "Nice to meet you."

I soon learned his name was Terry, and he was in prison for "Interstate Commerce fraud." He was a farmer in St. Louis and wanted to build a new barn on his land, but he had burned down the old barn.

As it burned, fire trucks showed up and fire fighters put out the fire. It turned out Terry didn't have a fire permit and thought he didn't need it since he burned down his own barn. He was wrong, and the fire marshal left. That was the end of it, or so he thought.

Four years later, a man showed up at Terry's door and introduced himself as a Federal Agent. Curious, Terry invited him in only to discover the topic involved his barn burning. The charge against Terry was insurance fraud. This was particularly strange since Terry had not taken out any insurance on his old barn.

Terry hired a lawyer, who spoke with the prosecutor to learn if he could make some sense of this case. After meeting with the Feds, Terry's lawyer returned with a proposal. Since no insurance had been taken out on the barn, the charge was changed to Interstate Commerce. Apparently, the fuel Terry used to start the fire came from the neighboring state, hence, it had been carried across state lines. So, without insurance fraud to charge him with, the Feds claimed Interstate Commerce Laws were violated. Once the Feds do any work on a case, someone is going to prison. Done and done.

Terry's lawyer worked out a plea bargain, a one-year and a day prison sentence. This meant Terry would spend approximately 8.5 months in prison. Although Terry was ready to fight back in court, his lawyer was quick to advise him that no one beats the Feds.

As it happened, Terry was a player in an unusual incident. I hadn't witnessed many fights at the camp, but he was involved in a major one. He was sitting on a footlocker in his room one day, looking much like any working farmer with a red neck and muscles, but he was soft-spoken and just wanted to go home like everybody else. We got along great and shared stories of our life before prison. I'd met his much-younger wife, who had a great sense of humor and seemed like a good down-to-earth person.

Ernie, another inmate was also in the room when all at once he stood up and told the farmer to get his ass off the footlocker. Ernie was a big guy, too, and only twenty-eight years old, but he had a big, rude mouth.

The farmer asked the owner of the footlocker if he minded him sitting on it, but Ernie suddenly grabbed the farmer and pushed him. But Terry surprised us all and pushed Ernie into the wall with such force he hit his head on the wall and fell to the floor.

Ernie got up, though, and jumped on the farmer. Both men were interlocked, not going anywhere. Finally, the farmer managed to get Ernie down on the floor again and stood up himself. Ernie got to his feet and walked out of the room.

We were all shocked by what we saw. It wasn't so strange for a young inmate to attack an elderly inmate, but this outcome was not the norm. The farmer became an overnight hero to all of us sixty-plus guys!

Still, Terry sat in prison counting the days until he could go home. After he learned the sentences other inmates received, he thanked God every night for his brief prison sentence.

These stories haunted me during my days in prison and continue to do so. For a time, it looked like these ridiculous sentencing guidelines were finally being changed. However, they are reverting back to the same mandatory minimums that do nothing but destroy lives. It's very sad.

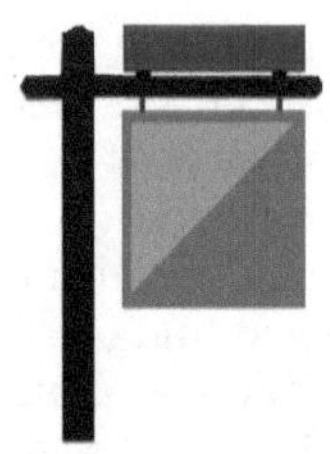

# Chapter Sixteen

## The Wizard and Me

Because of all the cell phones found in the Education Room, the administration took the TVs from the visitor's room away, leading us to take our "500" card game to Wizard's bedroom. Mike and I were becoming close and he was losing his roommate. I was still in my eight-man room and wanted to move to the housing unit where Mike lived. But it was impossible to get in without being at the camp for at least a few years and also have some years left to serve. These were two-men rooms and it was quiet. You could sleep and hear yourself think. This was the floor to be on.

During one of our card games, Mike asked me to become his celli. Any one of the 450 inmates in the camp would have jumped at that chance, and I did. It meant eating great, drinking great, and working for Wizard as my job. He paid better than the camp and I set my own hours, plus Mike would try to get me anything I needed.

He ran a casino where the inmates gambled, and I was the waiter. I served candy and cookies and drinks for 10 books of stamps per month. Much better than $2.00 per month. A book of stamps was $5.00 each.

Sometimes, I wouldn't even need to stand for count. Mike could put me on the out list and I could walk around the camp while others were standing for count.

190

What a cool feeling.

When I had trouble with a cop or a CO, Wizard made it right. One time, I had visitors (Julie's Aunt Rhonda and Uncle Sean) who were not on my list, so Julie asked Mike for help. They would've had to go back to Chicago if Mike hadn't helped.

Because the Wizard had clearance to be in the bubble, Julie was able to ask him for his help. He would hang in the bubble (which is where all the computers and administration stuff were kept) and help the guards during their shift. It was breaking Federal law for an inmate to touch the computer, let alone be in the bubble alone to look through the data. But he was not your everyday inmate. This was Wizard and he was powerful. He even had keys to get into places the guards couldn't enter. Some powerful gang members could control the inmates, but not on a Federal level, not like Mike. He controlled the prison guards and the COs. It was the craziest thing you could imagine.

What I gained for being a friend of Mike's sounds odd to people on the outside. But it meant a lot. For example, I was served first at the commissary and was in and out in five minutes instead of 30 minutes. I guess if you had to go to prison, this was the way to do it. Mike even threw me a big sixtieth birthday party. When we played cards, he got his hands on the snacks you'd buy for yourself at home, from chips to cookies, ice cream to pie. It was like a typical guys' poker night.

When the visitor's room TVs were removed, Mike promised he would have them back by the end of that week—and he made good on it. Just as he had for other privileges that were taken away from the inmates. Taking things and privileges away was one of the punishments we would endure when an inmate got caught breaking a rule. Then Wizard would talk to the warden and get the punishment cancelled. It was in Mike's interest to get the TVs back, because the camp started using his gambling room to watch TV instead of playing poker. Mike didn't make any money when the inmates watched TV, but he sure did when they played poker.

Mike's room was big at 15' x17' with two bunk beds. I'd be on the top bunk. I hadn't told Mike I snored, so I hoped he wouldn't call off our deal because of it. Mike had a lamp, not just the overhead light, plus he put a curtain over the room windows so no one could peer in. Mike used his floor locker as our card table.

Once, Mike pulled out a photo album and showed me photographs of his ex-wife and son. I was honored by this, because Mike seldom showed this personal side of himself to any inmate. Then, after he showed me his photo album, he brought out a bag of hamburgers and fries. The food is so terrible in the camp you can actually sell a hamburger in the camp for $50.00—or even more.


## My aching tooth


As I walked through the prison's main corridor, I glanced at the Call Out sheet posted on the main bulletin board. I saw my name posted as approved to see the dentist about replacing a filling rather than pulling the tooth. Four weeks had passed since I submitted a Cop Out requesting a dental appointment. An inmate can go through a period of pain until the dentist finally has a chance to see him. I had been continuing to press candle wax and temporary filling goo into my tooth. Unfortunately, as I was eating, the wax invariably came loose and went down my throat. I wondered if I swallowed a match, would my stomach burn like a candle!

When I met with the BOP Dentist, I explained I had lost a filling and needed a replacement. I asked him not to pull my tooth. From what inmates told me, if a problem with a tooth came up, even an ordinary cavity, the dentist pulled it. I'd had regular dental care my

192

whole life, including a cleaning every six months, but in prison, I wouldn't have that care. However, after the dentist checked my tooth, he agreed to fill the cavity and save my tooth.

While the dentist worked on my tooth, I heard a familiar voice—the Wizard! I found out later he had a bothersome tooth and walked in to see the dentist without an appointment. Sure enough, the dentist had him take a seat and agreed to look at his tooth. When my cavity was filled, I walked past Wizard's dental chair, and said, "Who do you think you are, the Wizard?"

He shot me a smile and gave me a thumbs up while the dentist put the drill in his mouth and the high-pitched whine began. I went on to the main corridor and showed off my saved tooth.

Mike soon approached. "What are you doing? Are you going to stand here all day long showing everyone your tooth? You've been showing off for 30 minutes.

I didn't care. I was delighted my tooth was still in my mouth.

Mike proceeded to the bubble and grabbed the loudspeaker microphone and announced, "*Attention!* If you haven't heard from Keith yet, he successfully got the dentist *to save his tooth!* Let's hear it for Keith!" His words echoed onto the entire prison, including the outside sports area.

I heard clapping all the way down the main corridor. It was a grand finale to my tooth escapade—even if he *had* announced my success, grinning and in a voice dripping with sarcasm.

I learned later that the Wizard was responsible for talking to the dentist and making sure he didn't pull my tooth.

## Mike makes his rounds

Because Mike regularly went to the bus station to pick

up arriving inmates and drop them off when they're released to go home, he had access to a prison car. Sometimes, his trips involved picking up inmates who are transferred from other prisons. That's why he was able to pick up fast food, and only a few inmates were ever given access to a car.

I went with Mike on one of his runs so he could take me through his typical day when he had a car. We got one foot outside our room door when Fin, the guy who ran the laundry stopped us. It seemed cases of chicken pox had broken out on my old floor unit S07 and the laundry had turned away their clothing.

Mike had heard about this from the inmates on the floor and took care of the problem as only he could. He went to the camp basement and turned off the cable TV in the laundry manager's area. When Fin complained about the cable not working, Mike offered his terms: accept S07's dirty laundry and get the cable service back.

I asked Mike if this broke a health rule, but he decided it was more prudent to get the inmates' clothes cleaned.

On one of Mike's rounds, we delivered papers to the USP. When a guard asked what I was doing there, Mike simply said I was with him. That made it okay. If I'd somehow been there by myself, my next stop would have been the hole.

That same day, we drove to a building where inmates repair tractors. Mike told one of the guys that he needed a tractor ready to go in about an hour. The inmate nodded and Mike got his tractor, which he used to get the softball field in perfect condition by smoothing out the infield. He wanted it safe for the players.

Curiously, on one of our drives to the USP, I saw Mike engaged in a 15-minute conversation with one of the COs.

I asked Mike what kind of services he provided for the USP. It was about the same as what he did for the camp: servicing computers, deliveries, whatever needed attention. If the COs were having a company party, Mike would be in charge of getting the food and the tables set up. If there was a stabbing at the USP and the COs called for lockdown, Mike was in charge of getting inmates from the camp over to the USP chow hall to help handout meals during lockdown. These meal workers started making lunches at 3:30 AM and sometimes worked in the kitchen as late as 6PM—on their feet all that time while they stuffed lunch bags.

When our floor had this duty, Mike made sure my name wasn't on the list to work in the kitchen bagging lunches. What a lifesaver. No one wanted that job. No one ever asked why I was never on the list to go to the USP to bag lunches because they knew I roomed with the Wizard.

That day with Mike at the USP, we drove to the prison warehouse where they store hundreds of brand-new flat screen TVs. Mike ordered a TV from one of the guards and asked him to deliver it to the commissary. Mike put an order in just like a CO. That's crazy shit!

Soon after, the warden punished the guards at the camp by taking away the TVs in the visitor's room, because they mixed up some of the "campers'" names on the count sheet. The guards couldn't watch TV when they were in the visitor's room watching the inmates. They punished the guards like they were children. Even when the guards got punished it affected the inmates. We also couldn't watch TV in the visitor's room. Mike just went back to the USP and replaced the TVs by ordering brand-new ones.

When we got back to the camp, we were both tired. We went back to our room to lie down, only to be awakened by the bubble guard yelling over the loudspeaker: "Wizard to the bubble!"

Uncomplaining, Mike slipped on his shoes again and went off to help. Seems he was always needed for something. To be honest, Wizard was the only person who actually did something in the prison.

## Wizard & his banker

Since I was his roommate, when Mike felt like talking late at night I was there to listen. He'd tell me things no one else knew. On one afternoon, Mike decided he was going to show me his case papers and explain why he was in prison. Mike never talked to anyone about his case, so I felt honored that he trusted me.

Mike's story started when he was introduced to a guy who wanted to sell his racecar track in Ohio. Although Mike already ran his own towing service, he was interested in the prospect of buying this racetrack. The racetrack was priced at $1 million, with a $200,000 down payment. Since Mike was already working with a bank, he approached the bank president with the solid business plan he knew the bank would need to do the deal. He did business with this bank primarily because his father had many years before.

Still, Mike knew he'd have to sell the idea hard. Mike's long dog & pony show worked, and within days the bank allowed the purchase, but only after arranging a 12-month leasing deal.

Mike called the current owner and cemented the deal, and had to add his wife's engagement ring, among other items, for collateral to the bank. After the initial 12-month lease period, the bank president kept his word, and Mike was the proud new owner of a racetrack.

Mike was a brilliant marketing guy, and in just three weeks he had thousands of customers visiting his track. He used airplane advertising all over Ohio, and his charter bus would pick people up and provide free admission tickets to the park.

He also had to rent an ambulance service to stand by at the track on Saturday nights. He saw the ambulance service as profitable if he rented it out to the County on the weekdays when he didn't need the service. Mike was always looking for ways to make a profit.

Mike diversified his businesses and needed more money to grow and persuaded the bank president to lend him money to grow his businesses. This was a small bank and the president was also an investor. He was a busy guy, so from time to time when Mike needed money immediately, and the bank president was out of town on business, the president would lend the money and have Mike "dot the I's and cross the T's" when he got back to town. If bank auditors were coming, the president always made sure Mike's finances were in order and papers were signed prior to a bank audit.

One afternoon, Mike learned the bank had gone into receivership. The Feds were investigating the bank president, and then Mike. Ultimately, the president was indicted for bank fraud, charged with altering and falsifying bank documents to deceive auditors. Mike was charged with aiding and abetting the fraud, along with borrowing money in amounts that exceeded the bank's legal lending limit. The Feds indicted Mike because he borrowed money over the lending limit of the bank. Why was it Mike's responsibility to know the bank's lending limit? If the bank exceeded their lending limit all they had to do was approach another bank and make arrangements to raise more capital. Why would he be concerned? Are you fucking joking with me?

Here they go again. All the Feds had to do was accuse Mike of exceeding the lending limit of the bank and he was going to be convicted of bank fraud. When Mike told them he never knew what the lending limit was, they said, "ignorance of the law is no excuse." Knowing all the details of the law regulating someone else's business isn't even possible, let alone typical. Can you believe this?

Mike wasn't related to the bank president, nor was he on the board of directors of the bank, so it didn't seem reasonable he'd be charged with criminal, fraudulent activities, and certainly not with anything related to the proceedings of a bank audit. As is typical, the Feds told Mike that a guilty plea would give him 12 months in prison. If he went to trial, they would make sure he got 11 years.

So, you have to be a gambling fool to go to trial with only a 2% chance of winning. But if you don't go to trial, they've got you and you're a felon the rest of your life.

Mike, not knowing that being innocent has nothing to do with a Federal case, decided to go to trial and prove his innocence. When he lost, he got an 11-year sentence, just as the Feds had warned.

I offered Mike my condolences and told him about the many inmates with similar stories. But as I looked at Mike, I was surprised to see the most powerful inmate in all the camp tear up. He asked me never to tell anyone in the camp what I saw.

I told him I was compelled to write a book to get this out to America. I was not into politics. I never even attended a political rally. I never took a stand in high school even against the Viet Nam war. But seeing and hearing this corruption turned my stomach. There is nothing worse than being put in prison for something you didn't do, either on purpose or by mistake and this camp was full of inmates that had the deck rigged against them. It's like picking a number on the roulette wheel and spinning. If the number comes up, you're innocent, but if your number does not come up and you dared to spin the wheel you are fucked.

An inmate later told Mike the bank president had admitted in prison that he was offered a shorter sentencing if he lied about Mike having knowledge of falsifying the bank records for the auditors. What a corrupt justice department. The Feds just force people (even criminals) to say what they tell them to say, and the defendant goes to prison.

Mike showed me an article in his local newspaper talking about the travesty of justice committed in this case. It was so touching to see a powerful person like

198

Mike cry. I couldn't help but look away.


## Patience is a virtue


No one was as patient as Wizard. He often slept whenever he got a chance, like he was a doctor on call. With no warning, inmates and guards alike entered his room with problems that had to be solved ASAP. He managed to wake up without a hint of a growl. And he'd be on his way down the hall in less than a minute. Mike was highly motivated, because he realized the camp couldn't run efficiently without him. It was nothing to hear an inmate needed a bed change *immediately*, even though the guy had nine years left to serve. Or, another inmate was fired from his job or someone stole his stamps. Maybe another inmate had been bullied, or a fight broke out. An inmate might need rescuing from the hole, or an inmate was caught smoking or was out of bounds. Whatever happened day or night, Mike got the call.

Since prior to going to prison Mike had taken courses to train as a paramedic, the administration even called him in emergencies, or even a sports injury.

One day, the bubble guard called Mike at 7 AM. "Wizard to the bubble!"

Mike smiled patiently and headed to the main office. A few minutes later, he was back, still smiling.

"How do you do it?" I asked.

"Do what?"

"How do you take care of everyone's problems from dawn to dusk without losing your patience?"

"I have a big heart and enjoy helping people," Mike said. "It's my way of trying to make this government blunder a positive experience."

He'd no more finished his explanation, when "Wizard, get to the bubble" came over the system again. And off he went.

When he came back that day, he found an inmate

waiting to discuss basketball with him. Mike had to okay every baseball or basketball game, tennis tournament, and so forth. He had to make sure the timing of the games didn't interfere with the timing of count. He also held the keys to the equipment closet. If we ran out of balls, gloves, bats, paddles, chalk, or anything else, he would go to the store and buy it. After that meeting ended, Mike tried to get some rest.

But it happened again. "Wizard to the bubble!"

"You have the patience of a saint," I said.

He glanced at me. "Keith, patience is a virtue." He opened the door and left like a cowboy riding into the sunset.

As he reached the middle of the corridor, I heard a scream loud as thunder "Fuck this place!" It was Wizard. Venting, I guess.

Mike saved the life of an inmate named Harry, who suffered from epileptic seizures. Other inmates would summon Mike—the medical staff didn't even bother showing up to help Harry with his seizures.

After he was released and when he got home, Harry sent a letter to the camp administrator praising Mike for taking care of him when he had seizures. He told the prison warden that if not for Mike, he would have died countless times.

Mike did more than help, too. He visited Harry in his room and asked how he was doing after his seizures. Sometimes, Wizard would help out and watch over Harry for the duration of the seizure, which sometimes lasted an hour.


## A cool miracle


The worse thing at the camp, other than longing for my family, had to be the summer heat. One July the temperature inside the prison reached a sweltering 110 degrees! There were only three air-conditioned rooms, but by the time everyone crowded into them, the temperature warmed again. And sometimes, guards didn't allow inmates in these AC rooms. If it was hot on a visitor day, inmates were screwed because they couldn't go in the air-conditioned visitor room without having a visitor. If the church was occupied by a group, we couldn't go there, either. At night, there was no air-conditioning when we were sleeping—definitely torture. You couldn't breathe, and there was nowhere to go for relief.

In my little world, if I'd been able to make a wish, I'd have wanted Wizard to install air-conditioning in our room. Mike heard a lot of my bitching when I was rooming with him. He tried to calm me down about the heat, but I was too far gone. Mike was thirty-eight and I was sixty-one, so maybe it was harder for me to cope.

He placed fans in each corner of the room, as well as by the window. I even had a fan over my head in bed. I would go into an air-conditioned room and then leave to go to sleep in our sweltering room. I took a shower before bed to help cool down. I even put a cold, wet towel around my neck in bed.

Finally, the unthinkable happened.

One night when I was headed to our room for bed, I saw the door closed, but the light was on, so I knew Mike was not sleeping. I opened the door and Mike said quietly, "Close the door, you're letting the cold air out."

I couldn't believe my eyes. In the middle of the room was an air-conditioner. I asked Mike where the hell he got it. He told me he'd gotten it from the bubble. He told the cop he needed it and would bring it back in a few days.

It was absolutely cool in the room. I could have died and gone to heaven right there. I hugged him, and he gave me a weird look. Then, he told me again it was only for a few days. That was fine with me.

We were able to keep the air-conditioner for three days and then Mike returned it. I'll never forget the look on the inmates' faces when they came into our room and felt the cool air. That was worth all the money in the world to me.

## Mike scared the piss out of me

If Mike liked you, there was nothing he wouldn't do for you. In my case, he was crazy about me because I made him laugh, a priceless ability in prison. He once told me I saved his life because I brought laughter into his prison.

On one occasion, Mike wanted to pull a prank on me. Once in a while the prison guards would say inmates' names over the loudspeaker, and the inmates would have to piss in a cup for a drug test.

I was just coming out of chow hall when I heard "Richard Keith to the bubble." What had I done? Each time Julie came to the prison, the inmates would run up to her to tell her the latest Keith story. She actually looked forward to hearing what crazy thing I got myself into each week. After laughing, she would be serious and lay the rules down again. "Do *not* get in trouble."

When I got there, the guard said, "Time for your urine test."

So now I had to go into the john and give urine. Some guys couldn't go if the guard stood there watching. I didn't mind him staying in the room but watching would have been a bit much.

We both walked into the john and he stood by the inside of the door. I pulled my pants down and got ready to go. I motioned to him to hand me the plastic urine cup, but to my surprise he held on to it.

I asked why he wouldn't hand it over and he replied, "We don't trust the inmates, so each guard is required to hold the cup while you urinate."

"Get the hell out of here," I said. "I won't be able to go if you are holding the cup while I piss into it."

Then he said in a loud voice, "I have to hold it while your penis is inside the cup. If you don't urinate within two hours, you go to the hole."

Now I was really riled up. "Get the hell away from me, you pervert. I'm not pissing in a cup while you hold it and I'm not going to the hole. I want to speak to the warden. If that doesn't work, I want to register a complaint to the BOP. I want you fired. This has to be in violation of something."

With that, the guard burst out laughing and opened the door while my penis was still out of my pants.

Looking in the hall, I saw 50 inmates rolling on the floor holding their stomachs. Some of them were turning blue because they couldn't take a breath. In front of everyone was (you guessed it) Wizard. That son of a bitch set the whole thing up and spread it around the camp.

I pulled my pants up and chased him through the hall, which made everyone laugh even harder.


**Step into my office**


I lifted weights and played softball for exercise, but was always careful to not push beyond my abilities. I didn't want to end up with a hernia or any debilitating issue. The medical staff was negligent and incompetent, so staying healthy and avoiding them altogether was a priority.

But, one night after playing softball, I felt a dull pain in my groin. Was that what a hernia felt like?

I sought out one of the inmate doctors, Dr. Ravi, whose name I remembered by associating it with George Harrison's friend (of The Beatles), the Indian musician Ravi Shankar. I described my symptoms, and he directed me to step inside his office, which was the shower room on his floor.

We both stepped into the shower stall, and I pulled the shower curtain closed. I dropped my shorts, so he could examine me while I turned and coughed. Since the water was not on, and no towels were hanging down over the stall, it would look to an inmate as if the shower were not in use.

It didn't take but a minute until an inmate pushed the shower curtain aside, and spotted the doctor holding my balls in his hand while I was told to turn my head and cough.

The inmate was standing in shorts with his towel and soap in hand. "Excuse me," he said, as he quickly shut the shower curtain.

The doctor and I knew we'd be the victims of upcoming rumors.

Thank God for Wizard, because he got the word out that it was a misunderstanding and Dr. Ravi was just giving me an examination. This finally dispelled the rumors, which had already circulated around the camp.

Of course, Wizard had to scare me. He told me he looked up the doctor and it turned out Dr. Ravi wasn't really a doctor.

That shocked me, because I knew Wizard had the records on everyone and knew their whole history.

After a few minutes of me freaking out, he told me the truth. Of course, Ravi was a legitimate doctor. As for the hernia, my injury amounted to only a pulled muscle.


**Casey at bat**


Top of the 7th and 2 outs, I was up. My team was losing by one run, and inmates took these softball games seriously. I played, but found out in a hurry I'm not as young as I used to be. Still, I'd done my best to stay fit, like many of the guys did.

I approached the plate, and suddenly the crowd yelled so loud it shocked the whole team. *"Keith, start a rally!" "Hit it past the pitcher!" "Come on, John*

*Lennon, get a hit!" "You're too fucking old to play ball!"*

Then everyone started stomping on the bleachers. I called time, and took a few steps away from the batter's box. The umpire asked me if I'd placed a bet on the game, but I hadn't. One of my teammates came out of the dugout, telling me to try to tune out the crowd and relax.

That was nuts. Relax in the midst of crass yelling inmates. I stepped back in box and waited for the pitch, too high and with a high ark.

I hate those pitches, but something made me swing. I belted the ball over the third baseman's head.

He tried, coming down from a leap empty-handed.

I stood on second base.

A few games later, we were back and inmates started gathering to find good seats. Coach Pete had his pencils and paper out, writing down the line-up. I batted sixth, as usual.

The game started, with our team scoring two runs, making the score 2-0. Next inning, I was first up.

Then the same yelling began again!

I tuned it out as best I could. I couldn't tell if the crowd was yelling *for* me or *against* me. When the umpire called the first pitch a strike, the crowd went wild!

*"You can't see the ball, old man!"*

*"Put on your glasses!"*

Unnerving. But I remembered Jackie Robinson and how much abuse he had taken from the crowd when he broke the color barrier in the major leagues. If Jackie could tune out the crowd, I certainly could. I was the oldest inmate to play softball and that's why I got so much shit for it.

The next yelling I heard was supposed to encourage me, so I had about 40% for me and 60% against. I managed a double, and my supporters clapped and yelled, "Way to go, Keith!"

It was good to hear the cheering, but I was glad I

was done batting for the game. The yelling had gotten to be too much. But game after game, it never stopped. I still don't know if they yelled because of my age or my sense of humor. But everyone knew when it was the "old guy's" turn to bat.

## You say it's your birthday

My birthday is June 20th. I'd decided to keep that to myself, but abandoned that idea around 3:00 PM. An hour later, the entire camp wished me Happy Birthday. When I spoke to Julie on the phone she asked if Mike was going to throw me a birthday party. The reason I told everyone it was my birthday was some of the guys would buy a guy a pizza if it was your birthday.

Mike asked how I'd feel about having a party. I was fine with that, especially if there was food. If there was anything Wizard could do well, it was throw a party. He assured me there'd be tons of food, and then he asked me for a list of 100 inmates I'd like to invite.

I started with a quick 20 and worked up to 100 inmates. When inmates heard about the party, they all wanted to be invited and offered little favors to ensure a place on the list. One inmate offered to throw out my lunch tray, another offered to go to the commissary for me. Inmates were bringing me candy bars and wishing me a Happy Birthday.

One inmate asked how it felt to turn fifty. I immediately added him to the list.

Of course, I invited all the doctors, and I definitely had to invite Dr. Ravi since my inquiry resulted in those rumors.

Everyone knew when Wizard threw a party, it would be big. Pizza. Burgers. Chicken, brownies, cookies, pie, and soft drinks everywhere. He usually conscripted a bouncer and the windows in his casino were blacked out with paper. The party was quite a shindig. Invited inmates received their invites on a playing card they showed to the bouncer to get in.

Wizard also often threw a farewell party for an inmate going home. My birthday party was different, but that meant I had to be careful not to offend anyone because I'd be living with them long after the party was over. When an inmate believed he should have been invited to the party and wasn't, I'd hear about it.

Sure enough, about thirty minutes after the invitations went out, word circulated throughout the camp and my birthday party became the hot topic: "Did *you* get invited to Keith's bash?" "How many people are going?" "What is Wizard serving?" "Who's cooking?" "How come Wizard didn't throw *me* a birthday party?"

My invitation list had grown to 125 inmates, but I had to cut down the list to 100. After all, the casino room had its limits.

As I started walking to the casino room, inmates greeted me and wished me a happy birthday all the way down the hall. The casino room was packed, not an empty seat in sight. Although the lights were off when I arrived, I could see trays of food—pizza, baked beans, fried chicken, green beans, and chicken burritos. Mounds of cheese nachos were stacked tall on the bar. On a table in the middle of the room, there sat a large white birthday cake topped with vanilla frosting and chocolate syrup—and 30 lit candles on top. He couldn't fit 60.

Mike quieted down the party invitees, and began an inmate "roast" by telling stories about me. How I made him nuts with the heat, worried about toilet paper when the warden regulated it, how I was always hungry, how I was hot, how loudly I snored, how I sat in my bed with my shoes on, how I smoked in our room, my tooth, the air-conditioner, how I made a mess with all the chips I ate in the room, how I invited the warden in my room to try and get my furlough, how many towels I used to shower, and how many times I lost my things. He went on and on until everyone was cracking up.

Mike also asked me to tell the story about my brother inviting me to visit the TV studio and sit behind him, so our parents could see me on TV.

I stood up and told the story of how I hammed it up behind my brother. I walked back and forth like Mick Jagger and the whole time my brother couldn't see me. When I went into my Jagger impression, all the guys started laughing and banging the table. My dad thought it was hilarious because he couldn't wait to see how mad my brother would be when he saw what I had done. When I was finished, I thanked Wizard for the party and everyone applauded.

As it turned out, no one seemed angry with me for not being invited. It was certainly a birthday to remember.


## A favor here, a favor there


I'd first approached Mike to ask a favor to see if he could help me get accepted into RDAP, the drug program. When that didn't happen, I asked if he could get me into a one-year halfway house. Hardly anyone got that. I would have been very lucky to get it. But even Wizard couldn't get an inmate home early.

One night as we were going to sleep, Mike asked me the question that made me realize he was not the Wizard, but an inmate who had his demons like the rest of us.

"What are you and I doing here? How and why did we get tangled up in the Federal web?" he asked.

I was taken aback by these questions that made him appear so vulnerable. You can really get to know someone when you talk with them while falling asleep. In my regular life, Julie was that person. When I first went to prison, Russ was my celli. He and I would have many conversations just before falling asleep.

Now Mike was my roomy. In one of our conversations, he said he was aware that while many inmates feared him, none really liked him. "Everyone knows I have the power to keep them at the camp and no one wants to get transferred to another camp or a tighter security prison."

Mike wasn't wrong in believing that. The way everyone ran to him nonstop made it appear they had regard only for themselves, not Mike. Knowing Mike wasn't a man who asked for help, I made sure to listen and talk with him as long as he wanted. In talking with me, he was reaching out for a friend who would hear him out.

Mike had a brother in law enforcement, but they weren't close. I spoke often about my brother, an attorney and media professional, but he never mentioned his. Mike had been married and had a ten-year-old son. I'd often hear Mike on the phone ordering a pizza for someone back home.

It was none of my business, so I didn't ask questions about it, but I realized he ordered the pizza for his son. He had to be the only inmate in the BOP that could order a pizza for his boy back home. Who would even think of doing that?

Just like most everyone else in prison for such a long time, Mike and his wife divorced right before he began his eleven-year stint. He wanted her to get on with her life. It was hard for me to imagine telling Julie to divorce me and get on with her life, but I didn't have 10 years to serve.

When it came to relationships, Mike and I were opposites. Maybe he wasn't allowing himself to miss anyone. In prison, people have a tendency to bottle up feelings and become numb to the outside world. Or, prison can spawn self-pity. Mike had already served five years in prison, and it had taken its toll.

I asked why he continued to help so many people after getting the short end of the stick. He answered that he saw the prison system as broken and he wasn't sure anyone could fix it. He pitied those inmates who may have done nothing to get thrown in here. Mike understood how heartbreaking it was to be without his wife and kids for years and years. He understood feeling helpless, and asked God for the power to help the inmates heal by giving them hope. He regarded the prison staff as people who weren't interested in what they did, but just showed up for work to collect a pension after 25 years.

I still believe many, if not most, of the employees who run prisons don't appear to know what they're doing. Mike believed that if he could step in and improve the administration of the camp while treating inmates respectfully, he could make a difference in the system.

I told him his intentions were worthwhile, and from what I could see, he'd done a superb job redirecting the camp and getting it on a better path.

If there was a meaningful reason Mike was sent to prison, then it would be to help the inmates get through their ordeals. It was no small task to be in that position. Come to think of it, the only other inmate I'd heard of who pulled this off was the biblical character, Joseph, who went to prison after his brothers gave him up. Joseph got his power because of his ability to predict the future by explaining dreams. Like Joseph, Mike not only ruled the inmates but the entire camp as well.


**I could make a difference, too**


My clout grew immensely after becoming Mike's celli. It only took a few weeks for me to realize I could make a difference at camp without using my gift of comedy. With Mike as my close friend, I had the eyes and ears to the throne. If something was going down at the camp, like a shakedown, I knew about it before the rest of the inmates. I had the power to intervene on disputes between new inmates and a camp veteran, or if an inmate needed a room change.

A new inmate approached me because he heard I could help. I was afraid and nervous when I first entered Franklin Prison Camp, and by comparison, now my situation as Mike's friend seemed incredible.

To think that defendants commit suicide when they learn they'll do time in a prison camp is horrible. No doubt my situation isn't the norm, but it has made me wonder why the public is unaware of the differences between a tight or medium security prison and a prison camp. True, once released from prison, I will still bear the stigma of having been incarcerated, an ex-felon, who has lost all my assets and certain rights as a citizen. However, at least I was able to make a major difference in inmates' lives while I was here. I could even help some inmates get food when the chow hall meal was terrible. It was like feeding the hungry.

## 500 showdown

One night, Wizard and I were up until 2:30 AM playing "500," and my partner Eric and I won most of the games. The next morning, I peered down at Mike in his bunk and asked how he liked losing to a sixty-year-old man?

He just shrugged. "If I want to win, I'll win. If I say so, you'll never win another game at the prison."

I asked if he meant he'd stack the deck or cheat in some manner. The Wizard could do tricks with cards like I have never seen in my life. It was like he knew where every card was at any given time in the deck.

"I'm a much better card player than you'll ever be," he responded, "and if I wanted to control the game, I would."

"You're full of shit," I said.

Then he made a remark he'd later regret. "If we play 500 until 2:30 AM tomorrow night, you won't win one game!" He made a bet to buy fast food hamburgers for the whole card room if he lost even one game.

"You're on," I answered, smiling. Then I took off to find Eric to tell him about our bet.

Eric knew Mike was ridiculous to make that bet, but sometimes that was just Mike. Next, I found Mike's partner, Pete, and told him about the bet. He also thought Mike was delusional. We figured we'd all come out fine and enjoy some hamburgers as a reward for playing well.

Sometimes, Mike put himself in precarious situations, and I knew he was puffed up about card playing, which is why I approached him to give him an out. He didn't accept it, because he truly felt sure he could stop me from taking even one game.

I told a few guys about the bet, and within an hour, the news was all over the prison. I even heard guards talking about the bet.

Finally, the next evening about 8 PM, Mike, Pete, Eric, and I sat down in the card room to battle at 500. The room was already crowded with inmates betting how long it would take for my team to win a game. We had until 2:30 AM to do it, so it was just a question of *when*. Since Mike was going to buy everyone in the room a hamburger, inmates were filling the room quick.

Wizard won the deal and dealt the cards. I discarded four cards instead of five, which was one of the rules, so Wizard penalized me in this first-hand, saying no mistakes were allowed. I won the second, third, and fourth hands. The game was over, and the room exploded with applause.

I got up, raised my shorts high to my shoulders like Peewee Herman, and announced, "My job is done here. I'll see everyone later." I walked out of the card room, leaving the whole place in hysterics.

There was no way Mike could buy everyone in the room a burger, but it was fun to beat him at his own game.

### Who's watching the hen house?


When the Franklin Camp's Administrator, Rains, got promoted to another prison, Teller became Acting Camp Administrator, but soon was promoted to the medium prison. This left the camp with two acting camp administrators: Pew and Squirrel.

Lucky for all of us, Wizard continued running the camp. With Wizard serving as the only administrator it felt like a breath of fresh air. Life with Teller, difficult at best, was finally over. No more running away from camp administrators because they wanted to change your job to one far worse.

In the summer, the camp administrator would tell the inmates to *picka da beans* in the field in 110-degree heat. It was a standing joke you must picka da beans, picka da beans. Teller would walk around looking for the culprit with an untucked shirt, and once found, send the hapless soul to the hole for sloppiness.

Teller would also make her rounds to individual cells to search under mattresses, finding and removing even one extra pillow or cushion that had helped an elderly inmate who had back problems cope with pain.

About every two weeks, she would get on her horse and confiscate all these "threatening devices." Inmates would replace the stolen items the next day, using them until she returned to snatch them away again. A revolving door of pillows going in and going out.

We'd also hide toilet paper, books, or anything else we had placed on our room shelf. Fans also had to be taken down in 95-degree heat. No coolers and no cooking. All that had to stop until the camp inspection had finished—which required as much as a week. Boy, did it get miserably hot!

## A close call

One day, as I got dressed in my room, Rain dropped by to say good-bye to me. He was leaving this camp to accept a promotion. I guess all in all Rain had been an okay administrator. In speeches he gave at town hall meetings in the gym, he'd say he thought of us as gentlemen who had made a mistake in the outside world. We weren't just inmates, but men who would soon return to that world. Although he preached about sanitation, the prison had asbestos (by law, it should have been removed), rusting pipes, leaking faucets, and dependably empty soap dispensers.

By allowing Wizard to carry the prison workload, the administrator didn't have to work as hard. Mike carried such authority with inmates and guards in the camp that early on when they first started working together, Rain had threatened to put Mike in the hole just to show him who was in charge. My thought? Rain had to prove it to himself.

We didn't have a replacement for Rain when the regional visit took place. I asked Mike if having no administrator would diminish his authority in the camp. But I'd mistakenly thought Mike derived his power from Rain. I learned that wasn't the case.

Not long after Rain left, we had another regional inspection. Mike took one of the TVs from the card room, along with an American flag, which he planned to ship to Rain because it was flying the day he left the camp. The TV would be stored in our room until after the inspection.

I didn't pay any attention to the TV stored in our room since Mike had placed it there, and after all, he was the Wizard. Because of Mike, I felt like I was golden and couldn't get in trouble, so anything he brought back to the room was fine with me.

A week later, a sergeant in a red shirt came into our unit to inspect the rooms. I stood in the hallway talking with other inmates and Mike was working somewhere else in the camp. The sergeant came into our room and asked whose room it was.

"Mine, Sir," I answered.

He motioned me into the room and pointed to the TV. "What's this?"

I panicked. I couldn't tell him Mike had brought it to the room. That would be snitching. Having been caught off guard, my mind went blank and I couldn't come up with an excuse. Where was Mike when I needed him? This could be a serious problem.

All I did was respond stupidly. "Huminah, huminah, huminah…it's a TV."

He glared at me. "I know what it is. What's it doing in your room?" He pointed to the flag. "What is *this*?"

"That's the American flag."

"I *know* what it is—why is it in your *room*?"

Still flustered, I couldn't come up with a good answer and bumbled my response. "Huminah, huminah, huminah. Wizard is sending it to Mr. Rain because it was flying on his last day here."

With that, the sergeant yelled, "Tell Wizard to see me if he wants these back." He grabbed the TV and flag, and left.

Boy, was I happy that was over. That sergeant was pissed off.

An hour later, Mike came back to the room and noticed what was missing. "Where's my TV and flag?"

Once again, I babbled before managing to say, "The sergeant took it. If you want them back, you'll have to contact him."

Mike's face got red as he stormed out of our room to go find the sergeant. About a half hour later, he came back carrying the TV and flag, complaining, "Why can't these idiots just stay out of my room and let me do my thing?"

I should have known not to waste time worrying Wizard would be sent to the hole. After all, it was *his* prison.

# Chapter Seventeen

## Ironies, Rumors, and Issues

While growing up, I believed doctors were heroes. As a child, doctors even made house calls. However, I was in prison with many doctors, most of whom had been convicted of Medicare fraud.

One such doctor named Stuart Taft, a cardiologist, had a busy practice before being sentenced. He'd performed many heart transplants, and no doubt saved many lives. Medicare rules require doctors to explain and determine treatment individual patients receive. It's about the insurance companies and what they want to be liable for. If the qualification of treatment is in a "gray" area, say, a variety of options exist, the onus is on the doctor.

If doctors make a mistake determining treatment for Medicare purposes, they've committed a Federal crime. Most of the doctors imprisoned at Franklin are not native to the U.S., so some don't speak English very well. It's possible this alone can account for how they can make mistakes in determining the correct levels of treatment.

I'd had a complete physical a few years before I entered prison and had been told the usual advice about avoiding saturated fats and increasing consumption of fruits and vegetables, along with exercising more often. On the other hand, my father-in-law, a doctor, looked at my test results and was extremely concerned. If two doctors' diagnoses can radically differ when reviewing the same report, is it any wonder a doctor could make a mistake with Medicare?

To me, putting these doctors in prison instead of doing community service seems ridiculous. They should be treating patients. Their skills and years of education are wasted when they're walking around in prison camp in their undershirts and shorts with nowhere to go. This makes me ashamed of the Federal Government.

Doctors might have jury trials, and the people judging them don't have medical expertise, but they determine the fate of these doctors. If gray areas in Medicare rules exist, how can a jury determine beyond a reasonable doubt Medical Fraud occurred?

In addition to Taft, another cardiologist, Steven Chess, was found guilty of Medicare fraud, along with the psychologist Ravi Abdul. I'm quite sure the jury of 12 had a difficult time understanding the premise of the fraud. How can they convict beyond a reasonable doubt when they themselves never went to medical school? Is this really a jury of their peers? Where is the justice in these trials?

Now, I'm not saying there are not doctors that are trying to use the Medicare system to defraud the government. I'm saying one would reasonably think that medical doctors' decisions should be judged by a panel of physicians in their field? Without this specific jury selection, how can a jury decide on the fate of a doctor? My mind screams, *"Where is the justice in these proceedings?"*

Blind justice does not mean blind as in deaf and dumb. It means seeing the truth through fair and just eyes. Shouldn't a jury have knowledge on the topic that is up for discussion before they make a decision that can ruin the carrier of a doctor?

## Rumors—and what the public doesn't see

Rumors have been rampant in the Federal prison system since its first days. Usually started by inmates and media picking them up, the rumors are often about new laws, which if passed, would allow many inmates to be released and go home. Overall, 99% of these rumors were false, but there is always hope the 1% will come true. After hearing Eric Holder's speech on Compassionate Release, inmates began writing letters requesting to go on Home Confinement to spend the balance of their sentences.

Sixty-one-year old Vern Marks was one of those inmates who suffered a stroke after he entered prison, and was never the same. He should've been eligible for the Compassionate Release program. After waiting eight weeks, he finally received a letter—*denying his request.*

After this, many inmates took Eric Holder's speech as just a bunch of bunk—something he had to say to appease Washington or the American public. I still think Holder meant what he said. Could the highest lawyer in the United States practically apologize to the public for the out-of-control Correctional System just to appease the public?

Then, I learned something that changed my thinking. Something I believe the people of this country would find unthinkable. When I was living in Unit S07, one of my roommates was a fifty-year-old man named Ed Sayer. Ed had been sent to prison for selling methamphetamines—like so many other inmates. He kept mostly to himself, but whenever I needed help, he stood by me.

One day, I saw Ed sitting in the hall. He looked sickly green and was pressing a blood-soaked cotton ball in his mouth. His hair had become long and stringy, and most alarming, he's been steadily losing weight, down from probably around 200 pounds to what now looked to me like almost 100 pounds. When I approached him to ask how he was feeling, he just stared into space as if I were not there.

I soon learned Ed had some kind of bacteria eating away at his body. The BOP wouldn't send him either to the hospital or home, even though the doctor had given him only three months to live. Everyone was terrified he was contagious. It was as though we had a zombie living among us.

I had no idea human skin could turn so green. This scared the entire inmate population, because if the BOP was not releasing Ed under the Compassionate Release program, no one was going home. This is how your mind works when you're incarcerated. You get the feeling the public doesn't care about you anymore. Your faith in the system gets even dimmer.

I did feel lucky sometimes because I knew the craziness would end and I would go home to my family.

Does being in prison justify less than basic humanitarian treatment? Even at a minimal security prison camp like Franklin Prison, where most are there because of white collar crimes, most often one mistake. Some didn't know they were doing anything wrong? Do these people not deserve medical treatment while incarcerated?

I've seen inmates who had cancer walk the halls of the prison. It's hard to witness their eyes, bloodshot from a lack of sleep, tearing up when they talk about their cancer. Some know they will never see their loved ones again because they will die in prison.

I asked one of these inmates what he was in prison for and he said bank fraud. Thinking of this person going through agony because he was a victim of predatory lenders is maddening. One day the public is going to learn that the banks were the reason the real estate market collapsed.

One day, the American public is going to learn the judiciary system has become like a black hole, sucking the life out of anyone who gets in its way.

## It's not always over when it's over

Toward the end of an inmates' prison sentence, the inmate is usually allowed to serve 10% of his time in home confinement or a halfway house. This is meant to give inmates time to find housing, if necessary, and a job, thereby gradually restoring his life on the "outside." A probation officer is assigned to monitor the inmate's progress by phone in order to confirm the freed inmate is working and paying his restitution to the government. Since the inmate is still technically serving a probationary period, various rules and regulations must be closely followed.

According to my lawyer, probation was not going to be a problem. But I came across an inmate from Tennessee, Gary Lock, who had considerable problems with his probation officer. In fact, the monitoring got so ridiculous, he ended up back in prison camp for 36 months.

Gary had three boys who played school sports in the private school Gary and his wife paid for—two years of tuition before Gary's indictment. His probation officer was from the same small town as Gary, but she couldn't afford to send her kids to the private school and was envious of Gary's family. Gary insisted his probation officer manipulated him out of jealousy, and that was the reason he was thrown back in prison for an additional 36 months.

I asked Gary to tell me why he blamed her jealousy for what happened. To prove his point, he explained the constraints she put on him. First, Gary and his wife had to keep a ledger of all expenses with receipts attached, even things like buying food at a baseball game. They had to get permission to eat at a restaurant and they had to save the receipts. Gary needed to travel to conduct his business, and his probation officer had to be informed each time he left town on business. She also wanted written information hand delivered to her office, a 90-minute round trip for Gary.

In one incident, Gary had approval to run an errand, and because it could be done in an allotted time, he didn't need to ask for additional permission. He decided to attend his son's baseball game and the probation officer followed him there and charged him with an infraction. Overall, she charged him with 60 infractions, which were frivolous, at best, and a judge ended up giving Gary an additional 36 months of prison time which sent him back to prison camp. However, the judge also dropped the restitution and lifted any further probation period after prison.

I'd never heard of anyone else having to ask permission for such petty things during probation. Gary had no reason to make up the story to me because he had already told me he was guilty of the fraud charge that put him in prison. He was another example of a good person sent to prison for a mistake and then treated unfairly while in prison or during the probation period, sometimes serving more time than some murderers.

Gary didn't care about the savings in restitution. He just wanted to be back with his family, and now he had three more years to go. Gary's story left me concerned about my probation period. I'd once assumed it would be easier, but now I had something else to worry about.


## The gangster


Denny's case highlights the way our Federal system relies on snitches to keep it going. Without snitches, many, if not most of their cases would likely fall apart. Denny was one of my cellmates for a time. He wasn't a tall guy, but he weighed about 250 pounds. Denny's main trait was his passionate hatred of snitches. He'd figured snitches made up about 75% of the inmate population, because prison camps partially exist to reward the snitches who cooperated with the Feds. Denny believed the first to talk would receive the lightest sentence.

That's what the judge told me prior to my plea hearing. Remember that in Ruttles' investigation of me, he asked if I'd help him indict the title company owner. He never asked me if I *knew* any facts that would lead to his indictment, and I told Ruttles I wasn't aware of any wrong doings he was guilty of. Angry about my answer, Ruttles then threatened to make Julie and me the masterminds of the scheme. He didn't bluff this threat, but rather, promoted this lie about Julie and me. This was how he conducted his witch trials.

I kind of understand the Feds need their harsh questioning and threats to sort out who's guilty in cases that involve murderers and rapists, but the Feds have no regard for those who have made honest mistakes for the first time in their lives.

I became guilty by association: the broker to whom I sent my customers had falsified mortgage documents and had been involved in other fraudulent financial activities. Only during the Feds questioning of the broker and his employees did I learn of the fraud running rampant in his company. Anyone who had dealings with this company became suspect.

*Suspicion* means, "An unsubstantiated belief that something is the case, especially something wrong that has happened or that somebody may have committed a crime..." And this is all you need to be *indicted.* And, as I have already noted, in 98% of legal cases indictment leads to conviction.

Denny always put down snitches. Even if he thought a guy *might* have been a snitch, he'd badger him at every opportunity. But Denny once made the mistake of getting on Wizard's bad side when he accused Wizard of being the police, and therefore, a snitch. The ironic thing was because Wizard knew everything about everyone in camp. Because he had access to the computer, he showed Denny the evidence that proved Denny himself had been a snitch and cooperated with the Feds on his case. That shut Denny up quick.

When I heard this, it was extremely difficult not to confront him directly. Every time I heard Denny call an inmate a snitch, his duplicity and hypocrisy made me sick to my stomach.

## The right to appeal

As I walked by the bubble to get to the chow hall, I saw a man with shoulder-length white hair and a long white beard and a skinny physique. He looked to be about seventy-five years old—and exhausted. When I got to the chow hall, another man ran toward me shouting, "Adam's back! He's in the bubble." (Adam, a lawyer, went to court and tried to win his appeal because the prosecutor shared some vital information with a party he shouldn't have. I advised him to go to court even though he had to ride with his hand and feet chained in the bus, the so-called "diesel therapy.")

I ran out of the chow hall and headed to the bubble. I couldn't believe the old man I saw was Adam. He grabbed my hand and said, "Do I have stories for you!" Then, he went off to shower and shave in his new room, which Mike had arranged for him.

Later that afternoon, Adam appeared at the door to our room, looking like a new person with his shave and haircut. He told me how he'd been treated going to and from court. It had been hell, and if he had to do it over, he'd have waived his right to a hearing and done his time at the camp. The Feds make a habit of forcing defendants to think long and hard before exercising their Constitutional rights. They make a farce of the Constitution.

Adam's ride to the first county jail had taken 14 hours. Cuffed, he'd shared his seat on the bus with another inmate who shared shackles with Adam, even when they used the bathroom. Only Houdini could clean up after using the facilities.

Since Adam had been in this low-security camp, where we could simply leave and hail a cab, so to speak, why would Adam try to escape on a moving bus? Adam stopped at five jails on that trip, waiting weeks at each one. He was locked in a cell with five other inmates, who weren't campers, so he never felt safe.

By the time Adam got to court, he looked like he'd lived on the streets. It was difficult to imagine him appearing in front of a judge looking like this. It's inconceivable to think this would not negatively influence a judge. A mistake made during trial that was prejudicial to Adam was heard by the same judge that wouldn't take the mistake into account during Adam's trial. So, Adam had to appear in front of that same judge, although the appellate judge ruled in favor of Adam in an appeal.

It was no surprise, the judge at this hearing ruled in favor of the government, and dismissed the mistake. So even though Adam won his appeal, he lost. The whole system is rigged.

## The jury dilemma

While I was away from home, I'd sometimes think about how lucky Julie was with her trial. In this country, we usually think that if we're innocent we choose a jury trial, rather than a bench trial, where one judge determines our fate. Most trials on television, real or fictional, are jury trials. It seems reasonable to trust twelve people to decide your fate, rather than one person. Judges work with the Federal prosecutors day in and day out, so we might wonder if they can remain impartial.

Juries have problems, too, however. First, in most cases, jurors don't want to be there, and most aren't well versed on the particular laws of the case, especially the details of white-collar criminal cases. For the most part, they presume guilt, not innocence. This tendency is made worse when a defendant is made to go to court in a bright orange jump suit.

Knowing what I know now, if I'd gone to trial, I'd have taken my chances with a judge, not a jury. Judges know pertinent laws and are more likely to understand the details of a case. In Julie's trial, the jury had absolutely no idea what she might have done wrong. They didn't understand her situation and weren't sophisticated enough to decide her case, based on the legal issues.

The jurors' facial expressions during the testimonies and attorney speeches of Julie's trial were, as the saying goes, like "a deer in the headlights," and from time to time, a juror even nodded off. The prosecutor attacked Julie in his closing arguments, since the jury needed something they could grab onto at the end of the proceedings—something to keep them awake. In his closing arguments, Ruttles called Julie "a bad mother, a bad lawyer, and a bag lady." This language was thrown at my wife, an attorney who had never been professionally disciplined or accused of any misconduct in all her years of practice.

I find it disturbing that the jury for Julie's second trial overwhelmingly would have convicted her, in spite of the judge having completely exonerated Julie regarding *all charges.*


**Let the punishment fit the crime**


Prior to President Ronald Reagan's war on drugs, crimes involving drugs usually were not Federal cases. Today, 209,000 prisoners, out of a total of 1,600,000, are in Federal prison, 13.5% of total crimes in the U.S. About 50% of these Federal prisoners were convicted on drug-related charges. I can't believe the number of times judges convicted inmates on drug charges, only based on one other defendant's finger-pointing. The person then received a benefit of lowering his or her sentence. Not only is the evidence bogus but the mandatory sentences are overly severe, and today, all but a few hardliners agree. Despite efforts to change the situation, Federal judges still don't have discretionary power in sentencing. This isn't likely to change for the next several years.

In 2018, President Donald Trump wanted to throw the death penalty at drug dealers. These people need help, not death sentences. Most of them come from poor areas and this is the only life they know. Many of these drug offenders come back to prison because dealing drugs is all they know. The drugs also influence their brains and they need counseling badly. These offenders should be sent to drug programs to get the help they need to recover—not be put to death.

One inmate got arrested for possession of $500 of marijuana. Because he also owned a gun, he got a 30-year Federal prison sentence. If this inmate had no pot on him and simply had shot someone, he would have served 5-7 years. Even if the public doesn't have any compassion for such a guy, they should at least care about the $40,000 cost per year they will spend keeping him in Federal prison. This annual prisoner expense may be the fact that grabs a taxpayer's attention.

There are legal discretionary differences in punishment for murder, depending on the intentions of the murderer. Involuntary manslaughter, often an accident, is distinguished from premeditated murder, which is planned. Thus, the punishment is substantially different between these two crimes, based on intent.

In my experience, white collar crime has no such legal distinctions. For example, when a criminal purposely embezzles large sums of money from a corporation, this is an intentional crime. However, if business owners make a mistake on their taxes or on a loan application, there appears to be no legal, judicial distinction in these crimes, nor difference in

226

punishment. Judicial sentences for financial mistakes nearly match those for persons committing intentional stealing.

There are inmates at Franklin Prison who made business mistakes that cost them ten years or longer prison sentences. There are young people serving *twenty years* for possession of marijuana—people who never hurt anyone or even showed violent tendencies.

Wisdom would allow these nonviolent persons an early release date, letting them go home, and no longer burden American taxpayers. If judges were given the power of distinguishing degrees of crime and degrees of intentionality, one would expect prison sentences to vary accordingly. The prison system could save U.S. taxpayers billions of dollars now spent on warehousing criminals.

As you probably know, there have been attempts to make these reforms at the Federal level, including at the Justice Department, many in Congress, and previously, at the White House level. Polls of average citizens show they want these changes. It's going to take voters telling their representatives to get these reforms in place.

## August 12, 2013, Eric Holder

The entire camp population desperately waited to hear Eric Holder, the U.S. Attorney General (at the time), speak to the American people. As I've said, most inmates in Franklin were incarcerated because a witness testified in court that the inmate had sold them drugs. I have spoken to highly educated, morally good, upstanding people who, because of mandatory minimums applying to drug laws, were incarcerated for ten or twenty or thirty years on conspiracy drug charges, based on hearsay.

This unjust and broken system has destroyed families. One inmate told me how hard it is to describe the sinking feeling when you are convicted of a crime in 1997 and receive a document showing an outdate of 2025. Would he even live that long?

Other inmates are serving twenty years for possessing or selling pot. Now they watch states decriminalize or legalize the drug, but that doesn't cancel their sentences.

This is why inmates hoped to hear Holder try to amend the policies that spell out the tragedy of mandatory minimum sentences. As Holder shared details, we heard him talk about the broken prison system. He confirmed the general belief in the country that the correctional system imposes sentences that are too severe on drug users or sellers, rather than focusing on reforming these people. He also claimed certain laws were so unclear, with so many gray areas, judges were forced to put good people who had made a mistake with drugs in the same category as drug lords and drug cartels that cause devastating harm to the country.

Holder wanted to fix this dinosaur of a correctional system, but rather than waiting for laws to be changed, his plan involved preventing Federal prosecutors placing the specific amount of drugs involved in the crime. This would speed up the legal process and remove the mandatory minimum, which would then allow judges to start sending first-time, non-violent offenders to hospital and drug programs rather than to prisons, or as President Trump desired, to be put to death.

Holder admitted that an astounding 5% of American citizens are incarcerated in Federal prisons. He continued that this represents 24% of the world's total prison population. Holder apologized to Federal inmates who have been thrown into the same bucket as drug cartel organizers and violent offenders.

It seems ridiculous to me that the only reason Holder was able to propose these changes was because so many families were touched by the unjust laws.

Society was finally waking up.

It's shameful that hundreds of thousands of inmates had to be subjected to such a travesty. In addition, we have far too many elderly inmates needing canes and walkers. Holder spoke about this as well, bringing it to the public's attention. He promised to expand the Compassionate Release Program, and revise this to include elderly inmates who did not commit violent crimes and have served significant portions of their sentences. Unfortunately, as I write this, Holder's ideas are not in favor.

I can still remember the prosecutor, Ruttles, threatening to throw my brother and father in prison with me, threats meant to pressure me into accepting a plea bargain. I was never worried about my father since he was eighty-eight years old. I believed the Feds wouldn't dare sentence him to prison. Was I ever mistaken!

The fact that relatives of mine invested in my real estate program meant the Feds could include them in the so-called conspiracy. My father's age was never a deterrent. In fact, when I arrived at Franklin, it occurred to me that in some ways it seemed I'd entered a nursing home.

At the time, I wasn't certain how far Holder was prepared to take the new policy ideas, but I prayed his public stance would help reverse the damage that continues in our system of unfair laws and sentencing guidelines. We're too great a country to allow this broken system to go on. We have to keep working for it, even if we experience setbacks.

## The Supreme Court ruling on Melvin Penn

I spoke to my friend, Melvin, whose case would be heard at the U.S. Supreme Court. I had no idea what a big deal this was until Julie told me this was the kind of case that sets precedent for future laws. Apparently,

District 7, the Northern District of Illinois, where his case was first tried, didn't follow proper sentencing guidelines. The sentencing guidelines range used at the time the crime had been committed were tougher than they should have been. Because the wrong guidelines were used, the defendant could have time taken off his sentence. Melvin and his attorney had been working on this, and the Supreme Court ruling was favorable.

When I heard this, I contacted Julie and she contacted my lawyer, Dan Purdom. We hoped that since my case was also handled by the 7th District, improperly used guidelines might also help me get time off my sentence.

After checking with Dan, he learned my range was 80-100 months. However, pleading guilty and being sentenced to 40 months meant the Supreme Court decision did not affect my case.

I was disappointed, of course. I'd never tried to get out of a place as desperately as I did this camp. I felt like I was clawing my way out of a caved-in mine shaft.

Still, if you have a loved one or friend in prison, the issue of sentencing guidelines is important. Some pardons have been granted based on the fact that what was a crime (involving marijuana, for example) at the time is no longer even a crime in that state. Therefore, no one should be in prison for it anymore. Of course, that's a state issue, but Federal sentencing guidelines could again become an issue.

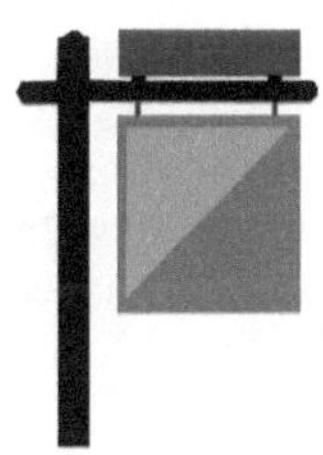

# Chapter Eighteen

## Everything Stays the Same, Everything Changes

Prison is a boring, unhappy place with a lot of time to fill. The secret is finding a daily routine. Inmates who like to read were fortunate, and arts and crafts were popular, too. I found myself talking with inmates about their crimes and their futures after prison. It wasn't unusual for an inmate to ask, "What am I doing here?" Usually, that was followed by the observation that the camp was meaningless.

An inmate might explain the specific reason he was sent here and for how long. If he were guilty of the crime, he'd complain about the length of the sentence. If the inmate were innocent, he would swear to me on a stack of Bibles he was innocent. Some inmates would state all the related laws they had broken during their lifetime. Admitting guilt somehow satisfies the inmate's thinking about undergoing prison punishment. If an inmate wasn't caught in possession of drugs at the time of arrest, in his mind, he was arraigned for all the times he *had* possessed drugs in his past.

Inmates often asked why someone would become a criminal at age fifty, when he had never committed a crime before. Wouldn't it be more understandable to believe he just made a mistake? It never ceases to amaze me how many inmates are *sentenced for over ten years for a first-time offense, a first conviction—* many for white collar crimes. In the drug classes I took in prison, the instructor asked, "Didn't you know you'd be caught?" "Weren't you aware you'd be punished if caught?"

What the instructor didn't appear to understand is that in many white collar crime cases, the person may not be aware he's even committed a crime. *Just because ignorance of the law is no excuse does not equate to the defendant being aware he was breaking a law.* That's why such an action should be called a "mistake" rather than a "crime."

When I found myself in such conversations, it's difficult not to think about my case. Truthfully, I realized I was bending the rules a bit, but I never realized the law isn't interested in hearing the word, "but," which includes extenuating circumstances.

Being in business involves solving problems. In some situations, solving a problem by breaking the law can lead to a serious result. For example, murdering a competitor to gain market advantage is a serious crime. On the other hand, I was losing my fixtures because they were stolen, *and* I was solving a crime problem by bending a rule. I wasn't blatantly harming any party involved. But I now realize Federal laws don't bend, they break. It seems to me that if the law is supposed to regulate the average citizen, then it should be flexible enough to understand human needs and motives.

When an appraisal and a contract are not congruent, this raises a legal red flag. What about what the contract says? It too is a legal document that goes to all parties. Is it not important that the contract said the fixtures will be put in the house after the closing? The red flag I raised cost me 40 months of my life, along with the anguish endured by my family and friends.

## Trivial Pursuit: the case of the missing dots

An announcement rang out, "Keith 4220 report to Squirrel's office."

My inmate number is 4220, and Squirrel is my case manager.

I'd been playing cards when I heard my name called and I hurried to Squirrels' office, standing outside until he motioned me to come in. He looked serious, even stern. I figured I was in trouble. My mind darted to how this might concern my furlough request to attend my son's wedding. Then I began to fear I'd be shipped to another camp because I kept pushing my case for a furlough. You can't push these people too hard.

But what happened next was unbelievable.

Squirrel opened his middle desk drawer and pulled out an empty box of Dot candies and put it on top of his desk. "What if I told you I found this in the trash can in your room?"

"I would tell you they were mine and I had eaten the contents."

"So, you're admitting they're yours?"

"Yes, my wife bought them at the candy machine in the visitor's room." I explained the whole trivial event, starting by describing food I ate during Julie's last visit. I didn't want the box of Dots, so I had brought them back to my room. I told Squirrel I asked the guard in the Visitors room if he wanted them. We weren't to bring candy from the machines back to our rooms, so I'd have to throw it out. But it seemed silly to discard a perfectly good box of candy. When the CO examined the box, he saw the unbroken original plastic intact, and let me take it to my cell. The empty box ended up in my trash can.

Squirrel asked again if I admitted they were mine, not Wizard's.

"Yes," I said. "I ate them and threw the box in the trash." This was like talking to the principal of a grammar school. I couldn't believe I was actually having this conversation.

Angry now, Squirrel ordered me out of his office. I figured he had to be acting. How could anyone get that mad at an adult for eating a box of candy?

This kind of trivia is part of the monotony of prison. It was one of the things that wore us down. Inmates like the Wizard could mix things up a little. There's a lot to be said for that.


## Downtown Houdinis


A couple of modern-day Houdinis offered a break in an otherwise dull day. Lucky for us, press coverage of an escape attempt at the MCC in Chicago turned up on TV stations around the country. Apparently, two men managed to escape through the window located on the 35$^{th}$ floor. The U.S. Marshals eventually found the guys. No Franklin Camp inmate could imagine how two men could escape the MCC medium security prison, let alone from the 35$^{th}$ floor. But, the whole camp was extremely happy for the escapees and cheered them on while their "freedom" lasted.

Medium security prisons are equipped with electrified middle fences that roast anyone touching them. Counts are done twice daily, with three counts in the middle of the night to curtail any escape attempt. Each inmate is allowed only two towels, two shirts, and two pair of red shorts, and after this escape, I began to realize why these rules existed.

I was talking with Kirk one afternoon and he told me he was at the MCC when the two men worked on their escape plan. The two inmates whispered to him and a few other inmates that they'd soon be making a run for it. No one, including Kirk, gave any credence to the talks, but he had seen an overabundance of bed sheets brought into the cell and put under the bed until needed.

A guard on the unit was called Baltimore. He wasn't a hall-walker, but was considered a lazy guy and close to 300 pounds. He carried out his duties sitting in his chair and never bothered to get up. The inmates considered him mean as well as lazy, and he was known to ignore prisoners' requests. While the two inmates planned their escape, lazy Baltimore never entered their room or inspected their cell. If the guard had done his job, the escape would have been impossible to pull off. No one noticed them obtaining the tools they needed.

At 4:30 AM, the two inmates dropped their sheet rope out the window and down the skyscraper prison building. The rope was 2-3 stories too short, because they couldn't wait any longer to escape. Apparently, there was going to be a guard change soon and these two guys did not want to take a chance on a new guard. Before leaving, they left a note:


*To Mr. Baltimore:*

*Thank you for being a fat and lazy fuck.*


Several hours later, a police officer driving downtown looked up and saw the sheet-rope hanging out of a window. This was the story told to the press.

After the escape, Federal Marshals interviewed inmates on the floor about what they'd heard or knew, but no one had anything to contribute. According to Kirk, one of the escapees talked to him on a couple of occasions and cancelled the escape, which is why Kirk was surprised the escape happened at all. When the two escapees hit the ground at 4:30 AM, they immediately hailed a cab. One guy went to a friend's house and the other went to hold up in an evacuated building. They weren't successful, but they captured attention.

**The new law**

Escape was one kind of fantasy, but many inmates were watching the more likely to happen legal developments. One morning, I found most all of the inmates crowded into the TV room to watch the news. We were waiting to learn the results of the vote in the House of Representatives to pass a 2-point reduction of the sentencing range for inmates convicted of drug charges. As it turned out, the vote was unanimous in favor of the change. *This was a great day at the prison.*

The new legislation applied to drug offenders who had received prison sentences of many years, like my roommate, Timmy, who had been sentenced 18 years for selling drugs, was ecstatic. This meant a reduction of four years for him. After deducting time already served and time off for good behavior, he now had only 41 months left to serve.

Although the law was not yet retroactive, inmates felt sure that because of prison overcrowding, another vote would adjust this law and make it retroactive. After many false rumors, after years and years of political discussions, relief had finally come.

But then, heartbreak for my friend Timmy when we found out the new law would not help repeat offenders—and that meant Timmy. Still, many other inmates got to go home early.


**Sandbagging against sandbagging**

It poured for three days. Listening to the radio in my bed, I heard that the river in town was overflowing and the town needed volunteers to help cope with the flooding. Usually, the administrator, Rain, volunteered the inmates to help with the sandbagging. It was Saturday morning and Rain came back from the USP where he had been the Acting Warden for the past few weeks.

236

On his return, Rain's first agenda item was to call a meeting in the cafeteria with all inmates having less than two years left on their sentence. Since this included me, I put on my uniform and headed to the chow hall.

Rain told us we were needed to fill sandbags for the community since there was major flooding at the riverbank. But inmates with health issues could leave. Almost all the inmates left. As for me, I figured since I was now sixty years old and had a bad back, I'd pass on filling sandbags and hauling them around.

About one hour later, another loudspeaker announcement came. "*All* inmates report to landscaping. We need you to sandbag."

Once again, I felt no guilt about staying in my room. But Rain walked through the camp, room by room, clearing out the inmates. I grabbed a book I'd been reading and slid down beside my locker. I could see out my window as the camp was emptying and heading out to a tall mound of sand that the inmates bagged and loaded onto waiting trucks.

As I sat reading in my room, I couldn't help thinking about Anne Frank sitting silently in their friends' attic, hiding from the Nazis. Although I wouldn't be murdered if someone caught me in my room, I could—and likely would—be sent to the hole.

A while later, Mac, one of my friends, knocked on my room door and startled me. I thought for sure it was a guard who'd catch me playing hooky. I let him hang out in my room as long as he kept quiet.

I still feel justified in my decision. Besides, the inmates hadn't been asked to help the community, they had been ordered to do so and Rain excluded no one. Age and physical condition didn't matter, and we had several inmates with heart conditions, and so on. It was ridiculous, not to mention dangerous, to expect these men to fill and lift 75 pound bags of sand onto a truck.

When the guys got back, I spoke to my close friend Pete. He explained that one of the inmates who suffered from seizures collapsed while lugging bags up onto a truck. The guards simply moved him to the side and continued yelling at the inmates to keep on bagging sand. Pete said it was like the movie *Cool Hand Luke*, when Luke was pissing in the woods and had to shake a tree to show the guard he was still there.

Reporters were also on the scene taking pictures and interviewing some of the inmates, commending then for helping the community. Little did the reporters know that anyone not reporting to help was reprimanded. This is even crazier when you consider that the Franklin Camp is a Level 3 Medical Camp, meaning that many inmates with medical conditions were often placed there. It made no sense to put them at risk in order to bag and carry sand. No sense at all.

**Success!**

Sometimes things change and don't necessarily have anything to do with prison. One afternoon I was checking my emails and saw one of the most important messages I have ever read. Over the years, I had written a couple of poems to my daughter Danielle, who was twenty years old at the time. Now she wrote one to me.

## What Makes A Hero?

### Danielle Keith

I know it is hard to see your situation as a positive,
But, if you take a step back, you can see what has come out of it.

How many hearts you have touched and lives you have changed.
The laughs that have risen, the smiles that remain.

You are a role model to so many, especially your children.
You have taught us the importance of family and to live every moment.

You've set an incredible example of what true love entails.
Anyone would be lucky to have the ship you and Mom sail.

You've brought families together by teaching forgiveness.
Strengthening bonds and creating memories to be cherished.

Your strength is inspiring to your daughters and your sons.
Your humor, love, and dedication shape the person I hope to become.

You've taught me to never give up and to stand up for what is right.
Even when it does seem hard, I'll never back down without a fight.

So while you endure this unjust battle that seems so damn unfair,
Remember the lives you've touched that would otherwise been left bare.

You are an inspiration and hero to everyone, not just to me alone.
I am so proud to call you Dad and can't wait for you to come home.

To say this poem changed my life would be an understatement. I started writing poetry in college, and a professor told me I had a knack for it. In prison, I seem to be writing poems non-stop. When I write my feelings, it gives me a sense of opening up my mind and heart, and a willingness to let my feelings be known. Writing poems gives me a sense of goodwill, knowing I'm sharing the love inside of me with whoever the poem is written for, such as my wife and kids.

What I hadn't felt was the rush of feelings on the part of the reader. I had an idea of how my poems might impact the reader, but had never experienced this first-hand. Now I had. Words can't do justice to the warm, magical feeling I experienced while reading Danielle's poem. I didn't want her words to stop. All my dreaming of riches, traveling to exotic places, owning cars, earning doctoral degrees, winning competitions, surrendering to lust or exulting in the highest pride could not compare to the feeling overwhelming me while reading Danielle's half-page poem. I was so happy she took the time to write me a poem. After all, I had plenty of free time to write, but she was busy with college.

I could now say to the world and myself: I made it. I achieved my goals. I am a loving father. I found a purpose for living. I am truly a success, and the government can never take that away from me.


## The Wizard gets shipped out


On another day, a sudden change left me pretty down. One afternoon, I went to the bubble to check my email. While walking down the hall, I noticed 22 cases of soda, five cases of candy, cookies, chips, and other snack foods on the floor of the bubble. Inmates had begun congregating in the hall and soon learned that Mike had been raided by the rookie "Night Cop."

Since this wasn't the first time he'd been raided, I wasn't concerned. He always seemed to find a way to get out of these situations and resume his recreation room a few days later. When a night guard confiscated Wizard's pizza oven, it was back the next morning.

He got air conditioning units back after Regional had them confiscated and then went back to Washington.

After the Wizard got up, he heard rumors circulating about the confiscated property in the casino and went to Mr. Swanson's office to make things right.

Normally, this would not even be a bump in the road. Later that day, my roommate Timmy told me about an article on the internet about the successful raid of the rec room and the inmate's cell. They found his cell phone—the kiss of death. Things that we took for granted with the Wizard, like the cable TV and the food were exposed. The verdict was "guilty" and that meant "ship out." Apparently, Wizard was going to be shipped to the Duluth, Minnesota camp, which was run like a low security prison.

Since I'd moved out as Mike's roommate and no longer worked in his rec room, my friend Eric had moved in and was also being shipped out. Wow. Had I continued to work for and live with Wizard I might have been headed to Duluth, too, which was much farther away from my family. Once again, I said, "There but for the grace of God, go I."

I thought it best to wait a day rather than rushing in to see Wizard. When I saw him the next morning, he was lying in bed writing on a note pad. I asked if he was doing all right. He looked a little pale but tried to play it off. He wasn't one to show his feelings, especially when he was sad. He said he would miss me, and that he was being shipped for political reasons.

Mike hoped we could stay in touch, even though he had another five years. I knew what he meant by "political reasons." He'd had way too much power at the camp for way too long. Inmates all over the country referred to the Franklin Prison as Wizard's prison.

I felt sorry for him, a guy who didn't belong here in the first place. He had to start all over in a new facility as a regular inmate with no perks. Seemed almost everyone came to say their good-byes, even all the inmates who Wizard had helped. It was like people paying their last respects to the godfather. We all knew the prison would be left in the hands of the commanding officers.

It didn't take long for some other inmates to realize how close I came to being shipped out, too. Eric had moved into my position and became Wizard's roommate at the wrong time. When I was working in the rec room, serving up snacks and drinks, I was under the assumption I was untouchable. After all, I was working and rooming with the Godfather, The Wizard.

Apparently when Rains left and Swanson arrived, Mike's power disintegrated, and it was just a matter of time. I still don't know what allowed me to escape punishment, but I am thankful I could finish out my time at the prison camp.

I asked Mike if his power was the reason he was being shipped to Duluth Prison. He agreed that was one of the reasons, but hamburger had been stolen from the kitchen. Swanson was trying to locate the stolen beef since the meal changed from meatloaf to fish sticks. The meat was nowhere to be found. A couple of days passed, and Mike walked into Swanson's office with a whole lot of raw meat.

To Swanson he said, "I'm sure you heard the name Wizard. Well, I'm him. I have been running the camp and if you want things to run smoothly, I suggest you leave things to me. I can get all the meat back to the chow hall."

That was the straw that broke the camel's back. Swanson was furious with Mike. "We'll see who runs this camp! I hope you like the cold, because that's where you're going tomorrow, pal."

Teller and another case manager tried to talk Swanson out of shipping out Mike, and even indicated that he could be a huge ally. Everyone knew Mike handled everything from rides to the bus station, sporting goods for recreation time, or computer help for bubble cops. Wizard also helped organize sand bagging by inmates when the town needed help because heavy rains caused flooding in town. Mike was in charge of Christmas decorations that brought a little cheer into the place. Any questions on furlough or policy or anything were directed by the inmates through Wizard, instead of bombarding COs with questions.

Wizard worked hard for both sides of the camp, but he was punished for having too much power.

# Chapter Nineteen

## Inspections, Food Strikes, Microwaves, and Wedding Watch

Every three years, Regional Prison Administrators visit Franklin Prison Camp and checked the way the camp used its funds. During these visits, the counselors and guards were nervous beyond belief. Seems ironic the inmates would give anything to leave the prison, but the prison staff was terrified of losing their $80,000 a year jobs.

The entire event was a big show. Every 15 minutes, an inmate was called to the bubble to do some cleaning around the camp. It's like the staff was on trial with their jobs at risk. Inmates were made to clean and paint. The COs would plead with the inmates to do a good cleaning job. The inmates were even promised perks if they passed the inspection, but the perks were never seen.

So, even though we had leaky plumbing and two floors didn't have working showers, the staff wanted everything spotless. One inmate dared to ask a commanding officer, "What would happen when Regional finds out we don't have a working shower on our floor?"

"Why don't you sweep up the area while he's going through it, so the inspector misses it," the CO told the inmate.

The prison employees accused inmates of deception and claimed they couldn't be trusted, yet this is exactly what the staff perpetrated on Regional inspectors. With an upcoming visit, suddenly our meals became almost edible and the ice machine actually dispensed ice. On the other hand, what thanks did the inmates receive for supporting the Regional visit? The inmates' ping-pong, softball, and card room were taken away.

The card room was important because it was the only air-conditioned room, so it was always filled with inmates any hour of the day. When the regional representative entered the card room, he was angry to see so many inmates crammed into such a small area. He immediately closed down the room and removed the air-conditioning unit.

The education area was closed, and the visiting room was being used for a job fair, supposedly held to help inmates get a job when they were released.

It was a sham. In all the time I went to the fair, no jobs were ever offered.

It was 100 degrees inside the prison on the day of the visit. But the air-conditioned room was gone, so inmates had nowhere to go for relief from the extreme heat. The local news station issued warnings to avoid going outside unless absolutely necessary, but the regional folks took away the inmates' only air-conditioned room other than the small library and church. Insane. Over half the camp's inmates had a medical problem and/or were over the age of fifty-five. It's also important to know that when it gets dark out, the church and library were closed.

So, was this cruel and unusual punishment? Isn't it inhumane to keep inmates in 100 degree conditions with no means of cooling off?

I saw any number of elderly inmates collapse from the heat, and the administration didn't seem to care. We had no one to call for help, no one to run to, and no one with the power to stop the nightmare. It was incredible that the Franklin Prison was a medical facility camp, whatever that meant.

## Camp Happy

For the regional visit, we cleaned for two weeks and they inspected for three days so the prison could be accredited by the testing group. Wizard wanted the rec room, which was also the casino, to pass, so he conscripted quite a few inmates to play miniature golf, tennis, and a board game, Risk. He was trying to make it look like the inmates needed someone to hand out sports equipment and board games so he could keep his so-called employees. He needed them for the poker table, making pizza, selling soft drinks, cookies, chips, and anything else he could manage to sell in the camp.

Mike asked me to resume my job behind the counter in the recreation room to hand out tennis racquets, golf clubs, and games. I even made the inmates sign out what they used. This was all staged for the regional representatives. If Mike made it look like we were all needed to keep records of the equipment, then we could continue working for him.

Two women and two men wearing suits were the representatives who came to the recreation room. One man walked over to me and thanked me for handing out the equipment to inmates and commented about what a great job I had. If he'd only known my real job was to sell soda, chips, cookies and candy! Sometimes, Mike even baked and sold pizza.

After shaking my hand, the rep strolled over to an inmate playing Scrabble. He shook that inmate's hand and asked, "Do you enjoy playing Scrabble and other word games?"

The inmate smiled and said, "Oh yes, Sir. I just love it here at Camp Happy!"

Teller had just come in and heard the inmate's comment. She gave him a funny look as if to say, "Don't be a wise guy." But the inmates in the room cracked up laughing.

The regional team left feeling pretty foolish. Let's face it; no one wants to be in prison.

## I invite the fox into the hen house

Unlike the guards, the camp administrator seldom came into the room hallway to look around. But one morning I heard a voice in the hall and went out to see who it could be. It was Swanson walking down the hall, popping into random rooms. I quickly awakened Mike so he could hide anything that shouldn't be found in our room. He said we were fine.

Since I'd spoken to Swanson in his office about my son's wedding, I thought it wise to invite him in to see my family photographs, so I called out a greeting and invited him inside. He went straight to the bulletin board where I'd put the photos.

Afterward, I learned that wasn't a good thing, because Mike had been sitting on his cell phone. I had forgotten I'd tacked a paper record that my kids gave me for my sixtieth birthday. They'd written clever spins on Beatles songs, each of which meant something that happened to me either in prison or prior to going. Swanson really liked The Beatles and wanted to know what some of the jokes on the card meant. Oh, no.

One of the messages was, "You're gonna lose that $100 bill." This was a joke about Julie dropping $100 on the visiting room floor. She never could find it. It had been for me, but I didn't say so or I could have been sent to the hole for having that much cash. Another was "Sexy Schmutzy after Sexy Sadie." Was "schmutzy" a Hebrew word, he asked.

Embarrassed, I explained that I called my cousin Danny, "Schmutzy." It's a Yiddish word for dirt.

Then there was, "Because you put in the furnace after the closing, after the song 'Because'." I explained this is the reason I got sentenced to prison, and he couldn't believe it.

"That's the dumbest thing I've heard yet," Swanson said, "and I thought I'd heard it all!"

There were other things, take-offs on various songs— "Got to Get You Into My Cell," "Don't Bother Me, I'm Hot," "I Should Have Loaned Better," "Roll Over Wizard," "She Escaped Through the Cell Window," "Mean Mr. Ruttles," "Happiness Is A Warm Visitors Room," and "Everybody's Trying to Be My Bunk Mate."

When Swanson was done with the paper record he looked at the pictures of my family and said, "Let's get you to that wedding."

"If I have to attend with an FBI agent," I said eagerly, "that's fine, but it's going to be hard to dance the "Satsky" chained to an agent."

Grinning, he asked, "What's the Satsky?"

"It's a Russian dance where the two men cross hands and hold on to each other while they kneel down and kick their feet out. Not easy to do cuffed to an agent."

When he left our hall corridor, the guys gave me a hard time, yelling, "Hey, Mr. Weeney, do you want to see *my* pictures, too? I'd like a furlough just like Keith."

Pretty funny. You're not supposed to be friends with the camp administrator, but I wanted to go to that wedding.


## Spun like a top


My son's wedding date was approaching fast. Although Swanson told me I would have my furlough, other inmates knew he was a liar. One afternoon, while standing in chow line, I asked Swanson to give me the respect I gave him and not forget about my furlough request.

"You got your furlough, now we're waiting for your team meeting to hash out the time you need for the wedding."

Because of all the rumors about him lying to inmates, I still couldn't be sure I was going on furlough. Our resident senator just barely got a furlough to attend his wife's funeral! Inmates generally don't get approval to attend the funerals of close relatives. I had to be patient and hope he wasn't spinning me.

The following Monday the temperature plummeted to 30 degrees below zero and no COs were in the camp. Since my last meeting with Pew had been disastrous, I didn't expect him to call me into his office anytime soon. Swanson was the person who could make my furlough happen, but Pew could try his best to make it difficult.

On Tuesday, I stood in the chow line thinking I'd screwed up my furlough by not accepting the hours originally offered, which wouldn't have allowed me to attend the wedding. Still, I'd have been able to take pictures with the wedding party and spend the day with the bride and groom.

Then, out of the blue, I heard my name over the loudspeaker and was told to report to Pew's office. But I'd begun to notice loss of my hearing acuity, so I didn't catch my name. Other inmates in line told me they'd heard my name, so I ran down to Pew's office and took a seat while he finished up some paperwork.

Finally, Pew asked, "Do you want an 8 AM to 8 PM furlough, or don't you? If not, you'll be turning down the result of a lot of Swanson's hard work. He got the warden to approve it, against my wishes. There has never been a single furlough approved in this camp that offered the inmate the luxury of leaving the county, let alone the state. You'd be looking a gift horse in the mouth."

Having already thought about my answer, I immediately accepted the hours and thanked him. So, I'd travel to Chicago and spend time with my family, take some photographs, and go back to prison. My prayers had been answered! Since it was a 3:00 PM wedding, I couldn't go to the ceremony, but I was able to acquire a groundbreaking furlough that could help inmates who came after me. I had been making my son and his fiancée crazy. First I'm going, then I'm not, and back and forth. They'd already put off the wedding a couple times. The wedding was getting closer and closer, and the bride's parents could no longer push the date.


## Are you joking?


I finished filling out the furlough request and handed it back to Pew. With a weird grin, he said, "Keep that form because Swanson is going to have a town hall meeting and he'll be discussing social furloughs."

Now what? What would Swanson say about furloughs? This time my son was sure I was going to his wedding. Swanson was making me look like an idiot. How can a system be so mean and corrupt? I'm starting to look like I'm losing my mind.

Wizard had some idea that we'd get family-related furloughs, including divorce counseling, but there'd be no more furloughs for a night out with our wives. How was this going to affect my wedding furlough? I was getting really angry, which was never a good thing in prison.

It bothered me that Pew had my Green Form (request form) sitting on his desk. Maybe he was waiting for the meeting to learn the guidelines, or maybe he knew exactly what would be said.

At the town hall meeting, Swanson started out with this: "I have a couple of rules to lay on you today. First, everyone will be expected to be dressed in full uniform during the day. Second, there will be no more furloughs given to inmates unless it's going to a court-ordered marriage counselor."

I raised my hand, and he added, "And no wedding furloughs."

What a son of a bitch. I wanted to choke him. I was screwed. What a mean thing to do to a family. I understand him setting me up, but he messed up my son's hopes at the same time.

Then, as if the furlough ban wasn't enough, he announced, "I'm taking away the visitor's room for your nightly entertainment."

That was terrible news. The entire camp watched TV every night, so now we'd have a camp filled with unhappy and angry inmates walking through the halls with nothing to do until bedtime.

An inmate challenged Swanson. "Why are you taking TV from us? That's an unjust punishment."

"Because you guys are throwing cell phones over the fence of the USP and that must stop."

This guy was a certifiable nut case.

"That's a lie," an inmate yelled. "Who would do such a stupid thing like that? Nobody is throwing anything over the USP fence."

"You're a moron," Swanson said. "Go sit in the bubble and wait for me."

The inmate headed for the bubble—and then everyone else headed out.

When Swanson approached the waiting inmate, he yelled, "You son of a bitch. I'll have you sucking cock at the USP."

Word immediately got out about what Swanson said. There were notices all over the prison warning about counselors showing their prejudices or saying anything derogatory about gays. Later that day, Wizard went to see Swanson to discuss the town hall meeting.

After reasoning with Swanson for forty-five minutes, the inmates finally got back the visitor's room TV time, but Swanson lost a ton of respect that day. We all saw him for who he was. The inmate went over Swanson's head to the prison warden, and man, did Swanson catch shit. Rumor was the warden severely reprimanded him.

I saw Swanson in the chow line at dinner, and he just nodded to me. So, Pew had me punished because I went over his head to Swanson, and now Swanson was nodding at me—gotcha, you're it. Like a first grader.

I wasn't used to these kinds of immature baby games.

## The food strike

Swanson arrived one year before I was due for release, and at first, I seemed to develop a strong rapport with him. Maybe that was because he had a sense of humor, or so it appeared. At least he'd laughed when I joked with him in the prison hallways, and he asked me Beatles' questions at lunch. Some inmates had heard of Swanson and had been warned he had bipolar disorder and could lose his temper at the drop of a hat.

I hadn't seen that side of him. I was so excited that he might be my ticket to the wedding and other benefits, I actually believed there was a possibility he could be a decent guy. After all, nobody in this place had killed anyone. Why not catch a break and get a fair camp administrator. However, over time, I began to see his sinister tendency to mess with inmates' minds.

Within a week of the wedding, I received legal mail from the warden unequivocally stating I *wasn't* allowed to attend the wedding. I initially assumed this was sent from outside the prison and from someone unfamiliar with Swanson's offer, so I was shocked to find *his* signature at the bottom of the letter.

I confronted him in his office. "Why did you lead me and my family to believe I could attend my son's wedding? You told me to call my wife with the news. Why would you do that?"

A weird, sinister expression came over his face. In an eerily calm voice, he said, "Don't take it personally."

Huh? There was no other way to take it.

My family was *livid.* Then, as the reality set in, they were depressed. There was nothing they could do. The stinging loss of my freedom led me to intense anger. Right along with my family, I was helpless. Swanson was cruelly toying with me and my family, just as I'd heard other inmates say he had done to them. I was down to 10 months and couldn't wait to get out of this funny farm. Swanson was the type of guy that should have been the administrator of the loony bin, not a prison camp.

I still have a hard time believing a man who reached that level of professional advancement would stoop so low. Did he really have time for this kind of game-playing?

Other inmates said he'd played with their trust as well, and once he had it, down came the hammer. What he'd done over the wedding was just plain mean. Obviously, many people abuse their power, but as I saw it, Swanson did this simply because he could. I felt stupid and betrayed, then soberly awakened to the man's controlling tendencies.

As I said, Swanson took away late-night TV for no reason. No more staying up until 2:00 AM on weekends. Like school kids, he sent us to bed at 9:00. He got rid of microwaves, our only way to cook legally. Things were getting bad. If I'd had to eat only prison food, I'd be dead in a month.

One of the rumors in the camp held the boxes on the food in the storage warehouse were labeled "not fit for human consumption." The inmate who told me this would know since he constantly was stealing food from the prison warehouse. This alone was enough to bother me.

I decided to speak to Swanson and see if I could reason with him, and he assured me the inmates would have late night TV back within a month. Only a week later, the *weekday* evening TV was gone again, and we had to head back to our cells at 9:00 PM.

Swanson soon had the outdoor visiting area locked, preventing family access to the outdoors on pleasant days, and instead inmates' visitors had to meet indoors—and he refused to turn on the air-conditioning. This room became so hot many inmates told their families not to come for visits. Jim, an older orthodontist, almost passed out, and others had similar issues. Since many inmates were in their sixties or seventies, some couldn't breathe in the heat. Swanson's decisions were beginning to seem sadistic.

Now the inmates were pissed.

Messing with inmates' visitors was the proverbial straw that broke the camel's back. Inmates began strategizing ways to effectively strike back. Many congregated in halls talking about the merits of a hunger strike. A hunger strike was considered the *only* way to get Regional's attention.

Even Wizard said, "If you want to get their attention, go on a hunger strike."

Fed up with the administrator jerking them around, inmates agreed the hunger strike would start on Monday. Many inmates had already gone through this ordeal, so they weren't hopeful to start with. They pointed out that when the inmates go on a hunger strike, they are likely to lose even more privileges.

We inmates finally figured that we would have to take this chance or things could get even worse. We'd heard rumors of Swanson taking away the weight pile and this would surely bring the morale down to rock bottom. We hoped Regional would get involved to make sure we got these privileges back. If a hunger strike lasts three days, Regional was required to come to the prison—and they weren't happy about it. It reflected poorly on the administration, because it would mean the camp administrator and warden couldn't handle the problems by themselves.

The inmates went ahead with the strike, but some inmates were selling burgers, pizza, and tacos, so no one went hungry. The inmates would steal food from the warehouse and then cook it and sell it. A few inmates still had frying pans and burners. We all ate enough to survive. We tried to keep this information among us, and let the camp COs think we were starving ourselves.

Two days into the purported hunger strike, the

warden drove to the camp from the USP with her captain. Inmates were ordered into lockdown mode, and we didn't know how long it would last.

The loudspeaker sprang to life, shouting instructions for specific inmates to report to specific rooms. The entire camp population was split into five large rooms. Once in our designated locations, we waited…and waited…and waited.

An hour went by, but it began feeling like a lifetime. Given the ominous waiting, we figured we were going to be seriously punished by the warden, maybe locked down for *months*.

Finally, after a half hour, the warden, assistant warden, and captain walked into our room. The assistant warden spoke first and presented eight grievances shared by the inmates the official visitors had met with prior to meeting with us. He expressed his concern and said he wanted us to be happy.

Of course, we knew he could care less about us, but he didn't want to bring attention to Regional. Nobody believed him until the warden took the microphone and informed us that she would see to it we got our late night TV back on weekends. But, as far as the restricted outdoor visiting area, it would remain locked because the inmates had been using the area to have sex with their visitors and *this had to stop*.

The warden also gave us back our microwaves. Each of these announcements lifted our spirits. Many of us had feared the worst, and maybe we didn't get all we wanted, but at least we had taken a stand. Maybe Swanson would think twice before taking away privileges in the future. During her speech the warden said she was unaware that certain privileges were being taken away. But we didn't buy it. We thought she was only trying to save face.

We were sent back to our cells and told we would meet individually with the counselors and staff. One by one, we waited in line outside offices to answer their questions.

Now it was time for the warden to find out who organized the hunger strike. I wasn't going to tell them anything. The inmates made a pact prior to the hunger strike that everyone would keep quiet.

When it was my turn, I met the guard alone in a room and answered a number of questions about the strike. Did I participate? Did I know which inmate gathered everyone together? I said I didn't, but *everyone* knew the organizers.

He also asked if I was happy with how it turned out, and my honest answer was no. As for other grievances, I wanted the outdoor visitation area opened, and I sure wanted better food. When asked if the guards treated me with respect, I again answered honestly and said no. I spoke so long about the heat in the camp that the guard cut me short and sent me back to my room.

Some inmate must have given up the names of the organizers, because two days later three inmates were sent to the hole and then shipped out of the camp. When you're dealing with the Feds, someone has to go to jail. They always look for a stool pigeon. That's how they work.

All in all, though, the hunger strike worked out well for the inmates. Sometimes, you have to stand together and fight even if the odds are against you. Although our freedom and rights were taken away when we were sent to prison, our personal worth still lived in our hearts and souls. Neither Swanson nor the warden could deny us that.


## Good-bye to our Jerry Lewis


I counted the days. What a rush. I'd be home with my family, friends, and my job, where I could actually make more than $2.50 a month very soon. I had left in charge a very good friend Bob, who was running a business I started when the Feds shut down my other company. Now, I couldn't wait to get back and feel like a person again. My self-worth had diminished and the thought of being back working was a thrill.

As I was thinking about the exciting days ahead, Pete, a friend, suggested we go to the basement to play 500. "We don't have much longer to play cards together."

I followed him down the unlit basement stairs, which was strange. Suddenly, I heard a loud "Surprise!"

Many of my friends were sitting at a long table that was covered with pizzas and a cake. I was really taken back. It was kind of weird that I would miss anything about this place, but these guys had made the time go by a little faster. They gave me a good-bye card that said in big bold letters:

*GOOD BY TO OUR JERRY LEWIS.*

They'd all written messages on the inside, telling me how I made a difference in their lives and how they wouldn't had made it without me. Each had a personal story in the card. I was deeply touched.

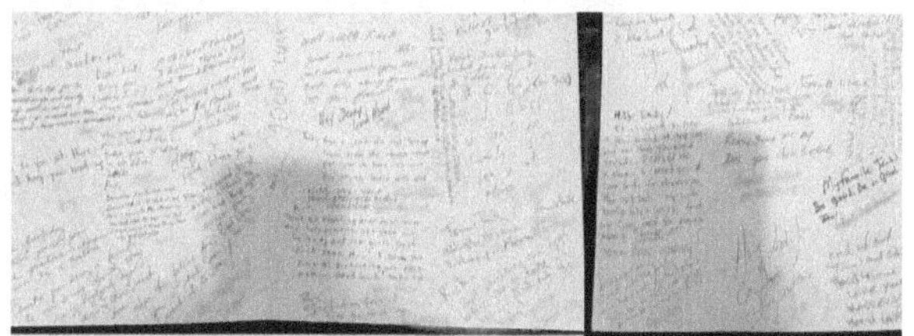

## My last USP lockdown

I was days away from going home, but I had a hard time believing it would actually happen. I was packing my books when I heard a list of inmates being called off on the loudspeaker. This usually happens when the USP goes on lockdown, often when one gang member stabbed another. (The USP was separate from the camp, and we didn't have that kind of violence.) For me, this meant some of us in the camp would have to go over to the USP and make bag lunches, and that could on for days.

I listened to the names being called off and hoped I wouldn't hear mine. Back in the good old days Wizard would keep my name off the list—he was the one who created the list in the first place. Finally, there it was, Keith 654. That was it; I was going over to pack lunches. My bad luck.

But then it occurred to me to ask Swanson for permission not to go since I needed time to pack and get ready to go home. I still had to do a merry-go-round, which is what happens when an inmate is about to leave and he has to go all around to all the staff members and get their signatures. Another stupid rule of the camp.

I knocked on Swanson's dreaded office door and he made some remark about my going home. I asked if I could be taken off the list to go to the USP and pack lunches because of what I had to do before I could go home.

Swanson asked if I had my ID on me. When I told him I didn't, he told me to go and get it. I left feeling great and hurried to get the ID and gave it him.

Then like something out of a weird movie, he stared into my eyes. "Okay, Keith, I'll take you off the list to go to the USP, but just remember one thing, you and me are through. There is nothing between us anymore. I guess you don't care about the safety of this prison, so we're done. Don't say hi to me in the hall. You're a stranger to me now. No more Beatles' trivia, no more jokes. We're done."

Huh? This guy was delusional. There was never a "you and me." He'd screwed me over with the wedding furlough, and now he wanted me to feel guilty about the safety of his prison. Because I didn't trust him, I offered to go to the USP and told him not to be upset.

"No, go do the things you need to do," he said. "You're not going. I'm taking your name off the list."

He sounded like a martyr.

I went back to my room and explained what happened. Timmy advised me to get into my uniform and be ready to go. They'd put me in the hole, otherwise, which was exactly what Swanson wanted.

I listened to Timmy, who turned out to be right. Remember, Swanson was a real maniac. Sure enough, my name was announced to board the bus to go to the USP. Swanson had set me up so I would miss the bus and it would look like I disobeyed a direct order. Another narrow escape from the hole.

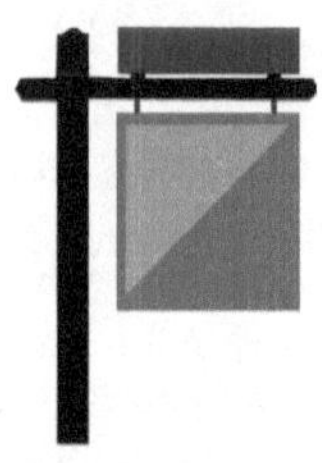

# Chapter Twenty

## I Return Home—Why Should You Care?

My life won't ever go back to so-called normal, but I was fortunate to have had a home and family to return to. Many don't. While I was in the camp and even after I came back home, I thought a great deal about what had happened. Not just to me, but to millions of others. I've included some of my conclusions in the story itself, but here are the primary reasons you should care about what happens to people every day in this country. And, I come full circle and say again: *If it can happen to me, it can happen to anyone.*

First, it's alarming, but losing poses little or no risk for the prosecution in an investigation or a trial at the U.S. Federal level. The worst and most ineffective and lazy prosecutors still maintain a high conviction percentage. No other endeavor can boast a 98% success rate. No baseball player has even come close to batting 98%, no politician gets 98% of the vote, and no one in sales sells to 98 out of 100 contacts. But our Federal prosecutors "bat" close to 98% because defendants are too scared by the system to take their chances in court. All prosecutors need to secure a conviction is to *indict* the person. No proof, no compelling evidence, no truth required.

This is allowed to happen because the entire system is unfair. For example, many convicted drug offenders were arrested without any drugs in their possession. They were arrested because someone claimed they purchased drugs from them—even several years prior to the arrest. So, whatever happened to presenting *required* evidence? *When the Feds get done manipulating the other defendants and witnesses, you can bet they will sing like canaries*, as the saying goes.

A Federal trial can be won on the basis of a conspiracy theory and without compelling evidence. The Feds use a conspiracy theory as a catchall device to throw everyone involved into the mix. They did this during the real estate crisis of 2007-2008, and they've been doing it with the drug issues for decades now.


**Grand juries**


Once the radar of Federal agents locks on you, you're in jeopardy. All Feds need to win an indictment is to present their case against you to a grand jury. During a grand jury trial, *no legal representation is allowed* for the defendant. However, the most skilled lawyer on the planet faces nearly insurmountable odds winning their case against Federal prosecutors. Most attorneys agree we can't put a price on freedom, but when representing defendants facing Federal charges, many of these same attorneys move to make plea agreements.

Many credible attorneys attest that Federal prosecution procedures are not about finding and disclosing the truth, but about the prosecution earning political points. Even if by some miracle the defendant is acquitted of Federal charges during their first trial, Federal agents have shown themselves perfectly capable of indicting people again on completely different charges, and the prosecutors almost always win the second trial.

If someone facing Federal charges asked me for

advice, I'd tell them to find an attorney who is an excellent negotiator, but *do not go to trial.*

I also talked about snitching, which forms the foundation of Federal cases. The person who "sings" the loudest and the quickest receives the shorter prison sentence and is sent to a prison camp rather than to a higher security prison. When I arrived at the camp, I learned many inmates received sentences of one year and one day. This could save two months because if you are sentenced to over a year you are entitled to good time. These "one year" inmates are viewed as snitches who benefitted greatly. They might have been the masterminds of the crime, but to the agents and prosecutors and the judge, snitching is considered your public duty and helping your government.

In my case, the mortgage broker got probation because he wore a wire against the other defendants who sent loans to him. The broker manipulated loan documents and took advantage of the banks predatory lending programs.

In many instances, the Feds will accept the testimony of a witness who knows *nothing* of the accused actions or inactions. The Feds will lead you in your "memory" to fill in the facts as they want them presented. Remember, the prosecutor wanted me to rat on a co-defendant in my case. But I hadn't witnessed any illegal activity on the co-defendant's part. After saying as much, the Feds regarded me as their enemy and told the judge that I didn't cooperate. I was put on notice: if I didn't help the Feds get their targeted guy, my wife and I would be at the top of the indictment list. And, as you have seen, they made good on their threat.

Since no other option existed, it was imperative the judge believe I truly thought I had committed a terrible crime. In other words, I had to convince the judge that I schemed to defraud. If the judge thought my guilty plea was bogus, as it really was, and I believed I was innocent, that would be deceit. I'd find myself in more trouble. Talk about having someone coming and going!

One of the major travesties of our current judicial system was put on display when the judge questioned me to ensure I understood I was forfeiting certain constitutional rights. He asked if I was high on anything or pleading under duress. Was I aware I couldn't change my mind later? Did I realize I waived the right to an appeal? The judge was making sure my plea wasn't directed by the lawyer, and that I was waiving my right to a trial with full understanding what that meant.

This part of the fiasco was especially difficult since I really wanted to prove my case, but simultaneously, I knew I had no chance at winning. So, while pleading guilty under duress, I was terrified of the consequences of going to trial and face the nearly inevitable conviction. If that were to occur, I'd not be with my family for 10 to 15 years. Even worse in terms of the system, the judge knows all this to be true, yet continues to ask the questions and acts as if the defendant is pleading because he is guilty or because he feels threatened.

As I've said, I met inmates incarcerated for possession of small quantities of drugs like pot and pills who received the minimum *ten-year* sentence! Some were sentenced to up to twenty years on these drug charges. Finally, in 2014, Attorney General Eric Holder issued a statement to the press apologizing for the lengthy prison sentences assigned these inmates. (That administration's work for reform was reversed in 2017.) The egregious minimum sentences and the use conspiracy laws resulted in overcrowded U.S. prisons. Even first-time offenders, the majority of these "soft drug" offenders, fell victim to a so-called zero tolerance policy. Alarmingly, these first-time offenders were receiving sentences once reserved for murders.

## What next?

Many inmates are like me; they never planned to break the law in the first place. But why should you care, or your neighbors care, or anyone out living normal lives? The reason you need to care involves the aggressive nature of the Federal judicial system and the ease with which law-abiding citizens may fall under their radar and become their victims. It's kind of like a spider watching a fly and waiting for it to get stuck in the web. Once the fly is stuck there is no hope.

Although I found information on the Wikipedia site, the research they report comes from government statistics and most of this information has been known by the general public for years, even decades. For the last two or three generations, prison is not an unfamiliar or even "foreign" concept. Crowded prisons aren't some odd phenomenon we see in foreign countries, you know, those places less enlightened than we are. No, when it comes to incarceration, the United States is the outlier.

Our prisons are not well-equipped to treat complex health conditions, especially those associated with aging. Some older inmates have prosthetics that need care and cleaning. It was appalling to see a parade of sick, older inmates walking the prison halls using crutches and walkers. Visitors come to the prison and see inmates who look like death itself. A program exists called Compassionate Release, but I never heard of an inmate granted this release.

FAMM (Families Against Mandatory Minimums) have long worked on behalf of inmates given long sentences for relatively minor and nonviolent crimes and sometimes grow old in prison. Right now, our prisons are also filled with professionals like doctors, dentists, lawyers, accountants, and psychologists. Many who have been convicted on conspiracy charges. None of these individuals received the benefit of "The Second Chance Act." (This bill, H.R. 1593, was passed in 2008) Only three parts of the bill may be able to affect how long a person stays in prison. These three parts only affect people in Federal prison.

The first lengthens the outer limits of the time an individual is guaranteed *consideration for* pre-release community corrections (halfway house) from six to 12 months. However, there is no new requirement that the BOP give every person the full 12 months in a halfway house at the end of their sentence.

The second section creates a limited pilot program called the "Elderly and Family Reunification for Certain Nonviolent Offenders" provision. As a pilot program, this provision will likely affect only one facility and is unlikely to provide relief for many individuals. As unlikely as it is to occur in the current political climate, the Second Chance Act should be re-written to release the elderly and the first-time offenders out early into a home confinement program. Finally, the bill increases slightly the percentage of a Federal sentence that can be served in home confinement. However, there is no requirement for the BOP to give prisoners any time in home confinement.

Almost every day, we see advocates talking about mandating drug treatment rather than prison for drug-related crimes. It's well accepted that treatment is less expensive than incarceration. Likewise, we'd have fewer people in prison if those convicted of white collar crimes, but which often were really mistakes and not planned schemes to defraud or deceive anyone, serve their sentences on home confinement and practice their jobs or professions and pay their fines. This would certainly reduce the prison population. Prison could be reserved for the handful of white collar criminals I met who deliberately set out to defraud individuals or illegally profited from businesses and institutions.

Our prisons are both extremely overcrowded and underfunded, which adds to the abuse of inmates in many ways. As I previously pointed out, the Franklin

Prison Camp continues functioning when temperatures inside the camp buildings reach over 95 degrees in the summer. The air conditioning systems remained unrepaired. This inevitably led to some elderly inmates fainting from heat exhaustion, as I've said I witnessed, with no proper medical assistance forthcoming.

Food served to inmates was sometimes years past its viability dates—much of it scared off rats. Protein portions were too small to meet daily requirements for the average man, and almost everything was poorly cooked, from the rubber-like meatloaf and stew that sure looked like dog food. Was it? Even worse, if an inmate desperately dared to use a snack machine to ease his weakness from the bad food served, he was sent to the hole.

Lack of funding and lack of humanity is at the root of these conditions, including the lack of healthcare. Incredibly, one of prison's physicians was convicted of *mass murder!* The staff attitude generally communicated that an inmate's life wasn't especially valuable—they didn't act as if they cared if any of us keeled over and died. I actually heard of inmates who passed out on the floor and died *after* asking for help.

Rather than help, they heard commanding officers yell at them to go back to their cells. I knew one inmate who turned purple, but it was too late. He died on the way to the hospital. This is wrong—a medical emergency inside a prison shouldn't be treated any differently than one occurring in an office or a store or inside a home. In any of these situations, coworkers or store employees would call for help. They wouldn't ignore someone who fell to the floor and lost consciousness.

## The threat of the hole

By now you realize that punishment meted out to prison inmates comes out of the Dark Ages. I know of first-time nonviolent offenders sent to the hole, a cement 8 x 10 foot cell, with only a cement slab for a bed and no pillow. Guards slid meals through a slot in the door. The overhead light was on 24 hours a day. This is a cold place, too, with prisoners released one hour per day for exercise. No visits. No phone calls. If this sounds like descriptions of prisons in other "less advanced" countries, you're right. And the families of the prisoners aren't told where they've been sent, so they don't know what their loved ones are enduring in solitary confinement.

Being sent to the hole was not reserved for egregious infractions. Anyone could get that punishment for everything from an untucked shirt or walking out of bounds, being late for work, caught with unauthorized food, or for smoking a cigarette. One of the COs working in Education, sent an inmate student to the hole for *three months* because she caught him feeding the birds. (It was likely she did that because these same happy seed-fed birds pooped all over her car.) I've known of inmates assigned to the hole for a full *year.*

## A captive market

Feds operate businesses out of prisons, which may contribute to so many unwarranted incarcerations. By the same token, inmates can't bring anything into the prison, under threat of the hole. We are a captive market. We can't bring our own toiletries, such as hairbrushes, shavers, and nail trimmers, shoes, shampoo, toothbrushes, watches, and so on, and we can't bring in food or even a bottle of aspirin. All phone calls must be made using prison landlines for profit and control. Vendors are not chosen for their quality or price, but for the profit from sales to inmates they bring to the Bureau of Prisons.

Unicore Corporation is one of the businesses owned and operated by the Bureau of Prisons. This company installs alarms and other electronic devices in Federal vehicles. The labor cost for thirty-five inmates who work for Unicore runs $5,000 per month, and you can do the math. I saw this particular situation up close because my roommate handled the payroll. This reminds me of IG Farbin, the pharmaceutical company the Nazis ran during World War II. Now we use the same prison labor today, although the conditions are not as terrible as they were in Nazi labor camps.


**It doesn't end**


Upon release, you would think inmates could put their nightmare behind them. However, for a period of time, inmates remain under Bureau of Prisons scrutiny. The BOP calls this being "on paper." Inmates must follow all rules or be sent back to prison. They must do certain things like get a job, live in a halfway house, or live on home confinement. Inmates must also pay restitution, which is an amount the Federal court assigns at trial. Ex-inmates must also submit to periodic drug testing. They have to stay in touch with the assigned parole officer, checking in with him or her when they do virtually anything, like moving, or even going out of town for a job or spending money in certain ways. A man I knew was sent back to camp because he sent his daughter to a private college. Other parole officers watch ex-inmates' spending on movies, meals, dwellings, clothes, cars, trips, and so forth. It's another form of control.

Of course, released inmates no longer return to the same status or are able to restore their reputations. I think of it as wearing a visible scarlet letter on my chest. When interviewing for a job, inmates must be prepared to discuss their "label" of convicted felon. This adds a great burden for finding a job and influences how supervisors or others they work with regard them. Many inmates are no longer able to support themselves or help support their families—at least that ability is jeopardized or eliminated. Former inmates aren't allowed to own a firearm. Most harmful, in many states, felons are still not allowed to vote again—ever.

A synopsis of the current judicial experience could read like this—and it could happen to you:

A United States business owner or employed taxpaying citizen on next to no evidence other than a conspiracy theory, is convicted of a nonviolent crime. This law makes it simple for the Feds to target nearly anyone and win a conviction. You are thrown into prison for a first offense and subject to a potential ten-year sentence. While in prison, you face living in a dungeon, eating terrible food, working slave labor, and receiving demoralizing—at best—treatment. Once convicted, the system regards you as subhuman, a worthless piece of garbage that needs to be treated like a five-year-old.

The bottom line? The Federal prison system and the judicial system are broken. Those sent to prison are not all violent people, and certainly not murderers or rapists, and not terrorists plotting attacks. I found that most prison inmates were first-time offenders and convicted of nonviolent crimes. They usually made a mistake in taking an action that turned out to be illegal. I believe nonviolent, taxpaying citizens of the United States deserve a second chance. I believe it is morally wrong to cripple an individual's life personally, financially, and psychologically or break what have become a plethora of poorly defined Federal criminal laws, imprecise in their interpretations.

Prior to incarceration, I had no interest in the prison system or the judiciary. Like most people, I was focused on my business and family. I believed if inmates were treated unfairly, they should have considered this before committing crimes. I also thought every accused person would have his or her day in court. The constitution says so, doesn't it? Justice would prevail, even if it took time and appeals. I knew no system is perfect, but ours is the best.

Right now, it's sad but true that most people in the U.S. have no idea about the current state of our judicial system. However, as more has been exposed and some attempts to reform the system have been put in place or have been seriously discussed, we will continue to backslide unless citizens-voters ask their representatives about this part of our justice system.

There are many ways average citizens can help make a difference. Some legal firms agree to represent an incarcerated client when they find inconsistencies in the case. There are people who write their congressional representatives and senators and state and local representatives to lobby to get laws passed to stop the inflated sentences for first time offenders. We can also contact media outlets to start a discussion with journalists who write investigative pieces or produce radio and TV features on prison conditions and reform.

Prison food should at the very least be edible and not past any reasonable expiration date. Drug users should be given help and treatment instead of long prison sentences. Ill inmates should be taken care of and treated like any other ill humans outside of prison. All religious groups should be allowed to work with inmates and conduct workshops in the prisons.

Unless people wake up, they won't be interested enough to promote change *until they come face-to-face with judicial issues themselves.*

But by then, it may be too late.

# The Track

A man feeds a ground squirrel
It looks so sublime
The same time each day
The same place each time.

Next, here come the birds
They keep their distance
They gather all together
They are very persistent

These things he does
Helps clean his mind
Adding up the hours
While doing his time

There is no fence
Just a walk in the park
Trying to finish this trail
Before it gets dark

No prison walls shown
To hold this man in
Only those in his head
He knows he can't win

The sky is bright blue
Over the happy camp
With clouds of powder
Heavy and damp

He thinks of his home
And days that have gone by
Having stayed here so long
Still not knowing what or why

You keep on counting
'Cause you're almost there
For your hopes and dreams
Are still waiting out there.

# Injustice

Oh, how ice cold
This world can be
When heads stay hidden
And eyes do not see.

He studied the paper
With a curious face
His future revealed
Confined to this place.

The date it was written
A tunnel thru time
So difficult to imagine
An injustice so unkind.

How could this happen
In his country, his home?
No one to turn to
He must sit all alone.

When will it be ended?
How many must be touched?
Until eyes will be opened
And injustice be crushed.

*Richard Keith*

# The Defendant (The Wizard)

They enter into her court room
Eager for an unfair fight
Acting the part with nose up
Knowing they rule his plight.

The judge, she enters from chambers
She's sporting her gown and crown
Peering out at the crowd
Knowing they'll win every round.

The twelve, they enter in silence
They turn and gaze at the sight
Of the lamb they've come to slaughter
Anxious to waste another life.

The burden of proof falls upon them
Though he knows it is his to bear
His face shows his anger
He's aware this won't be fair.

He feels so helpless and lonely
This tide he wants not to ride
The opposition knowing only contempt
Determined in proving their side.

The balance of power is tilted
The verdict is already done
The dice they have already fallen
He may never again see his son.

Oh, how he wishes he caved
To the cards, as they were dealt
Instead, he bucked the system
By standing by the convictions he felt.

So, wave as you see him exit
Not aware you've done him wrong
For you may soon walk in his shoes
And learn the words to his song.

*Richard Keith*

# Helpless Helpless

Out of the blue
They came into my life
A blast from the past
My day turned to night.

I went out searching
For someone to hear
A person to help
To lend me their ear.

It's not about truth
Or justice you see
It's more like a game
A team—you and me.

Don't whisper a word
Not to a soul
We'll win the game
This is the goal.

Fill in the blanks
The facts they will show
To prove their story
Them stooping so low.

Now you must plead
Throw in the towel
Make it look good
Or the judge, he will growl.

Now you are trash
You entered a plea
Trapped and helpless
Now a convict you'll be.

# Coming Home

Was I punished or did I learn?
I'll never really know
Only that now it's over
And I'm finally free to go.

My mind slowed down and paid the toll
Nothing in my power I could do
But, dream and hope of things to come
With mostly thoughts of you.

Was it fast or was it slow?
This interests me in the least
for what I learned and what I know
Will forever give me peace.

Now I come with open arms
Ready to dive back in
If I could just make one wish
I'd wish it will be as it's been.

# **Acknowledgements**

Writing a book takes years of effort. Without the help and support of friends and family, this book never would have been written.

I would not have persevered in all the accomplishments in life and business if not for the support of my mother, Sandra and father, Seymour. My mother passed away a year ago from Alzheimer's Disease, a disease I hope finds a cure in the not so distant future. I will never forget my mother and the importance she played in every part of my life. Through my life, my parents were always there to support whatever challenge I took on.

To my wife, who was always there when I needed her, words can't express my love. Your inspiration and belief in me when I didn't believe in myself gave me the confidence I needed to make this dream come true. I will love you forever with all my heart. Without you, I am nothing.

My children Gary, Barry and Heather, David, Mike and Lindsay, and Danielle and Jackie, who were my rock every step of the way while writing this book. For my brother, Paul who guided me through the trial and errors of writing a book and without, it never would have been edited and published. To my mother and father-in law Papa Roy and Loraine who always believed in me. Loraine left us for heaven five years ago and has left a legacy of love with everyone she touched.

To my brother and sister-in law Larry and Jodie and Uncle Dean and Aunt Joyce. My love goes out to every one of them. To Uncle Mike who was the caring rock and advisor with the knowledge and experience I needed to get me through the difficult times. To my daughter Lindsay who helped market my book online while she was raising my granddaughter Ella while being pregnant.

To Steve and Sue Arwady and Dan Purdom who helped me persevere and believed in me at all times. Steve has passed away, but I will never forget him as long as I live. He was there for me with pure love and never wanted anything in return. His friendship was precious, and he will be missed by many.

To my great friends Julie and Gary Keller who gave me the undying support I needed. They opened their hearts and home to me every day. Their support was unmeasurable and will never be forgotten. To my dear friends Laurie and Ken who gave me the idea and support to write this book. To my friend Jay, who named the book for me, and gave me the inspiration to follow it through.

To my friends Alex and Elsi, Paul and Stormy, Gary and Laurie, Eli and Leslie, Karen and Lon, Ted and Yvette, Bobby Engle, Danny and April, Marty and Judy, Jack and Gail, Howard and Nancy, Cliff and Adrian who helped make this book possible. Thank you all!

To Karen Moody who was there from the start. She took hundreds of thoughts and words written on scratch paper, organized them, and helped me put them into words in a book. Thank you for your hours and hours of work.

To Virginia McCullough, who took my book and polished it until it is what it is today. You made changes I was hesitant to make but was always correct. I will never forget the amount of work and time you extended to me as well as introducing me to Written Dreams Publishing. Your talent is never ending. I thank you with all my heart.

And finally, thank you to Brittiany Koren and the team at Written Dreams Publishing who took on this project. You always took time for me and gave me the guidance, experience, and professionalism I needed to market my book. I can't thank you enough for making this first attempt at my dream of being an author come true.


Richard Keith

April, 2020

# About the Author

R ichard Keith resides in Illinois and opened a steel distributorship after prison. He also works for a fuel company. In 2008, Richard had been selling real estate and got caught up in the subprime mortgage nightmare that brought the United States real estate market to its knees. Richard learned the right to a trial by jury was not what it was supposed to be. When he learned the truth on how the government, prison system, and judicial system worked, he used his stay in prison to write a book. Richard thought he would be doing a service by writing a book and getting his story out to the public. He had never had a run in with the law prior.

Graduated from Eastern Illinois University with a business degree, he opened a manufacturing company, steel import company, distributorship, powder metal factory, retail printing company, and worked as a shopping center developer. Favorite past times are tennis, racquetball, soft ball, ping pong, pool, and drumming in a Beatles cover band. Richard has four sons and two daughters.